Operation
FURY

BELFAST : NEW YORK : LONDON

WW MORRISON

Cedricwilson@live.co.uk

Published by Award Design & Print Northern Ireland

Copyright © WW Morrison 2010

The right of WW Morrison to be identified as the author of this work has been asserted by him in accordance with the Copyright, Designs and Patents Act 1988

All rights reserved. No part of this publication may be reproduced in a retrieval system or transmitted by any means, electronic or mechanical, photocopying or otherwise, without the prior permission of the copyright holders.

ISBN 978-0-9564515-52

Typesetting by wordzworth.com

This book is a work of fiction. Any references to historical events, real people, or real locales are used fictitiously. Any resemblance to actual events or locales or persons, living or dead, is entirely coincidental.

Dedicated to
'Artemis'
Personally courageous
and steadfast in duty.

Contents

Preface		iii
Introduction		v
1	An Average Day	1
2	Another Domestic Discussion	11
3	Tit-for-Tat Killing	21
4	Sniper at the Mill	35
5	One Armalite Doesn't Make a Provo War	47
6	Operation Ballymurphy	55
7	Feud	63
8	Another Possible Lead	71
9	Submarines	91
10	Ryan – Too Clever	103
11	Signal of Authorisation Operation FURY	117
12	The Three Bears	127
13	Operation JAZZ BAND	135
14	Artemis Arrives	151
15	Montgomery Arrives	159
16	Undercover For Drinks	167
17	Operation FURY Authorisation to be Rescinded	177
18	The Wrong Corpse	193
19	Epilogue	211
Acknowledgements		215
Notes		216

Preface

It is only through fiction that we may assemble the facts in order to arrive at the truth. And the truth is but a whisper, blowing on the wind of propaganda.

This narrative includes an account of a classified Top Secret operation sanctioned by the British government to eliminate a United States politician who was heavily involved in organising illegal finances and arms shipments to the Irish Republican Army (IRA).

The operation codename FURY involved the British Secret Intelligence Service (MI6), Armed Forces Unit (AFU) and others. FURY was overseen by the Defence Intelligence Staff in the Ministry of Defence. In a meticulously pre-planned follow-up operation codename SPEAKEASY, MI6 was to implement a disinformation programme to implicate and blame others for the assassination.

Astonishingly, to those involved at the time, FURY was called off hours before its completion. Following a general election, resulting in a change to the political party of government, the new Foreign and Commonwealth Secretary rescinded the 'Signet of authorisation' certificate issued by his predecessor. The ultimate chapter in this book speculates on the likely outcome of FURY not having been cancelled.

Operation FURY

I am convinced to this day that neither the American Central Intelligence Agency nor the Federal Bureau of Investigation had any knowledge of the existence of Operation FURY. More importantly, if FURY had been allowed to proceed to its ultimate conclusion, it would have greatly reduced the Irish Republican Army's capacity and will to murder members of the British Crown Forces and citizens of the United Kingdom of Great Britain and Northern Ireland.

Colonel (Retd) Peter Moore

In the early 1970s at the height of the Cold War an agent of the KGB, a senior intelligence officer of the German Democratic Republic's (East Germany) state security service Staatssicherheits-dienst (Stasi) made contact with the leaders of the IRA, believed by the British government to be a serious attempt by the Soviets to destabilise NATO. This culminated in an ill-conceived, but successful, long-range operation carried out by the Northern Fleet of the Soviet Navy. The operation in the deployment of submarines could have precipitated the splitting apart of the vast northern waters of the Atlantic Ocean – from which would have surfaced nuclear Armageddon.

> *...woe to the inhabitants of the earth and of the sea!*
> *for the devil come down unto you, having great wrath,*
> *because he knoweth that he has but a short time.*
> Revelation 12:12

In helping the IRA's 'armed struggle' to force the British to withdraw from Northern Ireland and subsequently Marxist Sinn Fein gaining overall political power, the Soviets were to secure the lease of a naval base at Lough Foyle.[1]

We, and indeed the southern Irish also, regard the Official IRA as a greater long-term threat to the UK and the Republic than the Provisionals, chiefly because of its greater political sophistication, its Marxist orientation, and its links abroad. [2]

MI5 Archive

Introduction

The Political Theologians

James Craig, Viscount Craigavon, first Prime Minister of Northern Ireland* and leader of the Ulster Unionist Party, said in April 1934:

> I have always said I am an Orangeman first and a politician and member of this Parliament afterwards...The Honourable Member must remember that in the south they boasted of a Catholic State. They still boast of Southern Ireland being a Catholic State. All I boast is that we are a Protestant Parliament and Protestant State.[3]

Eamon de Valera, leader of Fianna Fail and Taoiseach in his 1935 St Patrick's Day radio broadcast declared Ireland to be a Catholic nation:

> Since the coming of St Patrick 1,500 years ago, Ireland has been a Christian and a Catholic nation...she remains a Catholic nation.

By these statements both leaders set the mood of modern history for the two States. Only Eamon de Valera lived to see the inevitable consequence which ignited the passion that erupted in 1969 into bloody violence, spurred on by naked bigotry on the one side and innate hatred by the other. At this time, there were fewer than 600 British garrison troops in Northern Ireland. Within a few years the number of British troops was to grow to 27,000. Belfast became the main battleground for what was to become known as 'The Troubles' which lasted for three decades.

---

* *Northern Ireland also known as Ulster, the Province, the Six Counties and the North.*

Operation FURY

4.45pm**

From: The Inspector General, Royal Ulster Constabulary
To: The General Officer Commanding Northern Ireland.

/ In view of the continued worsening of the situation in Londonderry City on this date as outlined in the attached copy of a warning message sent to the Home Office, London, and the fact that this situation has deteriorated further since the timing of the message to the Home Office, I now request the assistance of forces under your command in Londonderry City.

(Signed)
14.8.69
4.45pm

Half a lifetime ago, as a young reporter I watched the first of them go in: bewildered British soldiers in steel helmets with bayonets fixed, deploying by companies amid the ravaged Bogside in Londonderry, then the Falls Road in Belfast.

Young squaddies gazed in disbelief at the shambles created by sectarian rioting: crowds of exhausted, frightened, bitter people.

The opening shots fired by the British army on that first August night of their Ulster commitment 38 years ago, were directed at Protestant incendiarists, not the IRA.

First, they faced rock-throwing mobs. By 1972, there were 10,000 shootings and hundreds of bombings. IRA gunmen learned to snipe the last man of a British patrol on the streets of Derry or Belfast; then to booby-trap the cars of judges and police officers; to murder soldiers at bases in Germany and politicians on the streets of Britain.[4]

** See Acknowledgements.

Introduction

1972 Negotiations - An Acceptable Level of Violence

On 13 March 1972, Harold Wilson, Labour leader of Her Majesty's Opposition held secret talks in the British Embassy in Dublin with the leadership of the IRA. On finding out about the talks, the government of the Republic of Ireland under Taoiseach Jack Lynch was incensed.

On 24 March, Prime Minister, Edward Health announced that the democratically elected Stormont government of Northern Ireland would be prorogued for twelve months. 'Direct Rule' was imposed by London on 30 March.

There were further secret talks in London on 7 July between the British government, involving the Conservatives, under Edward Health, with William Whitelaw, the first Secretary of State for Northern Ireland, now 'negotiating' with Provisional IRA representatives. The bottom line for the IRA was complete withdrawal by the British from Northern Ireland.

The Taoiseach Jack Lynch was well aware that in the Republic there was growing opposition to unity with the north. Lynch indicated in no uncertain terms the Irish government was not interested in a united Ireland under current circumstances and would in effect oppose it.

Operation FURY

The culmination of events had given the Provisional IRA/Sinn Fein the unprecedented position in negotiation with the British. Withdrawal became a probability rather than a possibility and the incredulous unionists could do nothing but look on from the sidelines. With the Stormont government prorogued the Unionist and Nationalist elected representatives were denied any direct input of the governance of Northern Ireland.

A temporary IRA ceasefire agreed prior to the Whitelaw/IRA negotiations was broken, either accidentally or deliberately, each side blaming the other and the IRA was back in business – the resumption of the 'armed struggle.'

On 10 July, the IRA Army Council made public that they had been in negotiations with the British government in London.

On 21 July, which became known as 'Bloody Friday', the Provisional IRA exploded 26 bombs across Belfast.

With the Republic's government displaying open antagonism to the British fraternising with the IRA; the Unionist and Nationalist politicians out in the cold; the Protestant paramilitaries, with few modern weapons and considered no more than an organised rabble, it is bewildering why the Provisional IRA leadership in a unique position, failed miserably to press home their demands with the British government. The IRA would not find itself in this strong position for another 25 years.

Introduction

For the Provisional IRA: the 'armed struggle' was no longer a means to an end but became simply a way of life to the backdrop of endless slogans and empty rhetoric.

For the British government(s): Northern Ireland and its people were to endure for another two and a half decades an acceptable level of violence.[5]

1
An Average Day

'There's that bastard O'Reilly; I wonder what the sleekit git's up to now? Pull over Sam. Park here and let's see,' said Inspector James Montgomery.

'OK Inspector,' was the reply from Sergeant Sam Smith.

O'Reilly was in his mid-twenties, from Ballymurphy in Belfast. A lout and petty criminal who had worked his way into the local brigade of the Provisional IRA, as a volunteer, only too eager to do the odd jobs required to advance the 'cause' and his own reputation. He had parked his car at the entrance to the petrol station forecourt, perfectly placed to deter other customers from squeezing past. He was now, full military style, walking towards the petrol station shop, playing Provo soldier. O'Reilly hadn't the wit to realise this inability to blend in with the crowd was a real give-away. Inspector Montgomery had instantly spotted him.

'Who's that with him?' Montgomery enquired.

'I don't know. Probably one of his ass wipes,' replied Sam, adjusting his gaze as if to make a definitive identification. 'There's another bugger sitting in the back seat,' added Sam.

'I see him Sam. It looks like 'Butcher' Wallace,' retorted Montgomery.

Operation FURY

Sean 'Butcher' Wallace was well up in the command structure of the Provos, believed by the RUC to be one of the main players in identifying possible targets – a serious malefactor. Wallace was in his early thirties. Stumpy in appearance, he was a man for all seasons when it came to killing. A top Provo yahoo.

'They are on a job Inspector,' said Sam, while instinctively cupping his hand around his revolver.

'Hold off,' said Montgomery, moving towards the back of the Land Rover to unlock the door while adjusting the flak jacket under his overcoat, in anticipation of his next move.

Montgomery had been in the RUC for almost fifteen years, having joined when normal police work was investigating the odd burglary or vehicle theft. He had worked his way up in CID and had recently been promoted to Inspector by diligent work as a Detective. A Roman Catholic from a small mixed town about seven miles from Belfast, which had seen little violence from the paramilitaries since the outbreak of terrorism in 1969; no doubt because it was a garrison town and too many squaddies about for any serious trouble. Montgomery was having one of his out of the office days with a patrol vehicle to relieve the burden of the ongoing paperwork which was a down-side for him and most of his team. He liked to be in the thick of it and Sam was his brother-in-law, good company and someone close and reliable.

'They are on their way out Inspector, heading back to their car.'

'OK Sam, let's just observe and stay put for the moment.'

O'Reilly was lighting up a cigarette and smirking, while his companion walked a few feet behind, somewhat taller and older than O'Reilly, Montgomery thought he seemed out of place.

'We need a closer look at O'Reilly's mate; drive closer Tommy,' instructed Montgomery.

'Damn, they have spotted us' retorted Tommy.

'Go on Tommy, just drive past and back to the station and make

An Average Day

sure they see us watching. It will make them think twice if they are up to no good,' said Montgomery. Tommy nodded while simultaneously forcing the gear stick into second with the usual rasp and accompanying expletives.

'Who taught you how to drive – Stirling Moss?' chuckled Sam.

'Back to the station for tea and crumpet you said Inspector.'

'Aye, OK, I'll have the tea, you can have the crumpet,' said Montgomery, smiling and patting Tommy on the shoulder.

As they drove past, Montgomery took a long look at O'Reilly's companion and thought to himself that's no dogsbody; he is clean shaven, hair tied back, in one of those daft pony-tails. Montgomery estimated his height with precision accuracy to half an inch less than six feet and was sure his mental image of O'Reilly's companion would be good enough to identify him from the mug-shots on file.

Sam broke Montgomery's concentration. 'Tea and crumpet it is then?'

'Yes, Sam, they'll be off back to Ballymurphy, no doubt to report our patrol – need to vary it tomorrow Sam, just in case.'

'Aye, Inspector, we always do.'

It was late afternoon as the Land Rover, with its three occupants drove into the station. One of those endless cold February days when the northern winter refused to relinquish its grip and the sun not having gained strength, lingered low in the pink ribbon cloudy sky, was about to dip below the top of the rusted security fence. On came the security lights as if to signal their arrival. At that moment, the Land Rover doors opened and all three stepped out to ease their stiffened limbs.

'See you lads tomorrow then.'

'Yes Inspector,' was the reply in unison.

'Check that registration number of O'Reilly' car, added Sam.

'Yea, Sam, I will,' replied Montgomery.

Operation FURY

More paper work, thought Montgomery, as he walked past the pillar box with the usual 'Hi,' to the squaddie standing inside and buzzing to release the lock for entry through the steel reinforced door. With the heave of his shoulder, he was inside and felt relief as the warm station air flowed across his cold face, tingling his ears and cheeks.

'It's damn cold, Stewart,' said Montgomery as he acknowledged the duty Sergeant.

'Don't know, Monty, I have been here all afternoon. You look foundered. The Chief Super is in the building and wants to see you as soon as you're back, Monty,' added the duty Sergeant.

'Aye, I noticed his car when we pulled in. What's up, Stewart?'

'I don't know. He's unlikely to tell me. Oh, he had a civilian with him. Someone with an English accent, very smart, Army type, I would guess. Better polish your shoes and smarten up. I expect you'll want to give a good impression, Monty,' quipped Sergeant Stewart White, relishing his remark.

'I'll have a cup of tea first,' replied Montgomery, as he set off along the corridor towards the locker room, undoing his overcoat in anticipation of removing his flak jacket underneath.

The locker room was at the end of the corridor, beyond the Chief's office – or rather the room he commandeered on his occasional visit, from more pressing matters at Headquarters. Montgomery gave a tired sigh and thought that hot tea was some way off.

'Hello Monty,' came a voice loudly from the half open door.

'Aye Sir, it's me. I believe you want to see me?'

'Yes, come in, come in Inspector. We have a visitor.'

'Right Sir,' was Montgomery's response as his bulk moved the door open wide giving the stranger a cursory glance as he spotted a tea pot and three cups on the Chief's desk, next to a single open file.

'You'll want tea Monty?' said the Chief as he eased the tray forward for Montgomery to help himself.

An Average Day

'This is Major Peter Moore from London, the Ministry of Defence – Army Intelligence' said the Chief lowering his tone and in his usual instructive manner, added: 'Close the door and take a seat, Inspector.' Montgomery gave a more searching look in the direction of the unexpected visitor, not quite sure if he was to treat him as friend or someone he should stand back from.

'Hello Peter, welcome to Grosvenor Road Police Station, we don't get many MoD visitors,' while extending his hand for the courtesy of a hand-shake.

'I suppose not, Inspector Montgomery, pleased to meet you.'

'James or Inspector will be fine,' replied Montgomery, in an obvious attempt on his part to soften the atmosphere. The Chief gestured with his hand, a silent instruction for the Inspector to sit down.

Opening the file in front of him, while moving closer to the desk, Chief Superintendent McClatchey began to explain to Montgomery.

'Peter has been here up at Headquarters for the past week. He is here to gather our opinions on closer cooperation, a coherent strategy and policy, between the Army and RUC on intelligence gathering and operational matters.

Yes, I know you are CID, not Special Branch, but your experience on the ground, in the pith of things, I feel would be of practical assistance to Peter and give him an overview of our difficulties and needs. This is to be kept from the lower ranks, treat it as confidential. Peter is on release from the Metropolitan Police CID for coal face experience here in Belfast, will be fine for cover. This is important, Inspector, the Chief Constable has agreed with the GOC Army in Ulster to their mutual cooperation. It's top level, Inspector.'

Montgomery's natural apprehension mellowed on hearing the mention of the Chief Constable.

'Yes Sir, I fully understand the importance of what you have said.'

Major Moore looked across at the Inspector and without

Operation FURY

speaking, nodded his head, signalling that an understanding had been reached between them.

With that silent pause, the Chief Superintendent was on his feet.

'OK, Major. I will leave you to explain your concerns to Inspector Montgomery. Can you arrange for Major Moore to have transport to the Europa Hotel? Perhaps Peter can use this office as a temporary base. It's only until Thursday when he is off back home to London.'

'Yes Sir, I'll look after the Major,' replied Montgomery.

As the Chief Superintendent made his way out of the office, he paused momentarily. 'I'll see you next week Peter, before you leave – perhaps Wednesday afternoon? You too, Inspector, we'll have a final get together.'

'Right Chief, Wednesday it is then,' replied Montgomery.

Montgomery rose to his feet.

'It's OK Major. I need to remove my flak jacket. I sometimes think it is more trouble than it is worth. It's a strain on the shoulders and my back. You do the talking Peter, and I'll do the listening,' added Montgomery, as he settled himself in a pose of relief disposing of his flak jacket with a thump onto the seat vacated by the Chief Superintendent.

'Inspector, I will give you some background as to what we know to date on what we believe is a serious developing situation, both for the Army and the RUC alike. What I am about to tell you Inspector, is to be kept confidential and I mean, strictly confidential.' Peter Moore continued and initiated what amounted to a briefing on information known only to a few members of senior ranks in both Army and RUC.

'Our intelligence service in the United States has found out that guns are being smuggled into Ireland, probably through the south, from the US via New York and by sea. But we don't know the exact details. We are a bit sketchy on dates, names; those sorts of details. What we do know is an armoury in Massachusetts was broken into a

An Average Day

few months ago, around Christmas time and weapons – mainly general issue Army assault rifles, ammunition, some explosives and detonators were stolen - a generous Christmas present for the IRA we believe. The American authorities of course have officially denied any such incident took place. Naturally it would be highly embarrassing for them if it became public and besides, they would be unlikely to tell us anything. But our intelligence people, MI6 to be specific, are adamant. Probably some Irish-American informant with more allegiance to a pocket full of dollars than to any far-off cause in some country he could not find on a map. They believe that the newly upgraded and modified Armalite[6] AR-15 automatic assault rifle was part of the haul. Around 500 were stolen, but they cannot be certain. This weapon, Inspector Montgomery, is a serious piece of equipment.' Peter Moore paused and removed from the file left behind by the Chief Superintendent, two photographs and one detail drawing showing and describing the rifle and its component parts. Pushing these forward for Montgomery to study in more detail, he continued.

'The new models, the AR-18/180 to be precise, can also be purchased on the civilian market in the United States over the counter quite easily. These assault rifles, we believe, are those as manufactured by Howa in Japan and imported into the States when the Japanese government granted an export licence after the Vietnam War. The modifications include a folding stock and lowered sights. Some variants come as a ten inch short barrel and can be fitted with a forty round capacity magazine - an ideal weapon for the urban gunman. There's also a sniper version with a Choate stock, top range Harris bipod, and a twenty-four inch heavy barrel.'

Realising Inspector Montgomery was not a ballistics expert; Peter Moore paused to allow him to grasp the full implications of these weapons and their devastating capabilities.

Operation FURY

Peter Moore continued. 'This weapon fires a .223 Remington, 5.56mm small calibre high-velocity bullet that can penetrate British standard issue body armour.' Pointing to the Inspector's flak jacket, Peter Moore added. 'I am sorry to say, your flak jacket wouldn't give you much protection under 300 yard fire. The bullets with full metal jacket used have a tumble effect on impact that can cause horrific injuries. Our own ballistic experts who have examined and tested these new models, have stated they are equal and in some respects, better than the FNLAR used by our troops here in Ulster.'

'Understandably, both the GOC and Chief Constable are very concerned. What we don't know is if the IRA has received these weapons. It is only a matter of time before they arrive in Belfast and by the crate load. Intelligence in the Republic has turned up nothing. The Garda Siochana is not interested so long as they are not affected and want the British to give them any intelligence information we have.'

'Well,' added Peter Moore, his voice raised in an aggressive tone displaying a loss of composure, 'If these guns fall into the hands of the IRA, then they will be affected. They will be forced to weigh-in. Our Ambassador in Dublin will have a few stern words for their government and the British government perhaps more in the way of persuasion.'

As Montgomery shifted back his chair, he rose to his feet.

'Come with me, Peter, to my office and I'll explain the RUC position. Well as far as it is from this station's control.'

Both men made their way out of the room and along the dimly lit corridor; Montgomery leading the way with Moore following. Montgomery unlocked his office door and walked in, directly moving to the soiled map pinned on the wall behind and above his desk. The map was of the greater Belfast area, colour-coded to show the demographics of the inhabitants. The map was emblazoned with 'orange' for the Protestants and 'green' for the Roman Catholics,

An Average Day

while those areas designated 'mixed' were alternative orange and green horizontal stripes.

'You will have seen this map before Peter. It's Army issue, fairly accurate in a broad sense, so we use it for briefings and organising patrols'.

'Yes, Inspector, I have.'

Montgomery began to explain.

'On this road, - moving his flattened out left hand sweeping from right to left, slowly and deliberately, as if to emphasise his point – everyone is called Liam. And on this road, everyone is called William. No difference between the gunmen from either side when it comes to killing. Just unimaginable what they do to one another. Like sabre-toothed tigers, a fight to the death in defending their domains.'

Peter Moore, without uttering a word, nodded in agreement and allowed the Inspector to continue.

'The situation keeps changing. We have quiet periods, then not so quiet. It comes in waves – it erupts – bombings, but mostly it is guns. Gun fights between the IRA and UVF this past couple of months. It's what the press and media are calling 'tit-for-tat' killings. And that is exactly what it is. It's random, nine this side of the city and five, I believe, over the river in East Belfast. It is out of control – an epidemic of slaughtering and impossible to stop. These murders take place at any time of the day or night; innocent people walking along the street or in pubs having a quiet drink. The Army mainly, and RUC vehicle patrols are not that effective. It would take a patrol on every street corner; an impossible deployment and even then these gunmen would find a way around them.'

'Yes Inspector, I have seen reports up at RUC HQ and the TV and newspaper reports over recent weeks back home.'

'Aye, Peter. Perhaps we both should be back home; you in England away from this place, and me out of here. Is that the time? 6.30: we can continue tomorrow if that's OK Peter.'

Operation FURY

'Yes, that's fine with me Inspector. It has been a long day of briefings and I could do with a few hours of rest and relaxation.'

'You're staying at the Europa Hotel, Peter? Someone has a sense of humour, not the most quiet of places on occasions. No sooner have they cleared up after one IED[7] then the IRA is back, usually every two or three weeks is their form. I suppose with you staying there, they can claim it is a military target.'

Peter gave the inspector a rum look, obviously not appreciating the Belfast sense of humour.

'Yes, Inspector, I am aware of the ongoing situation. But it is central and I have a room at the back. Besides, doesn't the IRA give a time warning before a bomb is to be detonated?'

'Yes,' replied Montgomery. 'But they like to play Provo games. Sometimes deliberately giving a wrong time. It's meant to catch out our people, and yours. We have learned to keep well back and try to get everyone clear in half the time they say – highly risky all round though. Then again, after a few hours, there's been no explosion and it's down to the Army – the bomb disposal unit.'

'What an awful job Major. Your people actually volunteer. If the RUC had to do it, I doubt there would be any willing souls.'

2

Another Domestic Discussion

As Montgomery drove out of the hotel forecourt onto Great Victoria Street to make his way home, he reflected on the day's events and felt uneasy by the issues raised with the visit from the Chief Superintendent and Major Peter Moore. He needed to follow up on O'Reilly, Wallace and their pony-tailed companion. In the morning he would ask Sam to check out the licence number of O'Reilly's vehicle while he would be free to check on the unidentified companion.

Turning his thoughts to the unusual briefing from Peter Moore, he was realising that the situation in Ulster may be getting out of control and unmanageable from a security aspect. While the Army presence had been gradually increased in numbers the RUC was below strength both in uniform and CID personnel. The long hours and double shifts give rise to inefficiency. While the CID kept up their professionalism in investigating the more serious crimes, it was at the expense of lesser incidents that were pushed to the bottom of the in-tray. Uniform helped when they could, but vehicle patrols had to be maintained during the daylight hours while at night, it was mainly the Army who patrolled the streets.

Belfast is a small city by British mainland standards of around 400,000 inhabitants. The city is confined to less than a dozen main

Operation FURY

thoroughfares, lending outwards along both sides of the River Lagan and the lower slopes of the Antrim Hills to the north, in endless rows of neat terrace houses, built for the influx of population during the rise of the linen industry in the nineteenth century. The Belfast shipyard had once been the largest employer, taking its main work force from the Protestant East Belfast. Since the ending of the Second World War these two mainstay industries has been in gradual decline and unemployment was rising into double figures. No more did the ocean going passenger liners with their towering funnels compete with the disused soot-stained red brick chimneys of the linen mills and factories for domination of the Belfast skyline.

The RUC and Ulster Special Constabulary, since their beginnings in the early 1920s had long and continual bitter experience in having to deal with the IRA. Montgomery was remembering and reflecting on his youth as a teenager. From a hillside he and his older brother had overlooked the scene of a gun battle between an IRA unit and a 'B' Special border patrol. The engagement of muzzle-flashing guns had lasted for about fifteen minutes before the cracks of the Lee Enfield Rifle fire and the rat-a-tat-tat from the Sten submachine guns went silent on that cold December evening of 1956 some two miles from the Irish border. It had been the prelude to a major and serious republican campaign of attacks, firstly along the border areas and then deeper into the six counties with IRA units in Belfast and Derry joining in, on orders from Dublin.

The Campaign had its roots in Dublin when after the Second World War IRA and the Republican Movement had been reduced to name only. Gradually revitalised by a half-dozen or so dedicated hardcore men, the IRA spent the following decade reorganising itself. Volunteers were recruited and trained at week-end camps, while armaments were acquired from raids on police barracks and military armouries both in Ulster and mainland England. Hundreds of bolt

Another Domestic Discussion

action rifles, dozens of Sten submachine guns and Bren machine guns along with tens of thousands of rounds of matching ammunition were obtained and subsequently hidden in bunkers on farms and in isolated wooded areas. Volunteers were uniformed in an assortment of battle dress and all had been issued with the ubiquitous black beret of unity. Added to this was the explosive of the day – gelignite, used to demolish previously identified targets. Without finance, nothing could be sustained indefinitely. Irish-America obliged with a constant flow of dollars raised from sympathisers and supporters. The Campaign had been launched on that night many years ago when Montgomery and his brother had watched from a safe distance, like a pair of wide-eyed inquisitive Irish hares from behind a clump of prickly gorse. Over time the sustained attacks fragmented into spasmodic hit and run operations which lasted for six years before the leadership of the 'IRA Army Council and Executive' in Dublin called off its campaign of resistance to 'British occupation in the North.' The IRA had been beaten back by the 'B-men,' police and Army security forces but refused to concede outright defeat.[8]

The IRA was back. But it was the new terror of the indigenous 'Provos' of Ulster that was making and leading the 'cause' to end once and for all, the foreign occupation of British rule. The 'cause' would take on new meaning for another generation of volunteers with unrelenting assault on civil society and acquired new methods of mass murder.

The parked car loaded with its home-made mixture of fertiliser and diesel fuel explosive, the hold-all surreptitiously heeled beneath the seat in a packed Friday night public bar, or the extra large hand bag discarded into the waste bin of the female lavatory in a restaurant and even the Royal Mail post box; office workers catching the evening post were the enemy. All rigged with a deadly cocktail timed to reap maximum human destruction with searing ferocity. It

Operation FURY

would not only be the civilian population terrorised by the armed struggle, but would include the RUC and the British army collectively who would take the republican onslaught. The Orangemen and Loyalist paramilitaries; the UVF and emerging UDA were lumped into the melee. All would be overcome by the revitalised Republican Movement. The gathering storm of the armed struggle would rage a hurricane that would not subside until the last Brit had vacated to the mainland. The Provisional IRA pogrom of the British of Ulster was now the new 'cause.'

A cold shuddering shiver ran through Montgomery's frame. It was as though he had just emptied his bladder on a cold day and his body was adjusting to the immediate loss of inner body heat. Some twenty minutes after dropping off Peter Moore, Montgomery turned into his driveway. As his car came to a halt, it was time to wind down from the day's events. Montgomery was home. Domestic matters would occupy his evening. As he locked his car, he felt the icy chill of the evening air; his cold breath condensing in puffs of vapour into the stillness of the night. His eyes followed his breath upwards into the clear evening darkness, only relieved by the silvery points of the stars, which reminded him once again of growing up on the family farm on the outskirts of Newtownhamilton. He knew exactly where to look as he found his boyhood friend Orion with his relucent belt and sword, just visible above the flat ridge of the Holywood Hills, some distance to the south at the rear of his house. Montgomery's nostalgia was interrupted by a long low miaow, more akin to the mystical cry of the Banshee, as Clancy the family cat emerged from beneath the shrubbery to accompany Montgomery up the path, through the outer and inner porch doors and into domesticity and safety.

'Hi dad,' came the voices in unison from his two young children, Claire and Conor. 'Mum has been looking for Clancy, he hasn't been

Another Domestic Discussion

fed yet,' added Claire, as she gave him a quick kiss on the cheek.

Conor interrupted. 'Can I watch the football match on TV dad?'

'Yes, of course Conor provided you have finished your school homework before kick-off tomorrow.'

'Yes, dad, I promise. Northern Ireland is going to win and George Best will score all the goals; at least two and maybe a hat trick. What do you think, dad?'

'Scotland will be hard to beat at home at Hampton Park. Don't forget Denis Law can score goals too.'

Claire, not to be left out of the two-way conversation, chirped up, 'Well then, it's going to be a draw.'

'Aye, love,' replied Montgomery, 'perhaps you are right. We boys will settle for a draw; two goals each from Best and Law, I reckon Conor.'

'No dad. Denis Law wouldn't score any and Northern Ireland will win three nil.'

As the children disappeared upstairs, Montgomery removed his overcoat, scarf and jacket and was now entering the kitchen with Clancy in the lead.

'Hello, love. The children seem in good form.'

'Yes, James. It's Friday and no school tomorrow. How was your day? You look cold. The children have had their tea. I have made dinner for us – liver and bacon with cabbage.'

'Sounds great. I haven't eaten since lunchtime. Just a cup of tea all day.'

The conversation continued as Montgomery made his way into the dining room. 'Is there any whisky left over from Christmas?'

'Yes, I think so. Try the back of the cabinet,' replied Catherine. Unlike some of his bibulous colleagues, Montgomery did not drink much, just on social occasions. He had been cold all day and was sure that a hot whisky was the quickest way to revive himself.

'What about you, Catherine?' 'Yes OK, just a small one with some water thanks. And by the way, I had a letter from your sister in Australia, or rather we had. She says things are quite good and Michael and she have bought a house. You can read the letter later. Sounds like they made the right decision to emigrate.'

'Yes.' Nothing more was said on the subject, it could wait.

It was twenty minutes later, with little intervening conversation and both had finished their meal.

'That was good,' I enjoyed that love.'

'Yes, I am glad you enjoyed it James. Would you like anything more?'

'No, not for the moment – I'll perhaps have a cup of tea later on.

'Don't forget to read your sister's letter.' Catherine reached across and lifting the letter from the cabinet top, she handed it directly to Montgomery.

'I'll clear up and start the dishes – it's almost half past eight.'

Montgomery was on the third page of the letter when Catherine interrupted from the kitchen.

'Perhaps we should think about emigrating to Australia or even Canada.'

Montgomery did not immediately respond. He thought to himself; was Catherine being rhetorical or was she in some way more serious – planting a seed for future discussion.

'And what would I do in Australia, stuck in the outback with nothing more to do than round up and arresting a few kangaroos for sheep worrying and being referred to by the locals as 'PC Dingo,' pissing into a billabong.'

'Oh, don't be disparaging James. We are just talking. And what are you referred to here? 'Inspector Mick' [9]

'All right, Catherine, that was one time only; besides that officer was transferred to Derry. He will end up being shot by his own side if he gets in their way.'

'I'm sure you wouldn't wish that upon him,' replied Catherine.

Another Domestic Discussion

'No, I don't, I'm just sounding off.'
'I'm sorry, James, I didn't mean to upset you love.'
'I know, I know you didn't – it's just me.'
Montgomery felt he needed to change the subject. He was not in any frame of mind for a lengthy in-depth discussion on any subject.
'It has been a long day and I am just tired and a bit agitated, Catherine. And how was night duty?'
Catherine was a Staff Nurse and worked three nights a week in the casualty unit in the Royal Hospital in Belfast. Night duty suited and gave her the flexibility she felt she needed. It meant that she would arrive home early enough each morning before the children left for school and would be there when they came home in the afternoon.
It was a few seconds before Catherine answered.
'Well James, last night was a bit distressing for the staff, for everyone. Even one of the Junior Doctors was, I suppose, distracted at having to deal with the situation – the injuries.'
Catherine didn't discuss her work, only in general terms on occasions. She seemed reluctant to elaborate further.
'What situation Catherine?' prompted Montgomery.
'It was a young soldier who was killed. He had been brought into casualty last night. Did you not hear about it?'
'Yes, Sam mentioned something about a soldier having been killed in an explosion. The Army had been searching a derelict building in West Belfast. Other than that he didn't know or hear any of the details. It was just a short piece on the lunch-time news to-day.'
Catherine sat down at the dining room table and continued in a hesitant voice, 'Oh James, he was so badly injured. He was almost naked. His clothes, his uniform, were in shreds and one of his legs was completely shattered below the knee and his lower body burned. But worst of all, everything was missing – blown off. There was blood

everywhere. It was horrible. Even the Junior Doctor didn't know how to treat the injury. He hadn't experienced anything like it before, nor for that matter, have any other members of staff. The poor boy was only twenty. It was a mercy he died and never regained consciousness. Why in God's name would anyone want to do such a thing James?'

'It's just raw hatred Catherine, nothing less. I would think it's like a drug, once hooked it progresses and eats away at these people. It probably occupies their whole existence; beyond comprehension.'

'I get concerned about your safety James. It could be you some day taken to casualty, badly injured or worse.'

'Don't worry Catherine. I know what to do and what not to do. It's the Army and uniform officers that check out derelict properties, not the CID; you know that's the position.'

It was Catherine's turn to change the subject.

'Conor was talking with some of the boys in his class. He asked me why Orangemen hate Catholics.'

'And what did you tell him?'

'What could I say? I just told him I didn't think so and the other boys were exaggerating. He seemed to be satisfied and hasn't mentioned it since.'

'Yes Catherine. I think the Orangemen are pretty well fixed to the notion. He is growing up and beginning to realise what's going on. He watches the news and picks up these things. We will just leave it and if he raises it again, I will have a talk with him. What about Claire does she…?'

'No James. Claire is more concerned with her school sports and Top of the Pops. She seems quite focused and has not mentioned anything, except she would sometimes say that she hopes you will be all right at work. Its just reassurance she needs on occasions.'

'Perhaps we should think about emigrating after all Catherine.'

'Oh! James, let's leave it for the moment. Are you going to work

Another Domestic Discussion

in the morning?'

'Yes, up until lunch time. I want to be home in time to watch the football with Conor. Saturday morning is usually quiet and I need to catch up on paperwork and reports. Besides, I have a visitor across from England, landed upon me by the Chief Super. He is over for a few days to see how we do things here. He will be off back home again on Wednesday next week if I can manage to keep him out of harms way.'

Catherine didn't ask questions about her husband's job. She knew that if there was anything she needed to know that wasn't confidential, then he would tell her; when he might be home and when he wouldn't be, not much more than that. It was difficult to plan anything in advance with the children being involved. It was just his job. Endless hours of overtime while domestic affairs were usually left to Catherine.

'By the way James, I picked up your new glasses with one of the new metal cases. They are on the sideboard. Try them on and if they are not right I can have them adjusted or you can call into the opticians yourself.'

James went to the sideboard to fetch the new spectacles trying them on and adjusting them as he looked in the mirror.

'Yes, they are fine and don't seem to need any adjustment. What do you think Catherine? I'll try them out and make good use of them tomorrow reading those damn reports.'

'Yes, they look good, they suit you Inspector,' replied Catherine with a broad smile. 'It's getting late and I want to be up early tomorrow as I am going shopping. Claire needs new shoes and Conor could do with a new shirt for school.'

'OK, Catherine. You are right – it's bedtime. I'll settle Clancy in the kitchen and you go on up and warm the bed!'

3
Tit-for-Tat Killing

It was 9.30 on a normal Saturday morning in the centre of Belfast. Traffic moved more smoothly than on weekdays. The air was cool and the morning shopper had not yet emerged on to the streets. Inspector Montgomery had picked up Peter Moore from outside the Europa Hotel as had been agreed between the two men the previous evening. Montgomery had driven a short distance and was now about to turn into Grosvenor Road Police Station. Suddenly a uniformed police officer emerged through the automatically opening gates. Recognising Montgomery's car, he signalled for him to slow up and stop. A serried line of police and Army Land Rovers drove on to the Grosvenor Road, turning westwards and sped off to the accompanying tremolo of their sirens. Montgomery realised it was more than a traffic accident, more serious. Perhaps it was a suspect vehicle containing an explosive device. Unusual for a Saturday morning he thought. No need for CID to be involved. It would be left for uniform and Army bomb squad to deal with, by now normal procedure. Besides, it's more than likely to be a false alarm.

'Inspector, he is waving you in!'
'Right Peter thanks.'

Operation FURY

Montgomery had parked the car and the two men were now passing the duty Sergeant's desk.

'Good morning Sergeant. What's all the commotion? Is it a suspect car?' Montgomery asked.

'No Inspector Montgomery. I'm afraid it is more serious. Two bodies have been discovered at Springfield Petrol Station. DS Mike Neill and DC Jill Humphries, along with uniform and Army are on their way to the scene.'

Montgomery did not answer. He seemed to become distant as he moved forward to support himself at the end of the counter. The Inspector's imagination had instinctively gone into overdrive as he realised it was the same petrol station the previous afternoon where he had encountered O'Reilly and 'Butcher' Wallace. Had these two, along with their companion been planning murder? Were they involved?

'Are you all right Inspector? You seem a bit distracted,' asked Peter Moore.

Without saying a word, Montgomery nodded indicating he was all right.

'Army rang it in, Inspector,' added the Sergeant. 'I passed the information through to the Incident Room as soon as it was reported. DS Mike Neill spoke to the Army and he organised our response. As I said, he has gone off to the scene.'

'Right Sergeant, we passed him on our way in. By the way, Sergeant, this is Peter Moore. He's come across from London and will be accompanying me for the next three or four days.'

'Right Peter, let's go through to my office. If there is any further information coming in, let me know immediately Sergeant.'

'Yes, Inspector, straight away; I'll put all calls through to the Incident Room.'

With an extra step to his pace and without speaking, Montgomery

Tit-for-Tat Killing

led the way along the corridor with Peter Moore following behind. Montgomery's mind was juggling with what he had just heard and relating it to the events of the previous day. Murder, a double killing by O'Reilly and company. He was sure both incidents had a direct connection, but he was not about to get ahead of himself. He was speculating but he needed to check his thought processes or he might go off in the wrong track and waste everyone's time and effort. Still, it was a possibility. Sergeant Neill should be at the scene by now. He is a first class detective so Montgomery decided he would allow him to deal initially with the investigation at the scene.

Montgomery had entered the Incident Room and had gestured to Moore to accompany him.

'Morning Colin, the desk Sergeant has just told me of the two bodies discovered at the petrol station.'

DC Colin Roberts had just set down the telephone and turned around to acknowledge Montgomery.

'Good morning Inspector. Yes, it is serious. Army patrol discovered the bodies and Corporal Anderson who led the patrol apparently checked the deceased. There is one male and one female. The Corporal believes they have been shot. I am just off the phone with the Coroner's Office and they are sending a medical examiner straight away.'

'Fine Colin, I need you to remain here and take charge of the Incident Room and deal with all the incoming calls please. You know the procedures. Nothing to the press or media other than we are investigating an incident. Nothing more than that.'

'As you wish Inspector.'

'I know it is Saturday, but it looks like we will be here for most of the day. We will need a full team on this one Colin. See if you can contact DCs Johnstone and Meharg and tell them I require them to be on duty before lunchtime. I need you to check a car registration, the full details from the vehicle registration office and ask them to let us have a copy of everything as soon as possible'.

It was from memory that Montgomery wrote down the number on the notepad beside DC Roberts. It was the registration of the car that Wallace and his two companions had been seen driving away from the petrol station the previous afternoon.

'Right Peter, let's go through to my office. It looks like our discussions will need to wait for the meantime. I am sure you can appreciate the urgency of the situation.'

'Of course I can Inspector Montgomery, of course.'

'You heard DC Roberts. It was an Army patrol who discovered the bodies. Perhaps you can accompany me to the crime scene. Army personnel are usually a bit reluctant to open up to the RUC before they have first spoken with their own people in the Military Police. I have experienced it a few times and it is a bit like extracting teeth with eye-brow tweezers. It can take nearly a week before we receive an official report and written statements from the Army. We require on-the-spot witness accounts. It is vitally important before memories fade. Army's more concerned about Army than giving first hand accounts of incidents to the RUC. If you have any influence Peter, it is one area of concern for us in CID.'

'Yes Inspector. I take your point, but it is Army procedure. It's purely precautionary. We need to protect our men from making any statements that might suggest they have gone overboard with their actions and perhaps contributed to escalating a situation, particularly when there has been an exchange of fire.'

Montgomery said nothing. He gestured with a nod of his head – an indication that Major Moore's response was fair comment. Montgomery turned and opened the door of the cupboard in the corner of his office. Taking out two flak jackets with one hand, he stretched across his desk handing a jacket to Moore.

Tit-for-Tat Killing

'Well Peter. You will need this. Can't have you attending an incident without a body protection jacket. I trust you have your own Army issue weapon.'

'Yes Inspector, I have and I am obliged for the use of the jacket.'

'I'll let DC Roberts know we are off to the petrol station.'

It was less than ten minutes after leaving the Grosvenor Road Police Station that Montgomery and Moore drove the short distance of just under a mile and were now pulling up at the petrol station forecourt. Sergeant Sam Smith was further along the footpath persuading a group of inquisitive onlookers to move along. Uniform on their arrival had immediately closed off the forecourt with police marker tape separating it along the back line of the public footpath designating it a potential crime scene which the public and press would not cross. Both men were now standing on the footpath. On seeing them, Sergeant Smith approached.

'Sam, it sounds bad from the information I received at the police station. Two dead is it?'

'Yes Inspector. Inside the shop in a store room at the back with access through the shop. DS Neill is inside along with Dr Perry, the medical examiner who arrived about five minutes ago. It was an Army vehicle patrol led by Corporal Anderson who discovered the bodies. DC Humphries is with the Corporal and his men at the moment, probably taking statements.'

'All right Sergeant. Look, Sam, the press no doubt will be here shortly so keep them back when they arrive. Line up the Land Rovers along the inside of the cordon at the front of the forecourt. It will help close off and mask the scene from the TV cameras. Nothing for the moment to the press other than we are investigating a potential crime scene and that a statement will be issued, probably later today.'

'Yes, Inspector, I'll organise it immediately.'

Montgomery moved off in the direction of the shop but decided to have a quick word with DC Humphries who had seen the Inspector approaching.

'Morning Jill,' said Montgomery as he gestured to Peter Moore to join him. 'What can you tell me?'

'Morning Inspector. A four-man Army vehicle patrol was coming off duty and had called into the shop for cigarettes and a newspaper. Apparently it is one of the few shops in the area that will serve them. It was Corporal Anderson who discovered the two bodies. When he went into the shop, there was no one about. No staff and no other customers, just quietness as he described it. It was then that he smelled what he knew as residual gun fire so he moved to the rear area of the shop to investigate. It was in the store room that he discovered the two bodies. He checked to see if they were alive, but they were not. He believes the bodies are those of two staff members, one male and one female whom he recognises from going in and out of the shop. The Corporal then immediately radioed it into his company command who in turn rang it through to Grosvenor Road.'

'At what time did the patrol arrive here?'

'Shortly after nine o'clock. No later than a quarter past according to the Corporal.'

Peter Moore broke into the conversation. 'If I may Inspector, the Army records all times when they receive radio messages. So you can check up and be sure of the exact time Corporal Anderson arrived here at the scene.'

'Thank you, Peter, times are always important in establishing facts. DC Humphries – I'll rely on you to check up on the precise time with the Corporal's Company.'

'Yes, Inspector, it's B-Company – the Royal Scots. There is one more piece of information Inspector.'

'Yes. What is it Detective Constable?'

'We might have a suspect, suspects or potential witnesses. When

Tit-for-Tat Killing

the patrol was pulling in to the petrol station, Corporal Anderson noticed what he assumed was a customer parked at the pumps. It was the vehicle that caught his attention. A white Ford Cortina with a grey vinyl roof. His brother in Scotland has a similar car; one of those two-litre jobs which is quite fast, somewhere around 100 mph. Unfortunately the Corporal didn't get the registration number. There was no reason to. PZ something, but he's not sure.'

It was that description of the vehicle – the same Ford Cortina which Montgomery had seen yesterday with its three occupants and the PZ registration letters matched.

Montgomery interrupted. 'It was definitely a grey vinyl roof, not black?'

'Yes, Inspector. Corporal Anderson is clear on that. I'll double check with him just to be sure. He also has stated there were two men in the vehicle. A driver and a passenger seated in the back. Sorry, no descriptions. They had their backs to the Corporal. One of the rear doors was half open obviously left for a third man who had come out of the shop and got in. With that, the Cortina drove off out of the petrol station and turned left in the direction of Ballymurphy. The Corporal describes the third man as around six feet tall with dark hair, tied back in a short pony tail. The Corporal cannot be sure of his dress – dark trousers and short jacket. He thinks it's called a bomber jacket. What he did notice was that he had black shoes highly polished – just like Army squaddies would have before kit and dress inspection, he said.'

Beyond a shadow of a doubt, thought Montgomery. That was what is required by the courts in all criminal cases. In his mind there was no shadow of a doubt that it had been O'Reilly, 'Butcher' Wallace and their companion, definite suspects – all three. The Corporal's description matched. The pony tail was the incontrovertible link and the Ford Cortina. There are not too many of those with their Lotus engines roaming around Belfast. A get-away car no doubt bought with IRA money.

'Right DC Humphries, finish off taking the statements from all four Army personnel. Have the statements typed up immediately you return to the station and have Corporal Anderson and the others sign them off today. If you need to go to the Army base later, do so. Ask the Corporal to remain for the time being. I'll speak to him shortly.'

As he headed off in the direction of the shop, Inspector Montgomery began to speculate in his mind. Was it another brutal and mindless tit-for-tat sectarian killing or a robbery somehow gone wrong? It was hardly cash they were after. Takings would be minimal so early in the morning so he ruled out
robbery. Montgomery pushed open the entrance door into the shop with the back of his lower arm making sure not to transfer his fingerprints. Inside, he had a cursory look around being careful not to disturb anything. Everything had to remain as it was for examination by forensics. There was no obvious signs of a struggle or that a fight had taken place. The small shop was well stocked and nothing appeared disturbed or out of place.

'If you wouldn't mind Peter remaining here for the moment while I go through to the back; the less people milling about the better.'

'Yes, Inspector, I'll stay here.'

'Hello Sergeant Neill. It's Montgomery,' said the Inspector in a raised tone as he opened the door marked 'Staff Only' and walked down the short corridor leading to the back of the building.

'Right Inspector, we are down at the end on the left. I am with Dr Perry,' replied DS Neill as he emerged from the doorway of the store room to meet Montgomery. This was Inspector Montgomery's fifth murder case since the violence had erupted on the Falls Road in 1969

Tit-for-Tat Killing

and the third time Dr Perry had attended a crime scene which he had been involved with as the leading investigating officer.

'I have spoken to DC Humphries and she has given me the basics; two dead, one male and one female.'

'Yes, Inspector, I am just waiting for Dr Perry to complete her initial examination.'

'Right Mike, I'll go in and have a few words. Any identification yet?'

'No Inspector, none, there is a staff room up the corridor. I had a quick look about when we came in. There are two or three lockers which I will check out.'

'Yes Mike, do that now and check everything in the remainder of the rooms.'

Inspector Montgomery was now standing in the doorway of the store room. Dr Perry had just completed her initial examination and was writing up her notes. Standing in the doorway, without stepping into the store room, Inspector Montgomery looked beyond Dr Perry. The two bodies were slumped, both on their knees and bent forward resting over what looked like cardboard storage boxes. The female was lying partly across the back of what was obviously the male; lifeless human beings huddled together in death.

'Hello Dr Perry, what can you tell me?'

'Hello Inspector Montgomery. What we have are two bodies, one male and one female. The male I estimate to be in his mid-twenties. He's of average height, around 5'9" and of average build, say, ten and a half stone. The female is younger and would be no more than twenty years of age. She is of slim build, about 5'4" in height and I would estimate around seven stone in weight. Both have been shot - the likely cause of death which would have occurred almost immediately. The young man has a bullet entry wound to the occipital bone, the lower part of the back of the skull, but there is no exit wound, probably the bullet has lodged inside. The young woman - Inspector she's only a child. She reminds me of my eldest daughter.'

Dr Perry moved forward towards the young woman as if she was about to hold her – a moment of compassion. It was Montgomery who broke into Dr Perry's humanity.

'Are you all right Doctor? Take a few moments.'

'Not very professional of me Inspector, I'm fine. The young woman has also been shot through the base of the scull, just above the first cervical vertebrae and there is gun residue around the entry wound. The gun was no further than six to ten inches when fired, an execution in your terms, Inspector. There is also an exit wound to the cheek bone area which has dislodged part of it. I have recovered the bullet which I need to retain for the autopsy.'

Dr Perry handed the evidence bag containing the spent bullet to the Inspector.

'You will want to have a look at it. It is slightly deformed but a .45 I would think Inspector.'

'Yes,' replied Montgomery. 'It is,' as he handed it back. You'll let forensics have it along with the other bullet when you recover it Doctor.'

Dr Perry continued. 'From the position of the bodies, it would appear that the young man was shot first and then the young woman. Both would have been on their knees rather than standing up when killed, unless the bodies were deliberately placed in their present positions and from the blood splatter patterns I would disregard it. I need to establish which blood belongs to whom from the samples I've taken to be definite.'

'Yes Doctor. I would agree with your conclusion – deliberate executions. Have you found any empty shell casings?'

'No I can't see any; perhaps when we move the bodies. I'll take the photographs and you can do your inspection before we remove the bodies to the mortuary.'

Tit-for-Tat Killing

'Can you estimate the time of death Doctor?'

'I can provisionally Inspector. Rigor mortis has not yet occurred and with the body temperatures and ambient temperature of the room I would estimate death for both occurred around one and a half hours ago, perhaps slightly longer.'

Montgomery looked at his watch. It was 10.35. That would make it around 9.00. This fitted in with what the Corporal has stated. He must have arrived shortly after the double killing had taken place. Montgomery was now sure in his own mind who carried out the murders. The evidence, only circumstantial for the moment, was stacking up in the direction of O'Reilly and company.

'I'll move out of your way Inspector and let you observe the scene.'

DS Neill returned from along the corridor.

'I have checked all the other rooms Inspector and have found a woman's small combined purse and wallet from one of the lockers which may be of help. There is a Northern Ireland provisional driving license in the wallet section.'

'Right Mike, let's have a look.' Montgomery opened the document and read out loud. 'Patricia Hamilton,' along with the deceased's address. Montgomery moved closer and bent down to make a comparison of the photograph on the licence and the young woman.

'Perhaps, Dr Perry, you would assist and raise the young woman's head for me.'

'Yes, Inspector.'

Dr Perry moved closer and turned the young woman's head as Montgomery studied both.

'You would agree Doctor that the photograph matches the deceased?'

'Yes, I do Inspector. The provisional driving licence may well place her at somewhere over seventeen years old. From the photograph and now with a closer look, she hardly seems much older than eighteen years of age. I'm more or less finished here Inspector.'

Dr Perry completed taking her photographs.

'I'll let you have a copy of the autopsy reports as quickly as possible and we will need positive identification also from the relatives.'

'Right, Dr Perry. If you would assist me once more – I need to check the pockets of the deceased male's coat to see if there is anything that might help identify him.'

Montgomery first checked the left hand jacket pocket and found nothing. Then, with the Doctor's aid, the right hand pocket and carefully removed a packet of Park Drive cigarettes, a lighter and a few coins in loose change.

'I'll just try the inside pocket of the jacket.'

Montgomery squeezed his hand underneath between the cardboard boxes and the still warm body and pulled out a thin wallet. On opening it, he discovered two single pound notes along with one five pound note and two photographs of a young female. His girlfriend or sister perhaps, thought Montgomery. No sign of a driving licence so perhaps the deceased did not drive. The last item was an envelope folded in half. Montgomery opened it out flat and read aloud the typed name of Mr J McKenna, along with a Belfast address.

'That's north of the city, Inspector, in no-man's land, separating the Protestants and Catholics,' added DS Mike Neill.

Montgomery did not respond. He carefully replaced the envelope into the black leather wallet and returned it to the inside pocket of the deceased's jacket.

'We need forensics. They should have been here by now. Perhaps you would check up on it Mike and see what's holding them up. I assume someone at the station has informed them?'

Tit-for-Tat Killing

'I'll attend to it right away Inspector,' replied DS Neill as he walked off back along the corridor towards the shop at the front of the building.

'Well if you don't need me further Inspector Montgomery?'

'Right Dr Perry and if you have completed your initial examination of the bodies, I will see you through to the shop as I need to speak with my DS.'

4

Sniper at the Mill

There was a sudden riveting thud from the bonnet of one of the police Land Rovers – followed immediately by a deep moan that startled and froze those within earshot. WPC Carol Phillips stumbled backwards, wrenching against the half open door of the vehicle and slumped to the ground, motionless and unconscious. Corporal Anderson and Sergeant Smith had been standing talking to one another and were closest to Carol Phillips. The Corporal was first to realise what had happened and both moved to Phillips' assistance while simultaneously shouting to his men.

'Officer down – incoming gun fire – sniper, sniper, sniper!'

The alarm that all soldiers dreaded was ringing out. The men instinctively moved to cover behind the nearest vehicle as did the RUC personnel, but somewhat slower. Within seconds, rifles were sited to all points of the compass.

Uncertainty and instinctive nervousness washed over and gripped everyone. Even 'Billy' the RUC Alsatian sensed the sudden tension from his handler, PC Rodgers, as he shortened the leash to a hand grip of Billy's collar and with more than the usual firmness of instruction 'lie down, Billy, stay.' Billy had not been issued with a protective jacket. His thick shiny coat was hardly adequate against a sniper's armour-piercing bullet.

Operation FURY

'It's the mill, Corp. There's movement second floor down, fourth window from left,' shouted Private Jimmy Dunbar. 'Do we open fire Corporal?'

Private Dunbar was the best shot in 'B' Company and was coming into his own as his finger tickled the trigger of his rifle. All weapons were now trained towards the disused mill, temporary home to Paddy sniper.

'Must be all of 400 yards Corp. At best we can engage with harassing fire – we might get lucky.'

It was a serious situation and Corporal Anderson measured his response.

'Well then lads, harassing fire it is. Identify the target and harass the bastard off the face of the earth.'

'Aye, Corporal,' came the reply in unison from the squaddies, or the 'Jocks' as they liked to be known in the Scottish regiments.

Peter Moore had been standing just inside the entrance door of the petrol station shop when the situation erupted. At an opportune moment, he moved outside and was now alongside Corporal Anderson.

'More like 430 yards Corporal.'

'Beg your pardon Sir, but are you not with the RUC?'

'Yes, Corporal, but I'm not in it,' replied Major Moore as he took out his ID and discreetly showed it to the Corporal.

Corporal Anderson was somewhat taken aback. 'Right Sir, I didn't know. I thought you were a detective.'

'That's all right, Corporal. There was no reason for you to know or think otherwise. I would prefer if you kept it low key, no need to broadcast.'

'Yes Sir, I understand.'

'I'm thinking Corporal, that you might consider contacting your company command. They may be able to trap the gunman if they moved quickly.'

Sniper at the Mill

'Yes, Sir – that sounds a fair move.'

With that, the Corporal was inside the Army Land Rover and on the radio phone explaining the situation. After a few minutes, he leaned out and advised the Major.

'I have spoken to Lieutenant McKay and he is up for it. Ten minutes at most and he is sending a platoon. Should be enough for the task I reckon Major – if Paddy obliges and stays put.'

Peter Moore acknowledged the Corporal with a nod of his head and thought it would need to be closer to five minutes. In ten minutes, Paddy will be up and long gone if he has any wit.

'OK Corporal. I suggest short bursts every thirty seconds or so might help to pin him down until the platoon is at the mill. Inform the Lieutenant and ask him to let you know when he arrives. Don't want any blue on blue incidents Corporal.'

'Yes Major. Listen up lads; Company's on its way to the mill. Harassing fire every thirty to forty five seconds. Keep a sharp eye as there might be more that one sniper. 'Right Private Dunbar; on your mark.'

Silence swept the petrol station forecourt. The RUC was not equipped for such a situation. The Sterling Police Carbine was a low-velocity weapon and its accuracy fell away drastically at over a hundred yards distance. The officers at the scene could do nothing other than wait it out until the situation was resolved by 'B' Company of the Second Battalion Royal Scots.

The first bursts of automatic fire rang out - the fusillade peppering the windows and adjoining brickwork of the top two floors. Glass cracked and splintered in all directions; red cornflakes of brickwork floated in the grey dust as the torrent of bullets ricocheted off the facade. A coven of pigeons flapped violently in rage as they exited from beneath the broken black slatted roof of the abandoned mill. A cast iron rainwater pipe broke free from its rotten fixings,

Operation FURY

losing its tenuous grip it bowed outwards and unable to defy gravity, crashed to earth. There was silence once more.

Meanwhile, it was Sergeant Smith who was attending to WPC Phillips. She had regained a semi-conscious state and was in considerable pain. A bullet had struck her, shattering her wrist bone and had ploughed along the back of her lower arm. Sergeant Smith's basic first aid was inadequate and all he could do was to apply a tourniquet with his neck-tie to her arm, just above the elbow which had only a minor affect in arresting the bleeding. What was he to do? He thought. There wasn't any point in calling for an ambulance. It would be impossible for it to come into a fire-fight zone. It would only be putting the civilian crew at an unacceptable risk. There was nothing else for it. WPC Phillips needed to be taken to hospital and in a police vehicle as quickly as possible.

Montgomery was still inside the petrol station shop as he shouted to the Sergeant. 'Sam, Sam, I'll bring Dr Perry across to you. Cover fire would help Sam!'

Although more familiar with attending to the dead, Dr Perry had concluded that she had no choice other than to help. From what she could see, the WPC looked in serious trouble. Montgomery had already removed his flak jacket and at his insistence put it around the Doctor.

Private Dunbar had heard Montgomery and signalled his understanding of Montgomery's and the Doctor's intentions.

'Right lads – on my mark, a five second burst.' As the Army rifles thundered out a second volley, the noise echoed around the forecourt. Montgomery, shielding the Doctor, made a dash. Both were now alongside WPC Phillips and the Sergeant, all crouched down against the Land Rover.

Dr Perry checked to see if there were other injuries apart from Phillip's arm. There were none. Airways were clear but breathing was erratic and pulse was slow. This was only to be expected under such circumstances. The bullet had not damaged any arteries and Dr Perry applied a tight fabric bandage to ligate the bleeding from the lower arm wound, provided by one of the PCs who had brought over a first aid kit from one of the police Land Rovers.

Dr Perry turned to Sergeant Smith 'What's the WPC's name?'

'It's Carol, Carol Phillips,' replied the Sergeant and looking directly at the WPC in order to gain her attention asked, 'Carol, you are going to be all right? Your wrist is broken and you have an open wound to your arm. The bullet did not penetrate your body. We need to get you to hospital so we are going to lift you to your feet.'

'OK, Sergeant.'

'That's fine Doctor.'

With that, both the Sergeant and Montgomery raised the WPC to her feet and helped her into the back of one of the police Land Rovers.

'Inspector, I will accompany Phillips to the hospital.'

'Thank you Doctor Perry, if you are sure. There is no telling how long we will be pinned down here. The sooner she is off to the hospital the better. There is nothing more we can do for her here.'

Montgomery signalled to Corporal Anderson that the Land Rover was ready to pull out. Corporal Anderson, along with the other squaddies sighted their rifles once again towards the mill. Triggers were squeezed simultaneously as another burst of automatic covering fire rang out. The Land Rover sped out from the forecourt onto the Springfield Road and on its way to the Royal Victoria Hospital less than a mile away.

As the gunfire ceased, DS Mike Neill shouted across to Inspector Montgomery.

'Forensics are on their way Inspector. I have told them to hold off about 200 yards or so back from the petrol station and we will let me know when it's all clear.'

Operation FURY

'Right Mike. Advise the station of our current position and emphasise nothing to the press. I will speak to DC Roberts shortly, and tell him to make sure we have a full team on duty straight away.'

'What a situation Sam, but don't worry, Carol Phillips will be OK. You will need to look to the other men and keep them under cover. I suppose there is little else we can do for the moment except wait it out until Army sorts out the sniper, and gives the all clear.'

'I'll go back across to the shop and wait for forensics to arrive and have another look around to see if there is anything more that might help in the way of evidence. Whoever did this Sam, it has been deliberate. No rhyme or reason, it's just brutal murder.'

'Right Monty. Be careful.'

Inspector Montgomery was now back inside the shop; somewhat relieved in relative safety as he endeavoured to sort out the situation in his mind. As he began to slowly move about, examining anything that looked odd or suspicious, he almost tripped over a small bundle of newspapers, the early morning delivery lying against the side of the counter. It was the 'Irish News' with its informative headline that caught the Inspector's attention: *'Internment[10] Adds Volunteers to IRA Ranks.'* That's stating the obvious; bound to happen thought Montgomery - another element added to the juggernaut of irreconcilable hatred. He had taken part in the republican round-up weeks earlier and at the time had mixed feelings. It had worked in the mid-1950s, but not this time. The Irish government did not follow suit, probably fearing a back-lash within its own jurisdiction and hoped that the Troubles could be contained within the North. Well it was done and the repercussions were all too evident. Montgomery did not have the time to dwell on the headline distraction. He had two brutal murders to solve.

The double killing at the shop and the ensuing sniper attack on the Army, and police and the wounding of WPC Phillips had now become two interwoven crime scenes and this made it number three, all interconnected within the short space of less than two hours.

Montgomery's thoughts were a jumble of emotion and the mental process of working out the logistics to control and manage the aftermath of death and attempted murder on what should have been a normal Saturday morning. A lull, but no, Saturday was now just another day of the week of endless days of brutality. Verbal accounts of witnesses needed to be taken before memories were diminished by the fog of time. Physical evidence gathered, finger prints, spent cartridges, bullets and even cigarette butts lying over the forecourt. There was the military police who would insist they would collect all the spent bullet casings and match them to the numbers of live rounds fired by the individual soldiers. Everything and anything that might be useful to connect the killers to the crime scenes and assist in court convictions. Montgomery could imagine some slick defence barrister in usual attire with thumbs tucked under his lapels, confidently undulating backwards on the heels of his shoes, then slowly forwards in rhythm to the staccato delivery of his cross-examination, searching questions resonating off the hard wall surfaces in the claustrophobic Crown courtroom on the Crumlin Road in Belfast…

…well, Inspector Montgomery, you have told the court in giving your evidence that forensics matched my client's blood group, B positive, to saliva found on a cigarette butt discovered at the scene. That you, along with two other uniformed officers in the RUC have stated that you saw my client – with others – the day before the discovery of the bodies of the two young adults inside the petrol station shop on the Saturday morning,. I put it to you, Inspector Montgomery, that what you most definitely cannot say, testify to this court, is that, that particular cigarette butt was discarded on the morning of the killings, on Saturday the 9th and not on the afternoon

Operation FURY

of the previous day, Friday the 8th of March when my client was seen by you going into the petrol station shop. I am correct on that Inspector, am I not? And that you have already stated that you observed the defendant smoking when he emerged from the shop, that it was then, my client discarded the cigarette end in question on the afternoon of Friday the 8th when the defendant called to buy an evening newspaper, an early edition of the Belfast Telegraph, my Lord.

Bollocks, thought Montgomery, every piece of evidence would need to be watertight, circumstantial elements could always play negatively, the doubts introduced by skilful defence Counsel in cross-examination. Montgomery had given court evidence before in three murder trials and one attempted murder. On each of these occasions the weapon was the main piece of evidence in securing a conviction. He knew that the recovery of the gun and linking it to the killers was vital. Without it, it would be difficult to secure convictions. The case would collapse. Montgomery would need to organise teams of detectives to gather the evidence with forensics kept separate to avoid cross-contamination of possible evidence. Montgomery's mind moved to a high gear. Everything was linked; the killings and the sniper attack. The sniper just didn't happen to come along. This was a well planned and organised terrorist operation. 'Butcher' Wallace was behind it. Montgomery imagined Wallace plotting the whole thing with the added bonus of killing members of the RUC and Army for good measure on top of the two dead within the shop. There was no obvious motive for the double murder. What the Loyalists could do would be matched by the Republicans in an endless cycle of sectarian tit-for-tat homicide. Inspector Montgomery knew it was necessary to establish the perceived religion of the two victims. The tell-tale sign to someone's religion, their names, William or Liam, Elizabeth or Mary, and the spelling was the mark of Cain by the opposing sides. 'How do

Sniper at the Mill

you spell that, Shaun or Sean?' No Orangeman in his right mind would saddle his son with this name, irrespective of how it was spelt. It was always the case 'who goes there?' Protestant or Catholic. Even the tiny Jewish community of Belfast could not escape by claiming neutrality. The standard was applied with obnoxious absurdity. 'Are you a Catholic Jew or a Protestant Jew?' Well, what an awful place, thought Montgomery, but religion needed to be established. Some prior knowledge was needed when having to tell the relatives of the circumstances surrounding the death of the deceased. There were no procedures, no ground rules. It was left to the senior officer investigating the crime to break the news. Inspector Montgomery had been there before, trial and error learned on the job. And it was for him to do it again with two more families.

***

A convoy of three Saracen personnel carriers drove at top speed along the Springfield Road in the direction of the disused mill. Lieutenant McKay was in the lead vehicle. As the convoy slowed to turn into the entrance, the Lieutenant, without speaking, signalled to his driver to crash through the locked heavy metal gates and on into the mill yard at the rear. As the Saracens slowed to stop, the men were already alighting from the vehicles, deploying themselves in harmonious military precision with all weapons targeted towards the mill windows and door. Sergeant Young was directing with his enthusiastic Scottish gurgle.

'Number one squad cover the top two floors; number two the next two floors down; three squad, the bottom two. Hold your fire and listen up laddies for the Lieutenant.'

'Sir.'

'Thank you Sergeant Young. Some ten minutes ago a woman

police constable was shot by what we know is a sniper operating from this building. As you are aware men, female police officers do not carry guns. So Paddy sniper isn't much fussed about the Geneva Convention. Yellow card rules, ultimate force becomes necessary will be on my orders only.'

Lieutenant McKay was now on the radio phone and speaking to Corporal Anderson at the petrol station to advise him that the platoon was at the mill and about to enter the building. The Corporal was to withhold fire and wait for further orders.

'Right Sergeant Young; enter and search the building. Use the Saracen. No time to check, the main doors for booby trap explosives. We will take the risk!'

'Yes Sir,' replied the Sergeant as he directed number two Saracen to drive through the double entrance doors leading into the ground floor of the mill.

The Saracen thumped the large timber doors which flattened on to the mill floor pulling with them the door frame and collapsing a section of arched brickwork which in turn tumbled on to the roof of the Saracen. The vehicle came to a halt, just inside the mill.

'Squads one and two with me and be alert lads, for booby traps,' instructed Sergeant Young.

As they entered, the Sergeant was leading and simultaneously checking with every pace advanced for any sign which might disguise or conceal an explosive device. As he approached the staircase door, he noticed a thin line glinting in the sunlight beaming through a gap in one of the partly boarded-up windows. The Sergeant's thoughts were that this is no strand of a spider's web - it is a trip wire. The wire was about a foot off the floor and stretched across the doorway leading into the staircase.

As the Sergeant's eye followed the wire, he could just see that it ran behind an old plywood tea chest to the left-hand side of the door.

He cautiously approached and looked behind the top of the chest and saw the concealed device strapped to the wall, perfectly placed, if detonated, to cause maximum injury at groin level.

'Hold up laddies; stand back. We have a trip wire and an explosive device. Corporal McIntyre, advise the Lieutenant and move the men back behind the Saracen.'

'Aye Sergeant,' replied the Corporal.

Sergeant Young was about to withdraw himself when he noticed a second wire concealed and running up the edge of the door frame, across the top and attached by a small eye hook to the door. Paddy's a sleekit git, he thought; he has made the device with a double trip wire. The one at ground level is obvious and has been placed to divert away from the overhead wire. Stepping over one wire and pushing open the door would detonate the explosives. As if to relieve the tension within himself, Sergeant Young spoke aloud, 'Well Paddy my boy – not this time.' There was no way through the door without disarming the explosive and the Sergeant knew to leave well alone. He ordered the men to move back outside and as he squeezed past the Saracen, he was met face on by the Lieutenant.

'What's your assessment Sergeant? I have called in the Bomb Disposal Unit. They will be here within ten to fifteen minutes.'

'I doubt if the sniper or anyone else is still in the mill, Lieutenant. There's no possible way he could have come out through the door at the stairs. He must have used a window. There's been more than one – the sniper and perhaps one or two others to set up the booby trap.'

'Aye, Sergeant that would be my assessment also. It's the stairs' window. We will have a closer look.'

As they moved towards the window they could see that the bottom sash was open about six inches. On closer observation they saw the outline of a hand print, left in the accumulated dust on the inside sill.

'I think we will leave it for the Bomb Disposal Unit Sergeant.'

'Yes Sir – it could be linked to the explosives as well or even a separate device fitted with a timer or mercury tilt switch.'

'Indeed Sergeant. Get the men back into the Saracens just in case. I will radio through to Corporal Anderson to let him know of the current situation. Nothing else for it but to wait.'

'Aye right, Sir.'

5
One Armalite Doesn't Make a Provo War

It was mid-afternoon when Montgomery arrived back at Grosvenor Road Police Station feeling both physically exhausted and mentally drained by having to deal with the complexity of the situation. He made a quick phone call to his wife Catherine, to explain he would not be home until possibly late evening and to let Conor know that he wouldn't be back to watch the international football match on television.

Montgomery was now sitting in the canteen along with some of his fellow officers who had returned for a quick break, along with DC Roberts who he had left on his own in the Incident Room earlier that morning when the call had been received about the suspicious deaths at the petrol station. The deaths were no longer suspicious; it was a straightforward double murder investigation and Montgomery knew he needed to keep up the momentum. Apprehending O'Reilly and the others and bringing them in for questioning was first priority. Montgomery turned to DC Roberts who was sitting next to him at an adjoining table.

'Colin, have you managed to obtain the details on the vehicle registration number I gave you this morning?'

'Yes Inspector, I have. There is a file copy and I left a further copy on your office desk as I thought it might be important.'

'Yes, it is. It could be a positive lead on the case which is now being treated as a murder investigation.'

Montgomery returned to his office to find the copy left by DC Roberts on his desk and immediately started to read it. The make of the vehicle and model, Ford Cortina Lotus, 1991cc. The registered keeper of the vehicle, Patrick James O'Reilly, address, Ardvara Avenue, Belfast. Montgomery turned around to study the map on his wall. Ardvara Avenue was off the Falls Road at the edge of Ballymurphy, an area by and large under paramilitary control of the First Battalion of the Provisional IRA Belfast Brigade.[11]

Inspector Montgomery was relieved and somewhat assured that he could link the vehicle directly to O'Reilly – a positive lead and a positive suspect. But Montgomery was a bit troubled in his mind. O'Reilly lived at Woodvale, off the Crumlin Road opposite Ardoyne in North Belfast, if memory served him correctly. Perhaps he had moved. Woodvale was alongside the Protestant paramilitary enclaves of the Shankill and Glencairn, virtually surrounded. The small Catholic population had to move out of their homes nine months earlier after continuous rioting in the area – a minor gain of territory for the Protestant paramilitaries.

Montgomery decided he would bring in O'Reilly and Wallace for questioning on the double murder and would do it without delay, but he needed to plan the operation and minimise the risks of walking into another ambush. Ballymurphy was becoming a 'no-go' area for RUC patrols and Montgomery concluded he would need the Army's presence for protection – a joint operation was essential. He knew the risks of an operation of going into Ballymurphy. In and out, in less than fifteen minutes; any longer and the petrol bombers would start followed by the gunmen shooting, was to be avoided. But it would be a risk worth taking if O'Reilly and the others were apprehended. Montgomery was crossing the corridor on his way to the Incident Room when he heard the now familiar voice of Peter

One Armalite Doesn't Make a Provo War

Moore in quiet tone from the far end of the corridor.

'Is it all right to come through Inspector Montgomery? I have cleared it with the desk Sergeant.'

'Yes, Peter of course. How did you get on at the mill? Anything positive?'

The Military Police are finishing up at the scene collecting whatever evidence there is. Your Sergeant Neill, along with uniform are with them. No sign of Paddy sniper when Lieutenant McKay and his men arrived, just a booby trap device. Bomb Disposal dealt with it; a nasty piece of equipment by all accounts. Can I introduce Lieutenant McKay, Royal Scots, James, and I think you know Corporal Anderson?'

Montgomery and the Lieutenant simultaneously extended their hands.

'We have met before Inspector Montgomery, last September when I first arrived in the province.'

'Yes, indeed we have Lieutenant. It is good to see you again despite the unfortunate circumstances. Look, I am on my way into the Incident Room. Why don't you join me for a quick briefing and re-cap on the situation so far?'

The four men were now standing inside the Incident Room. Desks, chairs, filing cabinets, wall charts and the paraphernalia of a busy office along with stale cigarette smoke, all added to the claustrophobic environment.

'May I have everyone's attention please? I know it has been a horrendous day and exhausting for everybody.'

Montgomery summarised the day's events and turned to Sergeant Smith.

'How is WPC Phillips, Sam, any news on her condition?'

Sergeant Smith, having visited Carol Phillips in hospital had just returned to the station.

Operation FURY

'Thank you Inspector,' replied Sergeant Smith, nodding his head in appreciation of the Inspector asking about his officer.

'Carol Phillips as you know sustained a bullet wound to her lower arm and was taken to the Royal Victoria Hospital. The doctor attending advised that her wrist bone has been shattered and she may lose slight use of her hand. Other than that, the doctor is confident she will recover from her injuries. She is stable and was sedated when I left the hospital. Her parents were with her and as you can appreciate she cannot receive visitors for the next few days.'

'Well Sam, if I may speak for CID and perhaps all in the room, please give WPC Phillips, Carol, our very best wishes for a full recovery and we all look forward to her returning to duty in due course. Perhaps I should also mention the Royal Scots, through First Lieutenant McKay and thank them for their professionalism in dealing with the sniper attack and in particular, Corporal Anderson and his squad for their quick thinking. They undoubtedly saved further injury and loss of live at the petrol station.'

Every RUC officer in the Incident Room acknowledged their appreciation of the Royal Scots.

'If I may say a few words Inspector Montgomery?'

'Yes, go ahead Lieutenant McKay.'

'On behalf of B Company, I also wish to express our best wishes for the speedy recovery of WPC Carol Phillips. Perhaps when she is fully recovered she will honour us by accepting an invitation to be guest of honour at our Battalion dinner later this year. An Irish, or is it an Ulster Rose amongst the prickly thistles of the Royal Scots. Unfortunately the Royal Scots were unable to apprehend the gunman operating from the mill. It was TFFO[12] before we had arrived which wasn't very sporting of him.'

Inspector Montgomery thanked the Lieutenant and continued with his briefing.

One Armalite Doesn't Make a Provo War

'I'll finish off by adding that everyone knows what we still need to do. We have unfortunately been here before. There are three definite suspects, two of which have known addresses in Ballymurphy so they need to be found and brought in for questioning. I will require a full CID team in here on Monday morning at 5.30 sharp for final briefing on details of the operation. Sam, I'll speak to your Inspector. We need uniform on this and hopefully Army will provide back-up once again. As normal, full protection gear; vests and weapons, ready to go, Monday morning.'

'Can I have a confidential word with you Inspector? It's in connection with the sniper attack and if I may have Lieutenant McKay join us.'

'Yes, Peter, you and the Lieutenant can come across to my office.'

'OK, Corporal Anderson you and your men can go off duty now and get some rest and relaxation. It sounds as though you will be needed on Monday morning. Oh! by the way, well done to you and the squad. The RUC seemed pleased with your performance. Tell my driver I'll be another twenty minutes or so.'

'Yes Sir,' replied the Corporal, relieved. He and the squad had been on continuous duty for almost eighteen hours.

All three men were now seated around Montgomery's desk. Montgomery turned around opening his cupboard door and taking out two glasses along with an almost full bottle of whiskey.

'I'm sorry it's not Scotch Lieutenant, but you will have a glass of Bushmills for medicinal purposes of course.'

Both the Major and Lieutenant nodded in the affirmative.

I'll sit this one out, duty unfortunately dictates. I don't want to encourage the CID, not that they need it on occasions. The sniper Peter, you were saying...'

'Military Police retrieved an empty shell casing on the floor below the window the sniper was operating from. It is a .223 bullet so it

Operation FURY

looks probable that the Armalite Assault Rifle has arrived in Belfast and in use by the IRA. Likely the AR-15. The casing, along with the spent bullets found at the petrol station – those lodged in the Land Rover and the one found on the ground which probably hit WPC Phillips, match this calibre and are to be sent over to Army ballistics in England for full identification. We need to bring in the American authorities to advise us if the ammunition used is military or civilian issue. Without waiting for a full report to arrive on the desks of the GOC and Chief Constable, I would conclude that if the terrorists have gotten hold of these weapons, then it's a serious situation for security forces here in Ulster. As you know James, even a few dozen of this type of weapon will be a lethal addition which will add greatly to the IRA's firepower and ability to kill, as this morning's incident demonstrated.'

'Well Peter, if a police or Army patrol was caught in crossfire by those weapons it would be slaughter. Is that what you are saying?'

'Yes Inspector. I have no experience in firing the Armalite but I understand they are as good as, and in some aspects, better weapons than the SLRs[13] issued to our troops. This is the first time Army in Ulster, let alone the Lieutenant, has encountered this weapon. The Lieutenant will inform his Battalion CO immediately he returns to his base, and of course the Brigade Command at Army HQ in Lisburn will be fully briefed. James, I need you to have a word with DS Neill on this. It is important to hold this information on the Armalite confidential, kept under wraps for the time being. If the press and the public are alerted, it would cause major concern and worry to the civilian population. I am sure you can fully appreciate the seriousness of the situation. Army as usual will have to cope – and they will.'

Inspector Montgomery did not immediately respond to the Major. He was somewhat numbed by what he had just heard.

'Yes Peter. I can appreciate the problems for all concerned. I will

One Armalite Doesn't Make a Provo War

have a word with DS Neill straight away before he goes off duty. I agree it is for the GOC and CC to advise the government on what the public should be informed about, but it is bound to leak out. The Republicans will do that to encourage support and recruit more volunteers. This is Northern Ireland and when a butterfly farts in Belfast, within five seconds, half the population knows about it. The IRA strategy and their propaganda is they are set up to protect the Nationalist people against the sectarian attacks by the Protestants. Peter, the situation seems to be escalating into an all-out offensive campaign. The Republican hard men are having their way, arming for a war against the British presence and about to take on the Army in all-out guerrilla warfare. It's history beginning to repeat itself. The IRA campaign of 1956 to 1962 all over again and it will not only be Armalites from America, but dollars by the bucket load flowing from across the Atlantic.

'Yes, James, that would be my initial assessment also. The IRA is upping the game and on their terms, but we cannot be absolutely certain on that. One Armalite doesn't make a Provo war.'

'No Major, I agree, it does not. But from what you have told me about the Armalite, it could make one Provo into a formidable killing machine. It's not for me, an Inspector in CID to assess what is likely or how the terrorists intend to act in the future, that's for others. It is Special Branch you need on this Peter.

Their intelligence network of ORs and PPs[14] informers is usually sound, providing accurate information. With this new development Peter, I am sure the RUC and Army will pull together under the cooperation and orders from the GOC and CC.'

'Yes James. As you know I intend to speak to Chief Superintendent McClatchey before returning to England and this new situation of the arrival of the Armalite in Belfast will top the agenda.'

6

Operation Ballymurphy

Inspector Montgomery walked into the briefing room with an air of determination and resolve.

'Can I have every one's attention please? Firstly, I thank everyone for coming in so early on a Monday morning. My apologies to your families, but as you will appreciate, it is essential to move positively and quickly on the brutal double murder of the two young persons at the petrol station and the attempted murder of WPC Phillips. There are essentially two operations this morning at different addresses in Ballymurphy: Operation Ballymurphy A and Operation B to apprehend and bring in for questioning the two, possibly three, main suspects. Sean Wallace sometimes known as 'Butcher' Wallace and the second suspect, Patrick James O'Reilly. There is one other suspect, identity unknown, who may be at either address. It is this third suspect who can definitely be placed at the murder scene on Saturday morning at the time of the shootings. So he is our prime suspect. I believe the other two were his accomplices. Details of all three are on the board which you should by now be familiar with. Operation A team will be led by DS Neill and Sergeant Adair and B team, by me, along with Sergeant Smith. Anything you wish to add Sergeant Adair?'

Operation FURY

'Yes Inspector. I remind everyone this is IRA we are dealing with and they will probably be armed. We could be in a fire fight, so full protection gear with all weapons checked and fully loaded. If we need to carry out a search of the premises, as is likely, then stay together in twos; one to do the search and the other to provide cover. But with caution, there may be other people on the premises who may not be armed.'

'Thank you Sergeant. One additional detail; Army, under the command of Lieutenant McKay, has agreed to assist. Army will cover the rear of both premises and will be on the street watching our backs against possible sniper attack. It's absolutely essential we are in and out with the suspects under arrest in less than ten minutes. Good luck to everyone for a successful outcome and stay alert at all times. Everyone ready and in your vehicles by 6.10 sharp. Last team back, buys the tea and toast.'

It was dawn and cold as Inspector Montgomery, accompanied by WDC Humphries along with RUC uniform were at the front door of O'Reilly's address, a two-up, two-down terrace house with a back return in a seemingly endless row of Belfast red brick dwellings. Montgomery rang the door bell for the third time. No one was answering. Perhaps no one was in – still it is only just after 6.30am. If there was anyone at home, they were probably asleep as anticipated, by Montgomery when planning their early morning operation. One more ring, coupled with a generous thumping and if there was still no answer, he would need to decide on whether the door would be forcibly opened by uniform – no chance of escape by O'Reilly, the rear alleyway was covered. As Montgomery signalled for the sledge hammer to be employed, he heard the door, at last, being unlocked. The door slowly opened to reveal a young woman in her dressing gown. Momentarily dazzled by its rainbow of red, green, blue and orange colours, his eyes had focussed on a fiery dragon. Either a

Operation Ballymurphy

memento from some Hong Kong brothel, or an irresistible purchase from Belfast's Smithfield Market, thought Montgomery.

'We are looking for Patrick James O'Reilly at this known address. Is he here?'

'Do youse know what friggin' time it is? It's the middle of the bloody night so it is,' was the reply in a broad Belfast accent, supported by its peppering of idiosyncratic provincial grammatical inaccuracies.

'I'm Inspector Montgomery, RUC – not the speaking clock.'

WDC Humphries lightly nudged the Inspector's elbow. A gesture for him to perhaps temper his approach and she could take over questioning.

'I'm his sister. My brorr's done nathin.' He doesn't live here any more so he doesn't.'

'We will just come in and check if you don't mind and see for ourselves, replied WDC Humphries. We have a warrant.'

Montgomery did not wait for an invitation. He was half way along the hall closely followed by uniform who proceeded to search the house room, by room, cupboard by cupboard.

'It hardly matters if I mind, you're bloody well in and suitin' yourselves. I told you he's not here. He lives in Dublin and he went there six months ago lookin' for work. So if you want to speak to him, yousins will have to go down there, so ya will.'

'And at what address in Dublin will he be found Miss O'Reilly?'

'I don't know. He doesn't bother us much. He tells us nothin what he does.'

'You say 'us,' Miss O'Reilly, is there anyone else living in the house?'

'Aye, me ma and da live here, it's their house. There in England visiting me ma's sister. I suppose yous'll want to speak to themins as well?'

'No, not for the moment; we don't need to. It's your brother we need to speak to.'

Montgomery broke in and took over the questioning. 'Well Miss O'Reilly – is it Miss, you're not married?'

'No, and what business is that of yours?'

'Well, Miss O'Reilly. Your brother Patrick was seen last week, last Friday in Belfast. Unless he has a twin brother,' added Montgomery sarcastically. And you are telling me he didn't bother to call and see you or his parents?'

There were a few seconds of silence before Miss O'Reilly responded. This time in a more measured tone. It was obvious to Montgomery she was thinking through her answer.

'Aye, he called in on Friday mornin' up from Dublin to buy car parts or somethin' to do with cars. He was only here for about half an hour and said he was in a bit of a hurry as he wanted to be back in Dublin that night. That's all I know. Nothin' else.'

'That's right; your brother's a motor mechanic. Does he still drive his white Ford Cortina?'

'Aye, he had it with him and a friend who didn't come in; he sat in the car.'

'Do you know your brother's friend, Miss O'Reilly?'

'No, I never seen him before, so I haven't. I think he must be from Dublin. Paddy said his name was Red Tom Ryan I think he said. He just sat in the car so he did.'

'Sounds like a nick-name 'Red Tom.' I suppose he had red hair?' asked Montgomery with a casual flair.

'No. I only seen him when Paddy was leavin.' I can't remember. I think it was black, tied back in one of those pony tails just like that American singer on TV.'

'Oh right. I know the one you mean – P J Proby on Top of the Pops.'

Operation Ballymurphy

'Aye him, J P Proby or whatever he's called.'

Sergeant Sam Smith was leaning against the balustrade at the top landing of the stairs, overseeing the search. There was no sign of anyone else in the house, as his men exiting in turn from each room shook their heads in the negative.

'Right, that's it, O'Reilly's not here,' said Sergeant Smith to his men as he turned to descend the stairs.

'Sarg, we haven't checked the attic,' replied one of the Constables.

'Aye you are right, Constable Irvine. He might be up there, holed up like the rat that he is, waiting for us to push off. Well, let's sniff about a bit more then.'

Constable Irvine went into the back bedroom, brought out a chair and placed it directly beneath the trap door in the ceiling. No one moved to perform the obvious, while all eyes rested on the Sergeant.

'This is a job for Billy,' leaning over the balustrade and shouting down 'bring up the dog PC Rogers. We have a job for him.'

In less than thirty seconds, Billy was standing on the upper landing with obvious alertness as he sensed his services were required. His handler, PC Rogers, removed Billy's lease and turned to the Sergeant.

'If O'Reilly is up there Sergeant, then he probably has a gun.'

'Yes Constable, you might be right. It's either the dog or one of us. I am not asking for volunteers, we will use the dog, PC Rogers. Wait a minute and let me see first.'

Sergeant Smith stepped up on to a chair. Stretching up, and with both hands, eased open the trap door, sliding it across into the attic.

'O'Reilly, this is the RUC. We need to have a few words with you. If you are up there, you will have to come down. There is no way you can escape and if you have a weapon, leave it and come down.'

Every one held his breath, waiting for some response to filter down through the square black hole in the ceiling - none came.

Operation FURY

'O'Reilly, we are sending up the Alsatian to escort you down. Billy's a big brute with a jaw grip like a ship yard vice, so it's up to you. If you have a gun and shoot the dog, then we will return fire with lethal force; make no mistake about that O'Reilly.'

There was another half minute of silence as everyone waited. No movement or sound came from the attic.

'Right Constable Rogers, give Billy his head.'

PC Rogers placed one knee on to the seat, steadied himself with both hands, gripping the back of the chair as he bent forward to brace himself in anticipation of taking the dog's full weight.

'Billy, come on boy, up you go,' came the firm command from PC Rogers.

The five stone Alsatian, leapt on to his handler's back, springing upwards in one continuous flowing movement and disappeared into the darkness of the roof-space. Billy would not be cowed by the muzzle flash of gunfire; he would do his duty. It was a good minute before PC Rogers switched on his torch, directing it upwards as he stepped onto the seat; startled as the beam of light reflected from Billy's yellow-green eyes as if a demon had suddenly immerged from the blackness.

PC Rogers felt a light thump on his shoulder. 'What the hell was that?'

'It's only a dead pigeon Constable. Did you not feed the animal this morning?' replied Sergeant Smith, while the rest of the men reacted with muffled sniggers in collective relief.

'OK Inspector, it's clear up hear. We have checked all the rooms, under the beds and the attic. No sign or anything to suggest he's been here.'

'OK, Miss O'Reilly. We need to interview your brother on an incident and eliminate him from our enquiries. If he happens to get in touch, you'll let us know at Grosvenor Road Police Station. Sorry to trouble you so early in the morning.'

Operation Ballymurphy

'Aye, I'm sure you bloody well are.'

Montgomery may not have been able to apprehend O'Reilly, but he did get unexpected information. The black hair tied back in a pony tail matched the description of the prime suspect, O'Reilly's companion – a name - Red Tom Ryan. It was another lead; another piece of the jigsaw added to the picture of gathering evidence. It was odd that O'Reilly's sister did not ask why he was wanted. Montgomery was fairly sure O'Reilly's sister didn't know or have any information on his activities and her answers to the questions were straightforward. There was nothing in her demeanour to suggest she was being evasive; just upset at having been awakened by the RUC so early in the morning and having to answer questions on the whereabouts of her brother.

'Right Sergeant Smith that's it. Back to the vehicles and return to the station for tea and toast and a bowl of dog biscuits for Billy.'

On the way back to the police station, Montgomery realised that the possibility of apprehending the suspects was diminishing by the hour. Unless DS Neill had a positive result in arresting Sean Wallace at his address, then it was most likely that the suspect trio had escaped over the border to a safe-house. Montgomery, with a forlorn sigh, realised the double murder would, for the immediate future, remain unsolved. There was now only one avenue open to pursuing the suspects. Montgomery would issue their details and ask An Garda Síochána to assist in their apprehension. But he knew from past experience that cooperation would be limited – piecemeal at best. It was an hour later when Montgomery had returned to the station that DS Neill came into the Inspector's office. The expression on the Sergeant's face reflected his obvious disappointment.

'Sorry, Inspector, we were too late. There was no one at the address but all signs led me to believe someone had been there recently. Whoever it was had left in a hurry. Unwashed dishes were on the kitchen table and an ashtray crammed with butts. The most telling item was a copy of the Belfast Telegraph with Friday's date. I called in forensics and went over what we needed; fingerprints of everything and the cigarette butts for saliva tests to establish blood groups. They raised a few moans when I asked for fingerprints on the newspaper.'

'That's good work Mike. Hopefully forensics can help establish who was at Wallace's address. I had no luck either. O'Reilly wasn't there but his sister was. On questioning her she stated that O'Reilly and a friend had visited her from Dublin on Friday morning. She unwittingly gave the name of the friend as Red Tom Ryan. What is positive is the sister's description of him with the distinctive ponytail, fits our third suspect. Not a name I know, so we will need to check the files to see if his turns up. Ask uniform for me Mike. They might know him. Red Tom could be a nickname. I am sure she knows nothing about the murders although I didn't question her too closely. I'm afraid Mike, the only conclusion we can reach is all three suspects have escaped over the border.'

'Yes Inspector, I would agree that's more than likely.'

'Nothing for it then, we will need the assistance of An Garda Síochána. If the suspects are in the Republic then we will have the whole process of trying to have them extradited[15]. How in God's name could any court treat these murders as politically motivated? First things first Sergeant, we will wait and see what forensics come up with.'

7
Feud

Charlie Goyle, IRA Chief of Staff, had agonised for months over what to do, in order to recover his waning influence over socialist republicanism.[16] Goyle reflected that it had been Jack Lynch who had attempted to take charge and placate those rattling their shillelaghs inside his government, with his RTÉ broadcast in August, on the 13th of all dates. His words still ringing in Goyle's ears...*the Irish government can no longer stand by and see innocent people injured and perhaps worse...that the re-unification of the national territory can provide the only permanent solution for the problem...* It was these words that not only sent the Belfast Orangemen incandescent with rage with their banner 'war cry,' *No surrender and not an inch to the Fenian Lynch*. For the idiot leprechaun Lynch had no wit. His words had sharpened the chisel that instantly re-engraved the armed struggle and breathed life into the emerging Belfast Provo warrior with a new idolatry for the Nationalist people to bow to and pray in homage. There were also rumours filtering out from Leinster House that senior figures within the Fianna Fail government[17] had taken an active interest in the deteriorating situation in the north; primarily to provide practical assistance in the defence of the Nationalist communities.

Goyle was equally peeved; money from the Irish government[18]

Operation FURY

for social relief of the Catholics in their Belfast enclaves had found its way into the hands of dubious elements operating out of Ballymurphy. Too much money had disappeared, filtered off by this new breed of infantile warlords whose only purpose was armed rebellion, void of any political strategy. Goyle was deeply suspicious, and with good reason that the money was to be used to purchase and bring arms from US sympathisers who had willingly assisted in previous campaigns. There was loose talk circulating on both sides of the border that guns, ammunition and gelignite had already arrived in Ireland from Irish- America; a first shipment with more to follow. He was not convinced by rumour.

Goyle had wrongly believed that the level of insurrection could not be sustained and would eventually subside. Through lack of manpower the RUC had lost control and despite the British army becoming involved, the Protestant working class of Belfast had nevertheless been drawn in, driven by their sectarian bigotry. Poorly organised, the Protestants were determined to confront the IRA at every opportunity, almost on a nightly basis of attack and counter-attack with varying levels of intensity. Goyle could see that any chance of involving and bringing the working class Protestants under his socialist revolution was diminishing by the week. He needed a counter strategy to subdue and eliminate the northern republican hot-heads from leading the Catholics into a civil war.

Goyle was acutely aware he needed to replenish the IRA's arsenal and acquire modern weapons. This would demonstrate to those in the wider Republican Movement that he had international support for the revolutionary struggle. His close associates within the Irish Communist Party had agreed to make contact with the Kremlin requesting, assistance of the most practical nature. An inventory of arms and munitions had made its way to the KGB by the Soviet Navy. As part of his counter measures to regain the political high ground, he had drawn up a list of around a dozen names of the gormless hot-heads as he had labelled them; those who had by some good fortune of fate, avoided internment in August 1971. His aim was to allow this list to make its way into the hands of RUC Special Branch, hoping for their subsequent arrest and imprisonment. This would remove them from the sphere of influence and ultimately he hoped to persuade the remaining volunteers to join his pathway to a united socialist and free Ireland. Suspicion, competing rivalry and simmering resentment had built up. Charlie Goyle believed that he was being sidelined by the northerners and was becoming irrelevant to the cause now sustained by continuous violence that would escalate through the barrel of the Armalite.

A meeting had been arranged between Goyle, along with his second in command from Dublin and Sean McMurray, the Officials' IRA Commander in Belfast. It was at a safe house in a cul-de-sac, off the lower Falls Road in Belfast, that the three leaders met to discuss the situation. The meeting got underway as the BBC Nine O'Clock News ended. As Goyle began to speak, a deafening crack from an explosion rang out. Glass from the windows catapulted in all directions in deadly razor sharp splinters. A rush of searing hot gas pressurised the small makeshift committee room at the return of the so-called 'safe house.' The ceiling hogged and split apart, relieving the pressure. The back wall next to the laneway had taken most of the thundering force but it did not collapse. There was no further sound as the thick choking fog of dust hovered in the warm oxygen-depleted air. All three occupants had been spun towards the opposite wall by the explosion; like rag dolls tossed away by an unruly child in a temper tantrum. All had survived, but ear drums thumped with pulsating pain and exposed skin had instantly blistered; spasms of shooting pain eased and gave way to disorientation. Jimmy 'Hard Ass' O'Hagan, Goyle's one man protection squad, look-out and driver, had burst through the front entrance door into the choking atmosphere. Fumbling along the narrow corridor making his way to his injured comrades, O'Hagan helped Goyle steady himself and along with the other two assisting each other, they managed to make their way out and into their car. Still coughing from the choking environment, all three had a large swig from a half bottle of whiskey that O'Hagan produced from his inside jacket pocket. The car drove off down the cul-de-sac on to the lower Falls Road minutes ahead of the arrival of a joint Army and police patrol on its way to investigate the scene of the explosion. First aid would be carried out on the move; on the road to Newry where all four would cross the border to relative safety. There, the injured would seek medical treatment under the pretext of having been involved in a road traffic accident north of the border. Even a first-year medical student would not be persuaded by such feeble deceit, but it would do. Injuries required proper attention and that is what mattered. If need be, O'Hagan would offer a suggestion of silent persuasion for treatment by opening his jacket to expose the butt of a 45 revolver - always guaranteed to induce compliance.

It was late afternoon the following day when Official Sinn Fein in Dublin issued a statement in response to questions from press and television journalists. In reply they had been made aware of an explosion at property owned by one of their members from Belfast. The member, they were informed, has been in Dublin over the past week visiting and staying with relatives. They had no knowledge of who had been responsible for the bombing. They understood there were unconfirmed reports by the security forces in the North that the device had been abandoned by the Provisionals whilst in transit. This fabrication by the Officials had two purposes. There were no reported causalities so any suggestion of a secret meeting would be treated as ridiculous, but more importantly it gave the impression the Provos had been involved to some degree. Nothing could be proved or disproved. It was only necessary to confuse and dilute the truth. The following day the Provos responded by denying involvement in abandoning the bomb and they passed the blame on to the Protestant Ulster Volunteer Force (UVF) who were happy to take credit for an attack on the Official IRA. But Charlie Goyle was not buying it. How could the UVF have known about the meeting unless the Provos had found out and tipped them off? If the Provos were in cahoots with the UVF, then retribution would follow to show there was no weakness on the part of the Goyle's leadership. He suspected Sean 'Butcher' Wallace as having a hand in it. Both men had disagreed at times in the past and there was animosity between them. The warring feud within the Republican Movement had begun in earnest between the Officials and Provisionals.

While Goyle was recovering from his injuries, he decided to find out the truth and a plan was hatched involving his wife's nephew, Red Tom. Red Tom who had met Patrick O'Reilly at a Sinn Fein rally in Dublin became friendly and it was O'Reilly who would be persuaded to accompany him to Belfast under the pretence that Red Tom wanted to offer his services and join the Belfast Provisionals because the Officials had no useful strategy. Sean 'Butcher' Wallace who was at the top of Goyle's list of hot-heads had gained his reputation as one of the hard men of republicanism at the outbreak of the Troubles. His natural abilities in tactics in repelling the Protestant mobs in the early days of rioting, along with organising and leading nightly attacks on the over-stretched RUC, gave him prominence well above lesser mortals. He was now second-in-command of the Provisional IRA Battalion in Ballymurphy. Nothing could be carried out, either defensive or offensive, without his approval. It was Wallace who personally organised and supervised the erection of the barricades throughout the Catholic Ballymurphy and upper Falls areas to the west of the city after his own home had been petrol-bombed in the riots at Woodvale and he was forced to move out.

Operation FURY

It had been six weeks since the bomb attack. Goyle had put together his plan, hoping to discover if the Provos had been behind the murder attempt on himself and his comrades. He was convinced that 'Butcher' Wallace had organised the whole operation. If it proved that the UVF were involved, then for every action there needed to be an equal reaction with the force of the gun and Red Tom pulling the trigger for revenge. The Republican feud had begun with lethal intent.

It was a cold winter's day when O'Reilly and Red Tom had driven the hundred miles from Dublin. By late afternoon they had made contact with the Ballymurphy Provos and arranged to meet Wallace the following afternoon at the Irish Rover pub on the Falls Road. Wallace had made discreet enquiries from a few trusted contacts in Dublin about Red Tom. It was his reputation as a marksman that persuaded O'Reilly to meet both men - Red Tom could light a match at 300 yards distance with a rifle bullet - a fanciful claim of course. It was the exaggerated reputation that separated the capable from the novice. But could he kill a man? An RUC bastard at half that distance? That was what 'Butcher' Wallace needed to know. The Provos had their assortment of willing gunmen, most learning on the job. One hit out of ten was not a good score - the Provisional IRA needed professionals and Red Tom by reputation, sounded the ideal volunteer. Wallace knew O'Reilly from the early days of the riots and knew him as a reliable foot soldier. It was Red Tom Ryan and his absolute commitment to the Provos that he needed to be sure of.

* * *

Red Tom was in no frame of mind to engage in conversation. What had been done was over. An end in itself that only twenty minutes earlier had resulted in two more deaths; the brutal slaughter of two young people at the shop who had no involvement with any paramilitary groups or engaged in anything remotely that could be considered terrorist activities. Sean 'Butcher' Wallace had casually devised the gruesome double murder to satisfy himself and prove that O'Reilly and Red Tom were totally committed. Two innocent victims, easy prey for the gunmen with their sanguinary thuggery, was the new mania added to the armed struggle. Later in the day Wallace would issue a statement to the press that the Provisional IRA had nothing whatever to do with the shooting and would encourage the word on the street that it had been the work of the Official IRA engaged in another killing. It would be the reaction by Red Tom and O'Reilly to his manipulation that would indicate their commitment, or otherwise, to the Provos.

O'Reilly was driving somewhat nervously along the Falls Road on the way to the Irish Rover pub. The other two men were calmly seated in the rear. In a few minutes they would be out of sight and safe. No-one had spoken since leaving the petrol station forecourt. Red Tom leaned forward and breaking the silence insisted O'Reilly drove him to the railway station. There was no disagreement from Wallace. Red Tom had no intention of being confined to some Provo safe-house in Ballymurphy for the next two or three weeks. There was the risk that some RUC tout would say something out of turn and the RUC would get lucky and locate the hide-out. Red Tom had calculated he could catch the mid-day intercity train to Dublin and be there by mid-afternoon – safe and in the clear from RUC activities. O'Reilly and Wallace could decide for themselves if they wanted to join him south of the border, or lie low in the north for weeks on end until the police had eased up on their investigation. Ryan was upset that he had no say in what had taken place. He resented his involvement being taken for granted. It would not happen again.

8
Another Possible Lead

It had been almost five months since the double murder and sniper attack at the petrol station on the Springfield Road. James Montgomery had been promoted to Chief Inspector and was now operating from Police Headquarters at Brooklyn, Knock in East Belfast. He headed up a new section – a small team of detectives whose main area of responsibility was to gather and co-ordinate information of attempted murder and murder carried out by the paramilitary terrorist groups operating within the greater Belfast area.

A new coordination group had been set up between the Army and RUC known as the Joint Intelligence Co-ordination and Operations Group. Major Peter Moore was now responsible for Army Intelligence Armed Forces Unit (AFU) in Northern Ireland. It had been long overdue that such a group was essential. Confusion had arisen on a number of occasions when both Army and RUC had mounted separate covert operations on the same terrorist factions and individuals. This earlier lack of understanding of who was doing what was inefficient. Sooner or later it would lead to security personnel being compromised and worse still, being killed. Ground rules needed to be agreed and put into place. It was also important to establish and coordinate all operations.

Operation FURY

It was established that Army Intelligence, along with MI6 when necessary, would lead and deal with matters relating to Republican paramilitaries, while RUC Special Branch and MI5 would have responsibility for dealing with the activities of the various Loyalist groups. The role of CID would not change from normal crime detection and evidence gathering for court prosecutions. The RUC had also realised that the terrorists had become better organised and that they too needed to keep up and if possible move ahead. The RUC was building up a picture of what the individual groups, both Republican and Loyalist, were capable of in the use of guns and explosives.

The new section of CID led by Chief Inspector Montgomery fed its information into Special Branch and this in turn gave the RUC a better assessment for counter-terrorism measures on covert operations in running surveillance teams and the difficult task of organising informants and agents. This was mostly a paper work exercise, but important. Montgomery was no longer investigating crime; he was gathering intelligence - a conduit between CID and Special Branch. It gave Montgomery the freedom to visit the various CID teams of the police stations in the Belfast Area Divisional Command.

Chief Inspector Montgomery was at his desk scrutinising evidence files when the telephone rang.

'Hello, Montgomery here.'

'Chief Inspector, there's a Peter Moore from London ringing, can you take the call?'

'Yes, Constable, put him through.'

Montgomery had not seen or spoken with Peter Moore for nearly two months and that was only briefly after both had attended a meeting at RUC Headquarters at which it had been confirmed that Montgomery was to head up the new section. Naturally he was curious why Moore was ringing.

'Hello Peter. How are you?'

Another Possible Lead

'I'm fine James. Still in the land of the living and keeping my head down; I trust you are doing the same?'

'Yes, Peter – just the usual unending paperwork at the moment. What can I do for you?'

'It may be more of what I can do for you Chief Inspector. The incident earlier this year at the petrol station with the two young people murdered. I have been going through, let's say, an unrelated tracing exercise with one of my colleagues and some rather odd details in our records came to light.'

'Yes, I am listening Peter. Go ahead.'

'Do you do crosswords Chief Inspector?'

'No Peter. It's just more paperwork as I see it.'

'Well, James. It's 'Red Tom.' Nothing to do with Mr Marx or communism. How can I put it? As the crossword clues would have it; it's an anagram – a man's name.'

Montgomery interrupted. 'Yes, Peter – that's obvious.'

'No James. You are not seeing it. Write it down in reverse; 'Tom Red' and read it as the Arabs do, from right to left.'

'Yes, Peter of course. It's Dermot – 'Red Tom' – it's a nickname or a cover name. What do you think?'

'Well James, from what we have, it's a nickname or both.'

'It sounds as if it could be a lead. Can you let me have a copy of what you have on record, Peter?'

There was a moment of silence before Peter Moore responded.

'Unfortunately I can't James. The file is classified – red tagged in our jargon. But look James I'm back in Belfast at the end of the week and I can talk to you unofficially and give you some more guidance. That's the best I can do. A chat out of hours perhaps would suit.'

'OK Peter. Will you contact me?'

'Yes, James, on Friday; I am staying out of town at the Crawfordsburn Inn and suggest Friday night.'

Operation FURY

'That suits me. I know the Inn. Sounds ideal and I'll wait to hear from you on Friday Peter.'

'Yes, I'll ring you Friday afternoon. Goodbye James.'

With that, Montgomery set down the phone.

It was clammy and hotter than usual for early evening; absent of any breeze that could cool the skin as Montgomery stepped out of his car. He had pulled up in the car park at the shady side of the Crawfordsburn Inn, situated less than a mile to the south side of Belfast Lough. Peter Moore had agreed to meet Montgomery at the Inn, located in the small and affluent village of Crawfordsburn, two miles off the main road leading from Belfast to the seaside town of Bangor. Montgomery quickly adjusted his jacket to conceal his firearm as he walked towards the main entrance. From his elevated position, he could just see over the distant tree line, the Isle of Man Ferry making full speed, shortly to round the Copeland Island at the mouth of the Lough and out of sight into the Irish Sea. It must be all of fifteen years since he visited the Manx holiday island with Catherine, shortly after they were married – quieter times he thought. The Scottish coast formed the backdrop and was quite visible in its gently undulating grey silhouette, floating on the sea and only broken by the Ailsa Craig rock, rising up like the conning tower of a nuclear submarine having left its naval base on the Clyde and on course to its secret mission into the depths of the northern waters of the Atlantic Ocean.

As Montgomery reached the Inn entrance, opposite the Orange Hall on the far side of the narrow Main Street, two couples tumbled out onto the footpath causing him to side step, allowing them to pass in their obvious high spirits and into a waiting taxi. Guests at a wedding party perhaps or office workers who had left Belfast by mid-afternoon to avoid being caught up in the chaos caused by the 'Friday bombers' and the ensuing evening of orchestrated rioting that

Another Possible Lead

usually followed in the numerous side streets surrounding the inner city in another now familiar weekend of spasmodic violence.

'Hello James how are you? It's good to see you again.'

Peter Moore had been sitting reading the evening newspaper in the lobby, waiting for his guest and now friend to arrive.

'Hello Peter. I am fine, except for this damned heat. I could do with a cool beer.'

'Certainly James. We can go through to the lounge bar. I'll lead the way and perhaps afterwards we can take a stroll along the shore and talk.' Moore lowered his voice away from listening ears.

'I have a great deal to tell you, unofficially of course as I mentioned on the phone.'

It was half an hour or so later when both men crossed the wooden foot-bridge leading over the stream to the path skirting along the shore. Montgomery was intrigued to know what Moore was anxious to tell him.

'Peter – it's Red Tom. You think you know his identity?'

'Yes, James. He's a bit of an enigma and of serious concern for all involved, Army and police alike.'

'Red Tom' whom we believe is in fact Dermot Patrick Ryan, a former British soldier, trained by us in the skills of marksmanship and covert techniques. In other words, a highly proficient sniper. Ryan was a first class soldier and reached the rank of Sergeant. What I am about to tell you and explain James, is five star top secret. Official Secrets Act, you understand.'

Montgomery nodded without adding comment. Peter Moore in his opening remarks had gained his full attention.

'Well. Dermot Ryan has met with – of all people – a Klaus Wolfe of the East German Stasi. For what purpose we do not altogether know. We have some ideas, only theories; nothing that can be firmed up as fact. What we do know, Klaus Wolfe, according to MI6 is an

Operation FURY

agent for the Soviet KGB. It was the Swedish Intelligence Service who first alerted MI6 to his existence. Wolfe was a Lieutenant in the Waffen-SS and in 1943 transferred to the Geheime Staatspolizei – the Gestapo secret state police. He was an undercover officer or one of the V-men as they were known who moved in German high society looking for anyone opposed to Herr Hitler. Wolfe was stationed at the Reich Security Headquarters and was captured as the Soviet Red Army entered Berlin. Why he wasn't executed is conjecture. Probably he turned on his countrymen and became quite valuable to the Russians as they purged East Germany of all dissidents and resistance to Uncle Joe Stalin's megalomania.

Before he transferred to the Gestapo, Wolfe was in the *'Nordland'* Waffen-SS Division which consisted of Scandinavian volunteers and some conscripts. He was attached to Regiment 23 Norge, mainly Swedes Norwegians and a few Dutch. His mother was Swedish and his father, a German Naval officer. We know all this due to the Germans' obsession for keeping records. It was to prove the downfall of many of the German military and Nazis in evidence presented at the Nuremburg Trials. The British Military Police had acquired his SS file but his name never appeared on any of the lists of German personnel brought before the Nuremburg Court and he was forgotten, but his file remains. So we were somewhat surprised when the FSI, the Swedish Military Intelligence brought him to MI6 attention, nearly thirty years later. It was their records of him that set the alarm bells ringing.

According to the Swedes, in 1950 Wolfe joined and helped to set up the East German Stasi secret police. Then in 1957 Wolfe headed up the HVA, its Foreign Intelligence Section which included Scandinavian countries. No doubt with the complete approval of the Russian KGB. Sweden is not a member of NATO but they do on occasions cooperate. The Swedes are well aware that neutrality is no

Another Possible Lead

guarantee against invasion. The military strategists in the MoD devise and develop war game scenarios involving both conventional and nuclear attacks by the Soviets and their Eastern Bloc allies. If Sweden, on its own, was overrun by the Soviets in an all-out invasion attack then it would have serious implications for NATO. The Soviet Baltic Fleet would have almost free access to the Atlantic. This coupled with the Soviet Northern Fleet would constitute a massive armada. The UK could become the next target. Royal Navy would be overwhelmed. The Americans, the Canadians, all the other member countries would have no option but to honour the Alliance. Even the French after discussing it over a two-day lunch would conclude they had to commit - a full-scale conventional engagement leading to probable nuclear war and the ensuing annihilation of the Northern Hemisphere. It's only war games, but still…

So James, you can grasp he is potentially a serious threat. His arrival in Ireland via the UK has caused major concern.

Colonel Wolfe arrived in Sweden from East Germany four weeks ago, apparently on a business trip. He then left from Gothenburg on the weekly ferry to Newcastle-upon-Tyne, using a false Swedish passport. The Swedish Military Intelligence and Security Service which is highly efficient and always suspicious had tailed him from his first arrival on Swedish soil. The Swedes advised the British Embassy of his movements and that he had booked passage to the UK. MI6's man immediately passed on the intelligence to London. In a hurriedly put together covert surveillance operation, MI6 tailed Wolfe from his arrival at Newcastle from where he caught the train for Carlisle and travelled down to Heysham. There, he had an overnight stay and the following day took the ferry to Belfast.

That's when we were brought in and asked to help out. Not to put too fine a point on it, when MI6 surveillance team realised his next destination was Belfast, they shit a brick and panic set in. Six had

Operation FURY

no people in Belfast who could carry out surveillance and above all, they did not want to lose him in the murk of Northern Ireland. They asked us for assistance as we knew the local scene. Army Intelligence immediately agreed to take over. I might add James, that RUC was not, and to date has not been informed of any aspect of the surveillance operation. Six insisted the RUC was to be left out and kept in the dark.'

Montgomery was now beginning to feel he was being sucked into a black hole and for no obvious reason. He interrupted with the obvious.

'Peter, why are you telling me all this when the RUC is unaware of the situation? Surely MI6 should have asked for some help from RUC Special Branch or at least told them of the surveillance operation.'

Peter responded in stark tone. 'James; it's the international elements - the East German Stasi and Russian KGB. I doubt there is anyone in the RUC Special Branch who would have any experience in these matters. Besides, there was no time to give a comprehensive brief, let alone to get clearance for the RUC to be involved. MI6 like to keep operations in-house. I don't think Six has even told MI5 about Wolfe. That is a matter for them. On rare occasions, there is the need for joint cooperation between Army Intelligence and the Secret Intelligence Service when operations are mounted in Europe. So I assume Six felt Army would be better tasked than RUC. The key and link to all of this is Red Tom. That's why I am bringing you in James. Bear with me for a little longer.

Army Intelligence had less than eight hours to organise our people in Belfast. The time it takes for the Heysham ferry to travel to Belfast. Well, we just about managed it. We took over the moment Wolfe was spotted stepping off the ferry. He made his way to the Midland Railway Station, caught the train and was in Londonderry by

Another Possible Lead

lunchtime. We had at this stage, no idea why Wolfe had arrived in Ulster. Was it on speculation or pre-arranged to make contact with Loyalist or Republican? We did not have long to wait until he showed his hand and we began to put the first pieces of the jigsaw on the tray.

Wolfe was met at the station by two males and one female and all four drove off with our people following at a discreet distance in a taxi. The taxi driver became a bit reluctant but it was only when the team offered to triple the fare and suggested that if he didn't cooperate, then he would receive a late night visit from the local Provos. It worked and he complied. Fortunately for our surveillance team, Wolfe and his friends went to a local hotel. It was late afternoon when the three left and drove off. Wolfe had obviously checked in. Meanwhile, one of our lads had gone off and organised an undercover vehicle from the local Army unit. The decision was made that as Wolfe was their primary target, they would not follow his contacts. Our lads managed to take a number of photographs of the three as they left the hotel.

The next morning, Wolfe was picked up at the hotel by the unidentified female. No sign of the other unidentified male contacts. Wolfe was driven off and the car crossed the border into Donegal followed by our surveillance team. Our people are not permitted to cross into the Republic of Ireland without prior permission and the GOC is made aware of any situation. They realised the importance of their operation and decided to continue to follow.

About half a mile south of the village of Moville, Wolfe's car pulled into a cottage overlooking Lough Foyle. The team decided to drive on past as they didn't want to be sussed. A few miles beyond Moville they turned and came back along the road. As they passed the cottage again a second car had just arrived with the two other unidentified males. They continued back to Londonderry and contacted their senior officer for further orders. It was decided that it was too risky to mount surveillance at the cottage. So Army border check point was given the vehicle registration numbers and told to immediately advise us if and when they crossed through the check-point and back into Northern Ireland.

It was six days ago when their surveillance report along with the photographs, landed on my desk. We have since identified two of the three. The female, we don't know her. Of the males, one is definitely Michael 'Bumpy' Duffy, one of the leaders in the Official IRA in Londonderry. From the descriptions by you and Corporal Anderson, we believe, or more to the point, I believe the other male is our mutual friend Red Tom.'

Peter Moore broke off his conversation while he produced a number of photographs from his inside jacket pocket and handed them to Montgomery.

'Have a look James, take your time. Can you identify anyone that looks like, or is your suspect for the double murder at the petrol station?'

Daylight was beginning to ebb into twilight. The early autumn sun had not quite dipped below the rocky outcrop known as Napoleon's Nose that formed part of the Antrim Hills, running along the opposite shore of Belfast Lough. The sun's pencil-thin orange reflection softly terminated as it mixed with the silver foam of the waves gently lapping in constant rhythm onto the sandy beach. There sat two surreal figures in silhouette against the backdrop of a Monet canvas.

Montgomery was now looking through the half dozen or so photographs produced by Peter Moore. In turn, he tilted each forward one by one to catch the fading rays of sunlight. Montgomery took his time, committing each image to memory and overlaying them in his mind to that day when he first encountered Red Tom.

'Yes, Peter. Even in this light I can say with certainty that in these two photographs, it is the same man whom I saw at the petrol station the previous day of the killings.'

Another Possible Lead

'Corporal Anderson has also confirmed to me from these photographs that it is the same person he saw on the Saturday morning.'

Peter Moore produced one more photograph. It was of a young man in British army uniform and without saying a word, handed it to Montgomery who, in turn studied it for a number of seconds.

'It's the same person. It's Red Tom – no mistake on that, Peter.'

'It's the official Army file photograph of Dermot Patrick Ryan taken when he joined the Irish Guards about thirteen years ago at the age of seventeen. Corporal Anderson confirmed it's of the same man he saw at the petrol station.

'Why Peter, would a former British army Sergeant get himself involved in such matters; the deliberate murder of two young people? It just doesn't make sense.'

'That's for a detective in the RUC to solve and with our help if we can.'

Montgomery's stomach churned and bubbled. He could not eliminate those images he had seen on that Saturday morning back in February. What it must have been for those young people when faced with immediate death – uncontrollable horror as the .45 revolver was pressed against the back of their heads.

'Peter. As far as Red Tom is concerned, he is up to his uxters in it. The case went cold. No one knew him. He had vanished until now and going on what you have told me of him it is hard to grasp. But in this hell-hole of terrorism, I suppose its par for the course. Everyone seems to want a slice of the action. There is enough hatred to last to the end of this century and beyond. We have been at it for over 280 years. Since King Billy – as he is affectionately known to many here - landed over there on the far side of the Lough at Carrickfergus and first stepped ashore in Ireland with his orange Protestant Army.'

Was it the tranquillity of the evening, or Montgomery's imagination unnerving his senses? His gaze had fixed to the long finger of the sun's orange reflection floating across from the far shore and pointing directly at him. Montgomery eased himself along the bench seat but the orange finger unrelentingly followed him.

'Aye James, the Nationalists blame the English for all their ills, instead of the Dutch!'

'Well it was the English who put him on the throne, along with Mary – The Glorious Revolution I think it is called. Glorious for the English, not so for the Irish.'

Peter Moore said nothing. He nodded once as if to give validity to Montgomery's remarks. He wasn't about to engage in debate over the historical events of the past 280 years. Neither man could change history. Like the entire population of Northern Ireland, whether on one side or the other, or no side, they had to endure history in the present and on a day to day basis. Not even when people returned home in the evening could they escape its blackness. There was always the 'knock on the door' and the sudden smashing of glass as the front door was sledge-hammered off its hinges, followed by the gunfire of the paramilitaries, or the concealed explosive device unwittingly detonated by the driver of the family car as they set off for their daily work; engulfed in a deadly fireball of searing heat welding their lower limbs to the twisted red hot metal and burning fabric of the interior.

'I sometimes think Peter that I should be off to the far side of the world, away from this place.'

'What! Australia? Sure it's full of convicts, who instead of tea or coffee, drink Wallaby piss for breakfast and when they can't get any milk, they pour it over their cornflakes.'

'Away with you Peter - who told you that yarn? I suppose you read it in one of those MI6 reports.'

Both men looked at one another and broke into rueful laughter - a moment of benign indifference to the whole ruinous quagmire of violence, murder and endless heartache that was Ulster.

Another Possible Lead

'I think we should make our way back to the Hotel, Peter.'

'Yes OK James'.

As the two men began to walk back to the car, a red setter came bounding along the narrow path towards them. Its wet stringy coat brushed against their trousers as they simultaneously parted to allow the dog uninterrupted passage. Perhaps exhilarated by its evening swim in the sea, it was oblivious to its female owner's instructions as she bellowed forth like some primary school teacher trying to calm an excited child.

'I'm so sorry. He's not normally like this. Did he soak you?'

'No. It's all right. I think he has spotted a rabbit in the field – just over there next to the gorse bushes.'

'Oh yes! That's what it has been. Thank you.'

Peter continued. 'There's a bit more you need to know about Wolfe and Ryan. There have been on and off contacts between the IRA and elements of the Soviet Union for decades. Nothing of a serious nature until now. Basically it has been the IRA trying to acquire arms rather than any attempt politically to establish a Marxist alliance.

In early 1971, an official of the Soviet Embassy in London was compromised by British Security Service. He had a passion for frequenting exclusively male clubs in and around London. One establishment called the Mountjoy YY Club was for exclusive members only; public school, civil servants and the odd Member of Parliament. Unfortunately it was not restricted to the more mature male. Members on occasions brought along their so-called 'nephews' as their guests, who were no more than sixteen or seventeen years old 'rents.' The Metropolitan Police kept more than a passing interest in the establishment and it was known by them as the 'Boy for Joy Club.' It was after one such 'nephew' was found at the rear of the premises, badly beaten up that the Met decided to clamp down on

Operation FURY

the place. There was a late night raid on the Club and a number of arrests were made, but no one was charged. One member caught with his pants down was a Soviet Embassy official who played the diplomatic immunity card. Their investigations of the young man beaten up revealed blackmail was behind the incident and involved the diplomat. Vice was uncertain whether or not to press charges, so they passed the file to Special Branch who in turn asked MI5 for guidance.

The official was a bit more than an embassy flunky. He was in fact Major Pyotr Anochkova of the Generalnovo Shtaba, the Russian military intelligence attaché at the Embassy. MI5 could not believe their good fortune. They told him there was no reason why the incident at the Club and his suspected involvement, along with his name, could not be released to the press. Well, there is no need to elaborate on Anochkova's reactions. Later codenamed by MI5 as Klondike he offered and agreed to provide details of espionage activities being run by the GRU and KGB within the United Kingdom. Before he was prepared to provide the information he insisted the British government would give him a new identify and he would be allowed to live in Canada. The Home Office agreed. Five treated the information with the usual scepticism but as they began to investigate the claims, it emerged that the information Klondike was providing was sound and high quality material. It was unbelievable the scale and extent of infiltration by the Soviets. They had successfully targeted the aerospace industry, nuclear weapons programme and naval development facilities which covered submarine sonar equipment and torpedo design. It didn't stop there. The MoD and FCO had also been compromised at a low level by Soviet moles. He also, and to the astonishment of MI5, provided information on the IRA. According to Klondike, two males walked into the Soviet Embassy and were seen by a senior KGB officer. He wasn't sure what exactly took place or what

Another Possible Lead

was discussed. He was asked at the time to provide a report from a military perspective on the IRA, which he did. Part of his report covered the prospect that the IRA could be useful and possibly obtain detailed information on the 'Seacat' and 'Blowpipe' guided missile weapons system being developed by Short Brothers & Harland in Belfast. The same KGB officer was on the plane to Moscow within the week of the IRA making contact. Klondike said that whatever the IRA wanted was taken and treated seriously. There was some gossip within the Embassy that the KGB officer went to Moscow to consult George Blake. Blake as you know and recall James, was sentenced to forty-two years for espionage and escaped from Wormwood Scrubs Prison in 1966, helped by Sean Bourke who had been convicted for sending a parcel bomb to a policeman in England. Bourke was out on parole and helped organise Blake's escape from the outside. Both men eventually ended up in Moscow a few months after the escape.

Subsequently, from the information and names provided by Klondike and as you know from the newspaper and media reports, the Foreign Secretary revoked the visas and expelled over a hundred Soviet Embassy staff and Russian nationals in order to close down the KGB spy network. British double agents were arrested by Special Branch and interrogated by Five and Naval Defence Intelligence section of the MoD. Other suspected moles were gradually reassigned to mundane jobs and closely monitored. Fortunately, my section was as clean as a penny whistle or even an orange flute!'

'Aye Peter, but it all depends whose blowing the orange flute. I suppose it is what you MoD intelligence people call 'whistleblowers''

'Not quite James. As far as Russian 'whistleblowers,' or 'flute players' as you refer to, Klondike was leading the parade on what he provided. I have seen the file section on the two IRA contacts. It's a bit scant on detail, except that there were at least three further meetings held over the following six weeks from the initial contact and all took place within the Embassy. There is one further piece of information noted in the file. Two codenames and descriptions and I will explain. I have been told the Russians love American cartoons. There is a bit of a black market in East Berlin and sometimes the Soviet Embassy got hold of them. I suppose they see the Americans as figures of fun – something along those lines, I presume. It sounds ridiculous, but that's what it's meant to be, unbelievable.'

Montgomery reacted like a pike about to strike at the hovering fly. 'What's not believable, Peter.'

'The two codenames – 'Tom' and 'Jerry'. Moore went silent, not prepared to say more, waiting for Montgomery's response. Montgomery's whole body slowly swivelled on the seat to catch Moore's facial expression. Somewhere between tense and sardonic as if he had just revealed one of the mysteries of the universe and nobody would believe him. There was a long pause before Montgomery spoke.

'What is it are you on Peter, L.S.D.? It's either that or Klondike is playing – how can I put it? – cat and mouse with MI5. It's pish. He is bullshitting all over MI5. It's a cocktail of nonsense, vodka and wallaby piss, I reckon Peter.'

'Yes James. That was my initial reaction – bolshy, baloney. But the extract from the file I saw convinced me to the contrary view. A footnote on who the IRA contacts were under the title: Source description: unsure sighting had Jerry 5'8" tall with wavy fair hair and of stocky build. Tom was described as 6'0" tall with dark brown or black hair tied at back in short pony tail and of slim build. Sounds as though it could be our man Red Tom.'

'I'll give you that Peter,' replied Montgomery. 'The Russians may like cartoons and Klondike seems to me that he could upstage Groucho Marx for one-liners. We will settle for possible, but not probable.'

Another Possible Lead

'And James, with the arrival of Wolfe in Ireland it may be more than an old comrades' get-together. We cannot have the Russians establishing a relationship with elements of the IRA operating from a country that borders with the UK. We are not sure if it is needle value for the Russians or another element added to the cold war, or they are testing our reaction – their favourite pastime of Russian roulette, using the IRA as the revolver. It may be cold revenge for the mass expulsion of their Embassy staff and wiping out their entire spying operations – well most of it in the UK. The Soviet Foreign Minister, Andrei Gromyko was a touch upset and accused the British police of 'hooliganism.'

As you are aware James, the cooperation between the British and Irish governments is mostly non existent. The burning down of our Embassy in Dublin by the IRA apparently in retaliation for Bloody Sunday is a prime example[19] while the Garda stood by and allowed it to happen. If we can convince the Americans that the KGB, through Wolfe, is conspiring with the IRA in Donegal to spy on the base in Londonderry and what ever else they are up to, then we may be able to persuade the Yanks to put pressure on the Irish government to genuinely co-operate with us. The alternative is for British troops to cross the border and eliminate IRA units operating from Donegal. It would be a major operation, but for the present not really an option. It is the diplomatic route through the Americans that is preferred. You can see we need to bring Ryan in for interrogation on what the IRA is up to with the Russians. It would be better if he is arrested and charged for the double murder. With a long jail sentence hanging over him then we should be able to persuade him to co-operate. That is why I am telling you about Wolfe and his connection with Ryan. I will give you all the help I can to catch him but I suspect he operates from Dublin. That is where he went when he left the Army. We have asked MI6 to assist us. It's a long shot, but we need to be active. Ryan needs to be caught or eliminated.'

Operation FURY

'You mean murdered, Peter?'

'No, James. Shot in an exchange of gunfire while resisting arrest. We have done our homework on Ryan. His father left Ireland for England just prior to the Second World War, probably looking for work. He met and married an English girl in Liverpool. Ryan was born the following year. He was ten years old when his mother died and his father moved back to Dublin with his son. Ryan moved across again and at the age of sixteen joined the British army. He can claim dual nationality but as far as we are concerned he's British, full stop and in our book a traitor. His association with Wolfe racks him up on that score. When British soldiers leave the Army they go on the reservist list and can be called up again. If he is caught spying for an enemy, then he could be brought before a military court. He wouldn't see the outside of the 'glasshouse' for thirty years if convicted.'

'Why don't you bring in the others Ryan was seen with in Derry?'

'If we do that James, then he will know we are onto him. Besides, we don't want the Russians to find out that we are aware of their involvement with the IRA until we have established an overview of their real intentions.'

'I am afraid Peter, the only way Ryan will be caught is with a bucket full of luck on our part and he makes a mistake, which is most unlikely.'

'I agree with you James. It is going to be difficult. If we involve RUC Special Branch or MI5 they will want to turn him as an agent and spend weeks or even months in this fruitless venture. Your CID investigation will be put into the unsolved drawer and forgotten about. What we need James, is Ryan behind bars, in prison, not playing double-dutch with Special Branch or MI5. It's down to you and with our help. Your main eyewitness, Corporal Anderson, along with the other jocks, have been transferred back to their base in Scotland. It is to avoid any risk to them being killed over here. I

Another Possible Lead

understand that Ryan would be facing a twenty-five year jail sentence.'

'Yes Peter that would be my estimate on conviction. These new Diplock Courts[20] are a bit unknown but I would expect the Judge would reach the conclusion on the evidence that the double murder was premeditated. There would be no deals on our part for the charges being reduced to manslaughter. What about Wolfe? Surely you can do something about him?'

'Unfortunately not; he is either back home in East Germany or still briefing the KGB after his visit to Ireland.'

'Why was he not arrested when he returned into Northern Ireland or on the mainland? After all, he first entered the UK on a false Swedish passport.'

'That's what MI6 intended to do and bring in Special Branch at that point, but Klaus Wolfe did not oblige. He never re-entered the UK. What we have concluded is that Wolfe departed from Donegal by courtesy of the Soviet Navy on one of their submarines.'

'You're pulling my leg Peter. Are you serious?'

9

Submarines

'Yes James. There is no service more committed to these matters than Her Majesty's Navy when operating in the north Atlantic. Their surveillance report was passed to us which also involved the RAF. The section in the Minister of Defence which I am attached to, deals with all intelligence gathering and assessment across all three services. Navy drew it to our attention as it covered an incident close to the Irish coast. I will explain in general terms on our conclusions.

It was two weeks – exact dates don't matter – after Wolfe entered the UK via Newcastle when two submarines of the Soviet Navy were picked up on satellite leaving the naval base of Severomorsk, in the Tuloma River estuary to the Barents Sea. Severomorsk is just north of the Soviet Northern Fleet Headquarters at Murmansk. Five days later they were seen again by RAF Air Reconnaissance off the Norwegian coast. What was unusual was that these boats were well into the Norwegian Sea – on a parallel course making full speed on a south westerly bearing. It is not normal for Soviet submarines to remain on the surface for so long. They usually go sub-surface just before they round the northern tip of Scandinavia at Mageroy Island. Navy thinks this was a deliberate ploy and they wanted us to know where they were. Soviet Navy on occasions like to break from routine in

Operation FURY

order to assess our tactical response. Within ten minutes of being spotted by the RAF, both boats submerged. Visibility was not good but from the assessment of the aerial photographs taken by the RAF, Navy was of the opinion that both submarines were of the Whiskey Class or more likely the upgraded version, Romeo Class. They are twin diesel/electric with twin propeller shafts and are designated long range attack submarines.

Royal Navy's closest submariner vessel was patrolling in deep water between the Faeroe and Shetland Island groups. HMS Rorqual was ordered to locate and shadow the Soviet submariners. If they diverged on separate bearings, then HMS Rorqual was to shadow the boat closest to the UK. HMS Rorqual failed to make sonar contact and it was assumed at the time that the Soviet boats squeezed past undetected or they changed course and headed west to the south of Iceland to play cat and mouse with the American Navy or even the Canadians.

I would add at this point James neither the Soviet nor British submarines carried nuclear weapons. The Soviet boats besides their torpedoes carry missiles for ship to ship engagement and need to surface to deploy. HMS Rorqual, a Porpoise class, is equipped as a patrol submarine with first class sonar and armed only with the Tigerfish torpedo.

The Commander of Rorqual decided to widen the area of search and moved south-west to a position mid-way between Saint Kilda and Rockall. His instinct and initiative proved positive. Sonar detected engine noise that could only have been from a Soviet submarine. Apparently the propellers on Romeo Class are noisy and have a unique cavitation signature – not too difficult to identify. Only one boat had been detected. Rorqual shadowed the boat, designated SNKl, for three days. It zigzagged occasionally to avoid detection but it was obvious to Rorqual that SNKl was heading for the Irish coastline.'

Submarines

'Well Peter, I am beginning to see the implications of what you are describing to me.'

'Indeed James. As you know there was a Navy base in Lough Foyle near Londonderry. During the Second World War this was a major allied forces naval base, strategically important for US convoys of the north-western Atlantic approaches. Most of the facilities are now long gone since the ending of the war. There is still an American communications installation in operation. If the Cold War was to warm up, then Lough Foyle may once again become strategically important for NATO.

What happened next was the Cold War was about to go red hot, if you will excuse the pun – and off the Irish coast of all places. SNK1 slowed to quarter speed, and then surfaced just after midnight on 24th of last month. This was eight days after Wolfe had crossed the border into the Republic of Ireland. Of course the Commander of Rorqual had no knowledge whatsoever of Comrade Wolfe.

The Soviets were on the surface for about five minutes when the Commander decided to bring Rorqual to periscope depth for a peek. He was somewhat surprised and intrigued when he spotted what looked distinctly like a small surface craft approaching alongside SNK1. It was then that Rorqual's sonar picked up a second submarine off its starboard. Well, the situation that Rorqual was in was explained to me in detail. I'll give you a shortened version.

It's what Navy call a Pythagoras mouse trap – a right-angle close attack formation which the submariners of the Soviet Navy have been perfecting; very risky but deadly for the mouse if an actual attack was carried through. Heaven knows what went through the Commander's mind. He's at periscope depth enjoying the night time view when suddenly he was under possible attack. Was it for real or the Russians having fun with the Navy? If Rorqual turned 90° to face SNK2 he would be presenting his port side to SNK1. If he surfaced,

Operation FURY

then he would also be presenting himself to missile attack from SNKl. Royal Navy Porpoise class don't have deck guns. They are now obsolete on all RN modern submarines. Not that a gun would have been a match for a missile attack. If Rorqual had surfaced it could also have indicated he was giving way to the Soviets' superior position. Simply not on, I would have thought! But I am Army, not navy. In the dark three dimensional world of Atlantic Ocean needs special abilities of judgement and a steady nerve. I suppose it's like playing three dimensional chess wearing a blindfold, but then it's the same for the opponent and the 'Reds' have first class chess players.

Rorqual's only other move was to make a tactical withdrawal. All three boats were in international waters. Rorqual was about three miles west of UK territorial waters – the twelve mile limit – and with the Soviets just beyond the viable range of Rorqual's torpedoes. The difficulty with a withdrawal was having to manoeuvre into unfamiliar and relatively shallow water and naval procedures dictated that the Rorqual would be required to surface. The Commander had already ruled out surfacing. He concluded his only solution was to stay steady and engage the Soviets if attacked. He kept Rorqual at periscope depth and maintained slow speed.

The Commander of Rorqual then gave the order – red alert – all crew to battle stations and rig for imminent attack, I understand is the usual jargon used in exercise. This time it was for real. He had no choice but to defend his submarine and its complement. What he did next must have sent deep cold shivers through the entire crew. He gave the orders to arm and load the starboard and port forward torpedoes, but he did not open the outer sea port tube doors, nor did the Commander alter speed or course. The Soviet boats being on full alert and via their sonar equipment would have realised what Rorqual was up to. It was for them to make the next move. And they did. Both Soviet submarines followed suit; loaded their torpedoes

Submarines

while maintaining the tube doors in the closed position. Well, nothing further happened and all three submarine Commanders must have come to the same conclusion that stalemate had been reached and that none was about to carry through an actual attack.

Rorqual was still at periscope depth and the Commander decided to have another look and double check his bearing relative to SNKl. He was now within torpedo range maintaining slow speed. It was at this point he observed the surface craft moving off from the Soviet submarine and it was just crossing his forward line and heading south towards Irish territorial waters. SNKl turned north-east gaining speed and went sub-surface shortly afterwards.

Rorqual's Commander concluded that whatever the purpose of SNK1 rendezvous with the small craft, it had completed its mission and he assumed it was probably heading back to its home port. As Rorqual was still under a potential threat from the second submarine, Rorqual increased to full speed and went to deeper water, making distance to reduce the risk of any potential attack. Rorqual was breaking off the engagement. Within ten minutes, the second Soviet boat had turned on a northward bearing. It too was heading home. Rorqual's Commander sent off a message to Naval Strategic Command giving the basic details of the encounter with the Soviets. Rorqual[21] was ordered to break off and cut short the patrol duty and return immediately to its naval base on the Clyde. As I said earlier James, we received a copy of the report. I subsequently spoke to the Commander hoping to establish every detail of the encounter between the Soviet sub and the surface craft. The Soviets had been on the surface for approximately sixteen minutes but the Commander was too far off to see what exactly was happening. I asked the Commander and he confirmed that it would have just been possible to transfer a passenger from one boat to the other. There was a slight swell and both the submarine and the surface craft had lights on.

Operation FURY

MoD, that is the top brass of Navy intelligence, Army Intelligence, together with the heads of MI6 have concluded that Comrade Wolfe was indeed shipped out from Donegal by the Soviet submarine in a well pre-planned and executed operation, and with the assistance of the IRA. The Soviets would not have gone to those lengths and used such a high-ranking and experienced agent if it was only a spying mission to assess the American base at Lough Foyle. There is more to it. We believe the Russians are about to add another piece to the Cold War chessboard and provide arms to the IRA.[22] This will depend on Wolfe's report to the KGB being favourable. We have no way of knowing, so we have decided to assume the worst and act immediately to be ahead of the game. It's that serious. There was also some mention of the possibility of MI6 re-activating the Zeta network; which raised eyebrows. It's an organisation of which I had no knowledge and was a highly secret network of exclusively foreign agents run from Basle, Switzerland during the war by MI6. After the meeting my CO told me – rather ordered me not to enquire further, but added Zeta was never mentioned as it was absolutely MI6 business. An undercover network within a secret organisation, which doesn't exist, I suppose. It was probably MI6 European agents who discovered O'Connell and McGuire trying to buy guns and whatever else for the IRA two years ago. There were never any CX reports, just word of mouth and always deniable of course.

MI6 is to step up its intelligence gathering – a priority for their agents operating in the Eastern Bloc to obtain information on movements of arms – anything unusual no matter how small. Six will be given additional funds and told to bribe and coerce government officials for information - high currency German marks and Swiss francs to seduce the poorly paid clerk and office worker into betraying their country whose government they probably despise anyway. The Russians are too astute to supply arms directly to the

Submarines

IRA. That's the difficult part, finding out in advance who will act as postman. It could be the upgraded Avtomat Kalashnikova – AKM59, or even the new AKS with state-of-the-art chrome-lined barrels for better accuracy and ranged up to 1,000 metres. East Germany could be the source but Bulgaria, Poland, Czechoslovakia, Romania, Yugoslavia or even Egypt who are now manufacturing AKMs. What links these weapons is they all use Soviet M43 calibre ammunition.

Like the American Armalite the Soviet Kalashnikova is a first-class assault rifle.[23] It is ideally suited for the guerrilla gunmen, simple to maintain and can withstand some abuse under battlefield conditions. The Russians know the value of close quarter engagements in urban areas learned at the Battle of Stalingrad.[24] It's what the German's referred to as 'Rattenkrieg.' If the Soviets provide the IRA with know-how on these tactics, then our troops will be hard pushed without specialist training themselves. The reason the 'B' Specials were disbanded was that they were outdated. They would have been outgunned and probably outclassed. That's why the Ulster Defence Regiment[25] was formed and properly trained by Army with modern equipment and weapons. The Enfield .303 with its manual bolt action used by the 'B' Specials is a fine weapon for the sharp shooter but it would be useless against a co-ordinated attack by the IRA terrorist using the modern assault rifle in the narrow streets and alleyways of Belfast. We cannot stop these weapons at source. If they are to be transported into the Republic of Ireland, then it will most likely be by sea. Overland is far too risky. There are too many border crossings and check points. We cannot rely on the Republic's navy coastal patrol. It is too small. So Royal Navy will become more active. Not quite piracy on the high seas, but close enough if and when necessary.

Middle East sources are a concern, particularly the Egyptians, so we have asked Israeli military intelligence 'Aman,' who have agreed to help out and provide us with information of any suspicious armament shipments heading west along the Mediterranean. It's not only these assault rifles falling to the hands of the IRA; it is also Czechoslovakian high explosive Semtex. If the terrorists get hold of this, they could cause major disruption and untold death to the civilian population. The Army and police would be stretched in having to cope and as usual the politicians would expect us to deal with it.

The government is at last beginning to realise that they need to take hold of the deteriorating situation and formulate an effective coherent political initiative. They are being forced to face up to the fact that they can no longer treat Ulster as 'that place over there' on the basis that the two islands are separated by twenty miles of sea. This business of the IRA contact with the Soviets has been discussed with the British Prime Minister and close Cabinet colleagues. They are in no doubt of its profound implications. As for the Stormont government; well, it is now beyond their capabilities to cope.[26] Their only answer to the solution is a military hard-line approach.

If the British government cannot turn the situation around and eliminate the terrorists then as I understand it, rumours only, the government will seriously consider some deal involving the Republic's government, which allows the British to disengage and withdraw from Ulster. The security requirements don't change for the moment. We are expected to ensure a manageable level of violence until the political initiatives begin to stabilise the province. The government will not, James, and I repeat, absolutely will not allow the situation to reach a stage where the IRA strategy moves to the British mainland, that British troops will be required to support the police and are deployed on the streets of London, Liverpool, Birmingham and elsewhere. It just can't happen.

A top-level meeting has been arranged for next week. My

Submarines

commanding officer along with the GOC Army in Ulster and a few senior staff members from the intelligence services will brief the Chief Constable of the developing and potentially seriousness of a Soviet intervention and its link-up with the IRA here in the province. The meeting is classified and limited to less than a dozen named personnel. James, I am here in advance of that meeting. I need you on board as the RUC direct link to me with the first priority to capture and bring down Dermot Patrick Ryan.'

'What are you saying to me Peter? What you are asking me Major, is to become a spy – an agent for your covert section of Army Intelligence. I am a detective in the RUC and not a donkey carrying information to the British army. I know, or at least I think we are on the same side and the need for general cooperation, but what you are expecting from me, is not on Major. It is not for me.'

Montgomery felt he was being played along into Major Moore's undercover operations; that all the talk and intelligence information about 'Red Tom' and the Soviets was a psychological onslaught to lock him into the plot. He also knew he wanted to apprehend 'Red Tom' as much as Major Moore.

'No Chief Inspector,' I don't see you as an Army agent as you put it. I see you exactly for what you are James - a first-class dedicated officer in the Royal Ulster Constabulary endeavouring to do your professional best in a situation not of your making in this hellhole of a province. Well James, at next week's meeting, my CO will speak to the Chief Constable and impress upon him that we need you to be involved directly at the highest level of input in bringing in Ryan. You will not be working without your Chief Constable's knowledge and official approval. I would not expect you to operate any other way.

I do not live here, you do. It is for the ordinary people men, women and children and your own colleagues in the RUC whom you have a duty to protect. Do it for them and not for the British government or for that matter, the Army. That is why I am here along with my fellow officers to do our best for the men under our command. The squaddies from the mill towns of Lancashire and Yorkshire, the hard-nosed Jocks from the Govan Road in Glasgow and the young men from the Welsh villages who have joined the British army rather than spend their lives underground in the damp blackness of the coalmines. Think on it James over the weekend. Let me ring you mid-morning on Monday. And I will leave it at that.

'If any of this Russian involvement with the IRA is correct, then answer one more question, Peter. I was reading an article recently about the American's suspicions of the Soviets engaged in developing biological bombs to disperse killer diseases such as small pox and bubonic plague. Is there any likelihood that the IRA could get their hands on this stuff?'

Moore did not respond immediately. He seemed thrown by the question.

'You have stumped me James. I don't know how to answer that. The section of the MoD that deals with this – germ warfare is highly secretive which I know absolutely nothing about. I doubt even my CO would be cleared or has knowledge on the subject. Damn it James! It doesn't bear thinking about. If the IRA got their hands on that stuff, then they could hold the government to ransom; demand whatever they wanted. They probably wouldn't have to use it. Just the threat would be enough. Even if they did get hold of it and used it, they would likely end up infecting and killing themselves.'

'Not necessarily Peter, just threaten to release it in London and a few other cities on the mainland. I agree. It is a horrifying thought. Well it is only a thought; let us forget I raised it.'

Moore gave a pensive nod in response, but how could he forget about it? The scenario slotted into his brain. A situation hopefully

Submarines

that would never arise. Surely the Russians would not be so senseless as to hand over lethal biological agents to any group not completely under their control. It was for the moment outside Moore's immediate concern, but still Montgomery had mentioned it. It was another possibility and the prospect of germ warfare which could be added to the terrorist arsenal was catastrophic.

Both men said little to one another as Montgomery drove them back to the hotel. Each silently reflecting on what had been discussed and the implications for the immediate future, which Montgomery knew was as unpredictable as ever. He understood the Major's need to capture Ryan, a man who knew a great deal of republican thinking. From what he had told him, Ryan was deeply involved in IRA strategy. If any of this Russian connection with the IRA was more than speculation – provable fact based on intelligence gathering, then the future terrorist campaign would be ominous, with endless cases of paramilitary crime; most of all murder and attempted murder for the RUC to deal with and solve. CID was already stretched and many cases were unlikely to see the inside of the Crown Court. Forensics played its part, but without the help from touts and casual informers providing solid information on likely suspects, it was a hard task to solve these crimes. Underworld information had virtually dried up. Anyone suspected of helping the RUC would be shot; adding more crime cases to the CID books in an endless spiral of hatred and revenge.

Inspector Montgomery was absolute in his determination to apprehend Ryan and the others to get a conviction for the double murder of the two young people at the petrol station. He felt in conflict, wrestling with the proper course to take. He knew that without Major Moore's help it would be difficult. There had to be cooperation, official and unofficial. Moore's psychology had worked. Montgomery was reluctantly now locked into the Army's world of intelligence operations.

Operation FURY

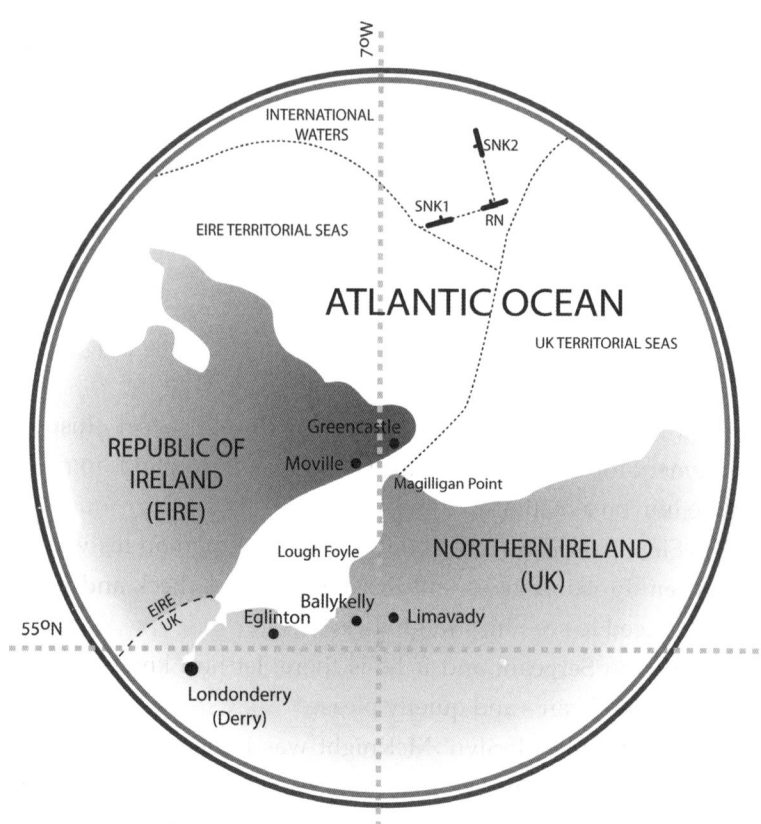

SOVIET NAVAL TACTICS - *Pythagoras mouse trap*

Submarines
Surface	Soviet Navy	SNK1
Submerged	Soviet Navy	SNK2
Submerged	British Navy	RN *HMS Rorqual*

Lough Foyle - *There never has been a formal agreement between the British and Irish governments on the delimitation of a territorial sea boundary between the two states.*

10

Ryan – Too Clever

'Sergeant McKnight, will you try and locate Chief Inspector Montgomery for me? He is not answering his phone and I do need to speak to him on a matter of urgency.'

'Yes Sir, I passed by him about five minutes ago on his way into the canteen. Probably he is still there. I'll go and check and let him know you need to see him straightaway.'

'Thank you Sergeant and if he is there, let him know it's about Dermot Patrick Ryan – and quietly please.'

Sergeant Judith 'Marilyn' McKnight was in her mid-thirties and had joined the RUC four years earlier on leaving the Royal Air Force Police, shortly after her husband had been killed in a road traffic accident. Sergeant McKnight was Chief Superintendent McClatchey's personal assistant and one of only three female RUC officers permitted to carry a firearm. Besides her general duties, she also acted on occasions as the Chief Superintendent's personal protection officer. It was not only her natural blonde hair, but everything else that seemed to be a mirror image of her famous namesake that she had acquired 'Marilyn' during her days in the RAF. It was those French curves travelling upwards, meeting those flowing down and terminating in sensual perfection. Sergeant McKnight never opened a door beyond the gap which allowed her to squeeze through, allowing herself the opportunity, subconscious or otherwise, to gently gyrate her curvaceous hips in seductive flowing movement which stopped just short of eroticism.

Why Chief Superintendent McClatchey seemed totally indifferent to her female perfection was somewhat bewildering to his male colleagues. Perhaps it was the intensity of the job. McClatchey, if he wasn't on the telephone or absorbed in the latest intelligence report in front of him was usually on the move organising and co-ordinating undercover operations at one of Belfast's police stations. There was also some talk amongst other female officers that Sergeant McKnight had taken a shine to Chief Inspector Montgomery, but nothing that could be quoted as evidence. Only circumstantial and human nature being what it is, flippant gossip was light relief from the intensity of the job and never discussed with male colleagues.

Chief Superintendent McClatchey was a determined man. His single-mindedness had secured his advance through the ranks to the position he now held as a senior officer of the RUC. He was not hard or tough in the ordinary sense; rather he displayed an unwavering strong approach to the tasks in hand. As a young sergeant stationed at Brookeborough RUC barracks in the early months of 1957, he had been ambushed by the IRA on the short bicycle ride to his home. Having been shot in both legs and unable to move to cover, he drew his .45 revolver and waited. As the three-man IRA unit approached for the kill, Sergeant McClatchey, with careful aim, shot dead one, wounding another while the third, not prepared to offer his life for the cause or in support of his comrades, fled in the direction of the border. That is how Brian McClatchey would describe it, if pressed by his colleagues. There was no reason to doubt his accurate recollection and he would finish the telling, by insisting that God had moved on that winter's night to protect him, so he owed God much in return. There were no areas of uncertainty, no shades of grey when briefing those under his command – black and white was his moral code of conduct. On occasions when summing up on a briefing, he would refer to some biblical quotation. Perhaps he felt his survival of the IRA attack gave him the privilege to pass on a few words of cautionary wisdom.

The IRA of the fifties and sixties had been replaced by the Provos; the new breed of volunteers to carry out the killings by ambush and set the booby trap car bombs. Every RUC officer was a target, a life to be taken and another man gunned down on the glory road to free Ireland from the jack-boot of the Crown and supplant it with the jack-boot of the IRA. Brian McClatchey had become all too aware of the pain, heartache and sorrow that hovered in the air at those funeral services of his fellow officers.

'It's Chief Inspector Montgomery, Chief Superintendent. Shall I show him in?'

'Yes Sergeant. Come in James. We have some news on Ryan from the Metropolitan Police of all people and it is sound information by all accounts. Sit down James and I'll go over what they have provided. It looks as if you were right by insisting that Ryan's description and details were circulated to Metropolitan Police Special Branch[27] as a suspect for the Springfield Road double murder and shooting of WPC Phillips. They have turned up a positive lead. According to Special Branch operating at Heathrow a Dermot Patrick Ryan passed through on his way to the US, on a New York flight two days ago. He is travelling on a British passport. Special Branch was routinely checking passenger lists mainly to North America. They assumed that Ryan was of Irish nationality and his name was only flagged on their list as a person of interest as opposed to a probable suspect.

It was the Met Anti-terrorist Squad, on double checking the lists who realised it could be the same person. So they cross-checked the

Operation FURY

identity kit sketch we provided against his duplicate passport photograph and are 90% sure it's our man, Ryan. The Met is sending us a copy of the passport photograph and as you have seen the whites of his eyes so to speak, Chief Inspector, it will be for you to positively identify him. They also contacted the American Embassy for his visa application details. The Americans have granted him a three-month stay and his reason given for entry is an extended holiday visit to relatives living in New York and Boston. Ryan travelled on a one-way ticket. SO13 is sending through his passport and visa details as quickly as possible. Apparently he has given his address as Liverpool. Special Branch is checking it out and will advise us on what they turn up. It sounds as though it could be an IRA cell.

'Surely Ryan is Irish from the Republic. How could he have obtained a British passport? These IRA terrorists are becoming a bit too sophisticated. More than likely a cover address or safe house in Liverpool from which they can plan and operate their mainland activities.'

'Yes, too clever Sir,' added Montgomery. Ryan's probably gone on the run and out of the picture for a few months to the States.'

In providing Ryan's suspect report details to the Metropolitan Police Special Branch, Montgomery had not mentioned that Ryan was born in Liverpool or any other information on his British army service. He had reluctantly agreed at Major Moore's insistence on that warm evening on the shore of Belfast Lough that Ryan's Army history was to be kept confidential. Montgomery felt uneasy but it had been agreed as Moore had put it 'Army red tagged and deniable.' Montgomery was not about to enlighten the Chief Superintendent. If it became absolutely necessary in apprehending Ryan then he could always contact Peter Moore and get his agreement to release the Army service information. If the Liverpool address given on Ryan's passport was indeed a safe house for IRA activity, then no doubt Special Branch would be predisposed to keep it under surveillance or arrest suspects and close it down. That was for mainland Special Branch, not the RUC. 'Red Tom,' that's a name Ryan will not be using in the US. It wouldn't open too many doors, thought Montgomery.

'James, you will need your passport. You are going to New York. This is a positive lead on Ryan. It's the best opportunity to apprehend him and you will need to be on the spot to sort out legal extradition matters. Ryan will have given an address of where he is staying in the US on his visa application, so when we receive the details from the Met it will be the place to start. The FBI has recently set up a special section to deal with illegal activities being organised by supporters in the US of Irish terrorists. Their office is based in New York and they have agreement from the RUC for full co-operation and exchange of information on wanted suspects who have entered the United States. You will need to contact them on arrival in New York for their assistance without which you cannot operate, James. I will advise them you are going and the RUC would be grateful and welcome their assistance to apprehend Ryan. The FBI will assist your entry into the US and will expedite your visa application. I will leave the paperwork up to you James. Update Ryan's file and arrange through our legal department for the issue of an international arrest warrant with Interpol. Without it, the FBI will not entertain an arrest let alone extradition by the US legal authorities.'

'Yes, Sir, it is well worth the trip if it leads to an arrest and extradition.'

'I will have Sergeant McKnight make all the travel arrangements and FBI contact name as quickly as possible. Let us say four or five days time if we can arrange everything necessary. Prestwick in Scotland may be your best bet for a flight, rather than London or Birmingham. Chief Inspector, I would prefer that you tell your wife it's a routine trip, fact finding, rather than anything specific. I am sorry to insist on this James.'

'That's fine Sir. Catherine knows I cannot discuss my job in any detail and accepts the situation.'

'OK, James, we will have a final get-together to tie up any loose ends and ensure everything is in place before you fly off to New York. I will have Sergeant McKnight liaise with you and she can help with the paperwork. We need to keep this confidential for the moment. No need to inform your team on any of the details.

'Yes Sir. I'll move on it straight away,' replied Montgomery.

Inspector Montgomery was now walking along the corridor on his way to his office. In his mind he was going over and dissecting the intelligence information that the Chief Superintendent had discussed with him. Ryan may not have been as clever as he thought. Travelling on a British passport is a mistake. Of course Ryan would have no way of knowing that the RUC had informed the Metropolitan Police that he was a wanted suspect or that Special Branch was monitoring passengers on international flights. Luck may have played its part, but it was sound police work along with the efficiency of the Met that had led to the known whereabouts of 'Red Tom Ryan.' It was the first positive lead that Montgomery and the RUC had.

Montgomery was now back in his office where he had earlier untidily left on his desk, the investigation files of a recent murder case, along with the only piece of physical evidence that had been recovered – the bullet that had been removed from the deceased. The case involved the killing of William John Dawson, a known loyalist UVF leader who had controlled the small Protestant enclave that lay between HM Crumlin Road gaol and Republican Ardoyne. Dawson had been in the lead colour party of an early July Orangemen's parade known as the 'mini-twelfth' when he was gunned down by a single shot. The shooting of the leading Orangeman sparked off two days and nights of serious rioting along the side streets and alleyways leading off the Crumlin Road which spread throughout North and West Belfast. The RUC undermanned and exhausted were unable to quell the warring factions and it was only when the Army moved in with force that an uneasy calm was returned to the area. The rioting had been so severe with one row of terrace houses having been fire-bombed and gutted that the Army decided to bring in an additional battalion of troops from the mainland the following week. It was now an emerging sequence that as the frequency of violence and rioting escalated, then the Army had no alternative other than fly in extra men and equipment before the situation developed into widespread disorder extending outwards like a fire-storm into the suburbs and effectively crippling the city.

The case was not one in which Chief Inspector Montgomery had direct involvement, but part of his job at Police HQ was to review cases that had hit a dead end, not closed, but those that had no immediate prospect of an arrest. He could not quite satisfy himself when reading the files; there appeared to be some conflict. He needed to clear the uncertainty out of the way before fully involving himself with the New York trip in pursuit of Ryan.

Removing his glasses and rubbing his eyes, Montgomery casually looked up to see Detective Jill Humphries watching Sergeant McKnight as she removed a file from one of the drawers of the filing cabinet. With a slow, horizontal sweeping movement of her hips, Sergeant McKnight closed the drawer. As the Sergeant turned to leave the office, she gave a knowing smile in the direction of Jill Humphries. It was as if she had sensed all along that Detective Humphries' eyes were watching her every move. Humphries gaze seemed intense to Montgomery. Somewhat personally intimate as if hypnotised by the very presence of the Sergeant. Detective

Operation FURY

Humphries turned her head to catch Montgomery's stare. He looked away with a hint of underlying embarrassment and feeling he had inadvertently encroached on his colleague's privacy. Had Jill Humphries caught the Monroe virus like many of the male personnel at Police Headquarters? Had he unwittingly discovered his colleague's secret – of sexual preference? This was the seventies and none of his business, thought Montgomery, awkwardly replacing his glasses as he endeavoured to return to the Dawson case file lying on his desk. It was there and then he decided he needed expert advice.

'Detective Humphries, I am going over to see Sergeant Young at the Armoury. If CS McClatchey is looking for me, perhaps you will ring over. I shouldn't be longer than half an hour with the Sergeant.

'Yes, of course Chief Inspector,' replied Detective Humphries.

Montgomery had brought Jill Humphries with him from Grosvenor Road Station when he moved to HQ to head up the new section. She was a first-class detective who had shown commitment and proved her ability on the double murder case at the petrol station.

'Hello,' it's Chief Inspector Montgomery wishing to see Sergeant Young.'

'Yes Chief Inspector. Come through please,' was the reply through the intercom.

'I'm Sergeant Young. What can I do for you Chief Inspector?'

'Yes, Sergeant. I am in charge of C Section here at HQ. I am overviewing a recent murder case of a William John Dawson, shot while taking part in an Orange parade at the beginning of July this year.'

'Indeed, Chief Inspector, I recall the shooting. How can I help'?

'Well Sergeant, it's the ballistics. I would welcome your input and advice. Nothing formal as far as a report, let's say.'

'Certainly Chief Inspector, give me the details. Have you the report with you?'

Montgomery handed the file containing the ballistic report to the Sergeant.

'As you can see there is little to go on,' added Montgomery, while simultaneously setting down the evidence envelope containing the spent bullet. Montgomery allowed the Sergeant time to read the report and examine the bullet.

'The ballistic report does not specifically state the type of weapon used; rather it only suggests possibilities.

'Yes, Chief Inspector. I would concur with the report. It is not possible to specify an exact type of weapon based on a single spent bullet. This is ammunition for use with semi-auto and fully automatic military assault rifles, the Armalite being the most widely known.'

'Yes Sergeant. I am familiar with the Armalite.'

'There are other weapons in addition to the Armalite that use .223 calibre bullets as the report correctly states. The Steyr AUG, manufactured by the Austrians, came onto the market some months ago and I understand a small quantity of these weapons has been exported for sale on the civilian market in the US. I would need to refer to the technical specifications in the catalogue on the weapon if you are interested Chief Inspector.'

'Yes, Sergeant Young if you wouldn't mind. I suppose I shouldn't rule anything out.'

'As you can see from the photographs, it's a bullpup design; different from the Armalite. The 30 or 42 magazine round is located behind the trigger grip mechanism and fits up underneath the stock. The rifle is fitted with an optical sight which has an integral range finder, all as standard. The other features are similar to the Armalite in capabilities; muzzle velocity, cycle rate, etcetera. The trigger's first stage fires semi-auto while pulling back further provides automatic fire. This weapon can be upgraded to provide a state-of-the-art sniper rifle. I have been told that the Special Air Service have started to use

Operation FURY

the Steyr AUG. Apparently there is a SAS unit operating undercover along the Armagh border area – well not officially, it's just a rumour, but that's British army business. You would need to speak to Army, but it's unlikely they would be forthcoming on the use of this type of weapon in Northern Ireland, Chief Inspector.'

'No Sergeant. I doubt the Army would provide details on SAS operations to an RUC Chief Inspector. It is hardly creditable to suggest the SAS had anything to do with the murder of William Dawson.'

Sergeant Smith said nothing. It was not for him to either agree or disagree with the thought processes spoken aloud by a CID Chief Inspector.

'Bear with me Sergeant Young. I would welcome your opinion on a few points relating to the case. I am trying to reconcile the autopsy report, ballistics report and witness statements. According to the autopsy the bullet entered the victim's body horizontally through the chest, passing between the sixth and seventh ribs below the heart, severing the descending aorta, and leading to haemorrhaging, heart-failure, resulting in death. The bullet travelled downwards, lodging against and fracturing the tenth rib without exiting the body. The bullet used and recovered by the autopsy, slightly deformed is .223 calibre and as ballistics suggest fired from an Armalite or similar type of weapon. It's the trajectory of the bullet that raises concern. If the gunman was operating some way back, say immediately behind the spectators, he would need to have fired over their heads. The ground where Dawson was shot rises up and is several feet above the gunman's assumed position on level ground behind the spectators. If the gunman fired from ground level, then the bullet in a straight line trajectory would have entered the body in an upward inclined direction.'

'Yes Chief Inspector. You are correct, both the Armalite and AUG fire a high velocity bullet. If we accept the conclusions of the autopsy report that the bullet entered horizontally, then I agree it would mean with the difference in ground level, the gunman – the sniper – was firing at a level several feet above the ground.'

'Thank you Sergeant. You have come to the same conclusion as I have. There are no eye witnesses who saw the gunman, well none who were prepared to come forward – all those spectators, and no one saw anything. Nevertheless, it does not explain the statements from two police constables who were on foot and crowd patrol. Both claim hearing gunfire coming from their left. At the time the constables were standing behind the spectators at the opposite side of the road looking upwards in the direction of the parade coming down Clifton Street, crossing on to Donegall Street when Dawson was shot, just before the parade reached St Patrick's Church.'

Sergeant Young did not respond immediately as he studied the sketch which Montgomery had drawn and was going over in his mind the possible combination of events.

'Well Chief Inspector, it is unlikely he used a step-ladder. The back of a lorry either lying down or in a crouched position would give the sniper the height to fire over the heads of those watching the parade, and it would be sensible for him to be some distance away from the back of the crowd to avoid being spotted. For the witnesses, the two constables hearing the sound, they could have got it wrong or misinterpreted. With noise of the parade bands, they might not have heard the bullet cracking over their heads on its way to the target. It is possible the thump of gunfire they heard was an echo bouncing off the buildings to their left. It's not always easy to tell for definite the direction where gunfire is coming from, unless you see the muzzle flashes.'

'No Sergeant, I agree, it isn't and I can confirm that from personal experience.'

'One further point Chief Inspector if I may. The bullet you have shown me is .223 calibre[28] designated by the US military as .224 FMJ,

Operation FURY

full metal jacket, as I understand, probably military issue as opposed to civilian. I am talking about the US market as the source. With the absence of the recovery of a spent shell casing which would have identification numbers or letters, I cannot be absolutely certain.'

'Thank you Sergeant Young. You have helped to clarify a number of points. Would you agree that from what we have discussed that the gunman knows his business, a professional?'

'Yes Chief Inspector. He has done his homework in all aspects, setting up the firing position and choice of weapon and ammunition, perhaps someone with military training, or dare I say someone who was in the 'B' Specials. As you know they regularly trained in target practice.'

'Sergeant, I doubt I will be able to interview all 8,500 ex B-men. Besides, none would have had training on automatic rifles like the Armalite or the Steyr you have described. But I take your point.'

'Yes, Chief Inspector, I think it reasonable to discount anyone from the former B-Specials. If you work backwards from the spot Dawson was shot and with a distance of say 300 to 400 yards, it will give the general range from where the gunman pulled the trigger. You could refine that distance if you speculate and take into account the gunman would not want to be too close to the spectators in case he was observed. There are many factors to consider. It is not only accuracy but velocity which matters and can make the difference between fatality and surviving a bullet wound. As the range is increased, there is naturally a corresponding drop-off in velocity. So Chief Inspector, I would make a calculated guess – your sniper was probably 300 to 325 yards range when he fired the fatal shot that ended the life of William Dawson.'

Montgomery thanked the Sergeant and left the Armoury. Making his way back to his office, he reflected upon whether or not he had advanced the case in any meaningful way and felt he had at best established the likely method of operation. It was what Sergeant Young had said 'military training background in marksmanship' that Montgomery thought Ryan could be the sniper who had brought the life of William John Dawson to a violent end. Unless someone came forward with reliable information, this case of homicide would like others, remain unsolved.

11

Signal of Authorisation
Operation FURY

'Yes sir, you are on the left' advised the stewardess as Peter Moore made his way to his seat in executive class. His destination was New York to meet with Colonel Frederick Jones, recently appointed Military Attaché to the UK Mission to the United Nations. 'Freddie' Jones had been Moore's commanding officer when he was first assigned to oversee intelligence gathering operations in Northern Ireland, some fifteen months earlier working from the MoD Army Intelligence Corps. Their experience, knowledge and commitment in Northern Ireland operations had given both men a unique overview of the paramilitaries, particularly the more active IRA and its international connections. Top of the list was the US involvement. The weapons smuggled into Ireland had made their way north into the hands of the Belfast Brigades of the IRA and were being used to deadly effect against the Army and police. Casualties were rising at an alarming rate to the dismay of the GOC and Chief Constable. The British government was becoming more agitated as the weeks and months passed. A policy of containment was no longer working. It needed to be supported by direct action, positive and effective counter measures.

Operation FURY

Jones and Moore had been seconded to the Defence Intelligence Staff, to the Armed Forces Section. Defence Intelligence's main function was to provide intelligence analysis to MI5, MI6, GCHQ and of prime importance, to advise the Joint Intelligence Committee (JIC) which in turn was directly responsible to the Prime Minister.

It was Jones and Moore who had been quietly developing a hypothesis of likely paramilitary future activity and their plan to counter such activity. The IRA in its Provo form was becoming a Hydra. Not so much an army in the true sense, more a private militia; secret, cunning and lethal in operation. It had expanded its covert efficiency to mainland Britain with attacks on military establishments and bombing atrocities aimed at civilian targets – a campaign of terror against the daily shopper. The Provos were armed, not only with modern assault rifles, explosives and sophisticated timers and detonators. Added to this, was finance from America. Irish-America had joined in through the front organisation of the Irish Relief and Aid Fund. MI6 had advised in a number of their CX intelligence reports that dollars were being collected on a large scale. Bucket loads of hard cash were the only commodity. Book-keeping was minimal; only necessary for the veneer of legality and to satisfy the revenue authorities. Through a series of bank accounts, the money was being transferred to the IRA Dublin headquarters for their command to distribute as they felt necessary. There were reliable reports from MI5 in Dublin that not all the funds raised in the United States were being sent to the IRA in Dublin but that considerable sums were being diverted directly to the Belfast Provos, who were effectively becoming battle ready. If the egotism of the leadership became overpowering then the Provo Army was well on its way to engage the British army and RUC in an all or nothing sustained campaign. There was always just one more push that would see the British withdraw and finally leave Ireland.

Signal of Authorisation

Both Colonel Jones and Major Moore had concluded that in such an event, hostility would be widespread, bringing in the Protestant paramilitary gunmen in a three-way war. The fabric of Northern Ireland society would most likely disintegrate. Anarchy would ensue throughout the Province. The eventual and humiliating prospect of London having to agree terms for a gradual withdrawal and abandoning the unionists was, for the moment, not an option. The government needed a strategy and was looking to the Army for a solution in the short term to counter the escalating violence.

It was back in London at a meeting held at the Foreign and Commonwealth Office two months earlier that authorisation approval for the implementation of FURY had finally been given by the Foreign Secretary. It was the JIC Chairman, Sir Cunningham Smyth and Director-General of MI6 who had finally convinced the Foreign Secretary of the necessity of Moore's New York operation. Moore knew the rules of persuasion and had in his report included MI6 as an essential part of the operation. MI6 had obliged with positive enthusiasm. It had been MI6 New York Station that operated out of the United Nations under cover of the UK Mission that initially provided high grade CX reports. Over a number of months, Six was gradually building up an overview of Irish-Americans, which included a number of politicians taking an interest in the Irish troubles. Known republicans from Dublin and Belfast had arrived in the US and made contact with supporters, not only in New York, but also other cities with sizeable Irish immigrant populations. The main concern of MI6 was that US support was growing alarmingly. It was one such report that set the alarm bells ringing back in London.

It is my firm belief in evidence acquired by our well-placed source (Bellhop) that the organisation (with its identified targets) for Irish Relief and Aid is covertly dedicated to providing whatever is

Operation FURY

necessary – firearms and finances to the IRA in Ireland. This organisation is disguised as supposedly concerned in only 'providing relief aid to the Irish people who are suffering from oppression and discrimination under British rule in Ireland.' Source (Agent) report attached.

Max Westcott, head of New York Station, operating undercover as First Secretary (Political) was immediately recalled to London and a full briefing was given to the Director-General MI6 and Chief of Defence Intelligence. It had been the result of this briefing that a counter-strategy operation was initiated – firstly a suggestion, then a detailed proposal and eventually executive authority. From this meeting it had been agreed that Colonel Jones, along with Major Moore would draw up proposals for a counter-strategy operation. Their 'Plan of Necessity' report, as it was titled, concluded in their recommendations that the heads of the Hydra controlling the Provisional IRA required to be severed one by one and without delay. FURY was the operation by which the first head would be severed. Moore was now on his way to New York to ensure a successful outcome. It was imperative that the operation would not fail. Moore needed to be on the spot to ensure every aspect of the operation was foolproof. This was a military planned operation which required Major Moore's constant input and attention. FURY was no business for JIC and it was never briefed beforehand nor would it be explained after completion of the operation, particularly when the CIA[29] head of London Station or his deputy, on occasions attended meetings. The American presence at such meetings had continued on from WWII when at that time it was vitally important to co-ordinate allied undercover missions throughout Nazi occupied Europe. The Cold War validated and extended the Americans attendance – felt necessary for exchange of information on the Soviet

Signal of Authorisation

Union and its allies in the new stand-off era of nuclear superpowers. Cunningham Smith with his outstanding military record and subsequent diplomatic experience was an essential member of the planning group overseeing FURY. Smith's influence with the Prime Minister, to whom he had direct access, proved invaluable in helping to obtain executive authority. The Prime Minister was not told of the details of the operation, or the name of the intended target, other than being advised the target was a leading US citizen heavily involved with providing practical support to the IRA in Ireland and therefore was considered an enemy of the British state.

The planning group had met *sub rosa* in a secure room within the labyrinth of the Defence Ministry. At these meetings there were no formal minutes ever taken. Discussion and agreement were committed to memory with each person taking their own short notes on their area of responsibility. Absolute trust and secrecy unified the group of less than half a dozen people – codename the 'Hades Group.' Colonel Jones had been at the final 'Hades' briefing meeting the previous month before returning to his post at the UN. Confirmation details of the operation had already been sent in the diplomatic bag to Colonel Jones three days before Moore's departure for New York. The sealed file, stamped in blue 'Top Secret' with the inside single sheet authorisation order cover hidden from all eyes and both further placed inside a plain envelope. The order cover was clear and exact. It read:

Operation FURY

Ministry Of Defence
Military Zone: Defence Intelligence

SIGNAL OF AUTHORISATION AND ORDER
MEMO: OPERATION OVERSEAS (Non-United Kingdom jurisdiction)

To Colonel Frederick Thomas Jones MC
UK Military Attaché, UK Mission to the UN
United Nations, New York City

Authorisation: Foreign and Commonwealth Office
Certificate Number: Code XXXXXX IRA (US only)

Order: Subject HYDRA to be rendered permanently ineffective
In all events operation ultimately deniable.

Operation Designated Codename: FURY
Operational Control: GS02 Major Peter H. Moore (DIS)
Operational Duty: Armed Forces Section (Task force SAS)
Operational Staff Codename: ARTEMIS (transferred Special Air Service)

* * *

Operational Support: MI6 Stations: New York and Washington US
Operation Codenames: JAZZ BAND and SPEAKEASY
Authorisation: *Green Ink*.

Signed: _____ Date: _____

MAJOR GENERAL PATRICK WINGFIELD, GCB, DSO.
Chief of Defence Intelligence.

Certified original: issued. Duplicate retained.
No other copies.

Operation FURY

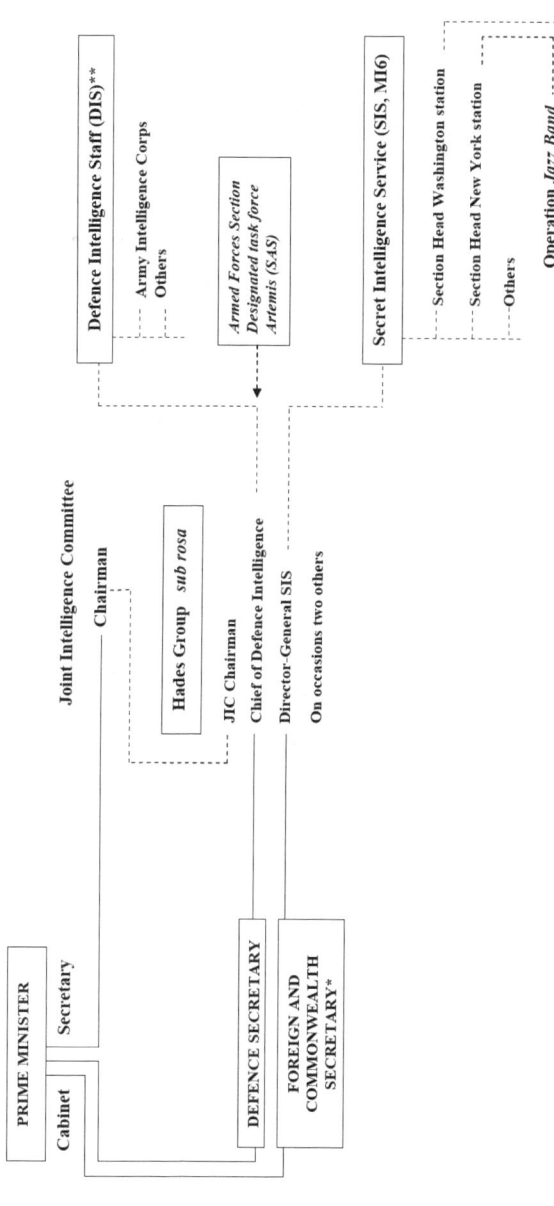

*The killing by an MI6 officer (or agent) of a foreign citizen within their own national territory was not unlawful under British law, provided it was authorised by the Foreign Secretary; commonly known as a 'licence to kill.' The Intelligence Services Act 1994 formally recognises the Intelligence Service. 'Authorisation of acts outside the British Islands' presumably covers an act of assassination. Authorisation (if given) under the hand of the Secretary of State is called Class Seven (7) certification.

** DIS has overall responsibility for providing expert analysis on received intelligence, for the various intelligence organisations including the armed forces.

Operation FURY

The flight from London to New York had been uneventful and Major Moore was glad to be on terra firma as he passed through immigration and customs. He was travelling under his own name and his cover occupation had been provided by MI6 from its standard list of innocuous professions. Major Moore was temporarily in the publishing business and was visiting New York to establish contact in this wide and varied industry. It was for MI6 field officer Debra Rutherford to recognise and make contact with Moore rather than the other way about. It was late afternoon when he emerged into the arrivals concourse. With perfect composure, Debra Rutherford greeted him as if he were her brother whom she had not seen for some time.

'Hello Peter, it is great to see you,' throwing her arms around him in a hugging embrace and whispered in his ear, 'I am your 'sister,' Debbie, whom you have not seen for two years.'

Moore, slightly taken aback, then responded in equally warming terms.

'I am so glad to see you Debbie after such a long time. You are looking well. Mum and Dad send their love.'

This exchange of coded greetings established contact.

'Let me help you with your luggage Peter. I have my car waiting to take you to the hotel.'

Major Moore's only MI6 contact in New York would be Debra Rutherford and would be limited to the carrying out of the operation. There was no need for clandestine briefing meetings. Everyone involved knew what was required with critical dates and timings committed to memory.

Debra Rutherford had been assigned to the MI6 New York Station eighteen months earlier and had quickly acquainted herself with the temperament of the New Yorkers. She had blended into the social life of hedonistic Mid-town Manhattan and always cautious as any prudent field officer would be. This was the

Signal of Authorisation

seventies and liberal Manhattan where social experiment was the new sporting life. Temptation was the risk of being compromised. A cover once blown could not be retrieved. Of course there was always the get out of gaol option and straight into the pit and the pendulum of becoming a double agent.

Rutherford's cover was her administrative job in the UK contingent at the United Nations - one of hundreds of international support staff who floated daily in and out amongst the administration offices and committee rooms of the UN. There was nothing extraordinary that would attract attention to her covert position, but Debbie 'Maggie' Rutherford was exceptional. Her natural easy-going femininity gave her a sophisticated and self-assured persona; perfect to represent her nation at the numerous official social events and diplomatic gatherings where she could mingle. She knew when to smile with her disarming dark eyes, when to accidently bump into a diplomatic 'target' and not least of her attributes – she knew when to gyrate her ass when everything else failed. Male and occasionally female targets when rare necessity required a more intimate engagement. Debra Rutherford was no fool and was aware she needed to be in full control at all times. Alcohol was always sipped in public and sniffing *lady snow* was taboo, even in private. MI6 had a small and dedicated team assigned to New York. There was no room for wannabe slackers and every member had been vetted accordingly by London. Any MI6 staff member who even dabbled in drugs, if caught, would be instantly recalled and either suspended or more than likely dismissed from the service. 'Maggie' Rutherford had been selected above others by her head of Section for FURY, the MI6 support operation codename JAZZ BAND. 'C' back in London, wanted his own man for the job but Max Westcott had convinced him that Rutherford was solid and knew the Manhattan scene intimately. Besides, anyone flown in would need to acclimatise and this could take weeks. 'C' finally agreed.

On the journey from the airport, conversation between them had been limited to a few incidentals of the operation. Rutherford had given Moore a telephone contact number which he committed to memory. It was only to be used in emergency or if an unforeseen development occurred that would impact on the operation. Moore was not to use his hotel phone; only call from a pay phone, ask for Maggie and he would be told when to receive a reply call. Rutherford would only contact Moore at his hotel if anything went wrong or an unforeseen change was required to the operation, otherwise no further contact between them would be made. Debbie Rutherford knew Peter Moore was from the MoD but nothing more as to his role in the operation. Everything was limited. There was no necessity for everyone to know everything or everyone else involved. It was standard security procedures in the unlikely event that somebody would be compromised or caught by the US intelligence services. On his departure from New York, Moore was to travel to Canada and back to the UK. It was almost an hour later when Debbie Rutherford dropped off Peter Moore at his hotel on East 42nd Street,

'Goodbye Peter. I trust everything will go according to plan.'

Peter Moore leaned forward, putting one arm around Debbie's waist and brought her gently closer.

'And for you, with your JAZZ BAND engagement Debbie, nice to see you again – no goodbye kiss for your brother?'

Smiling, Debra eased Moore's hand, which had moved to her hip. With a flick of her flowing nut-brown hair, she was inside the car and drove off into the Manhattan traffic. Rutherford knew JAZZ BAND was a vital support operation sanctioned at the highest level from London; but what she did not know and was not told, that her endeavours would be essential to the end-game of assassination, a licence to kill, as she would shortly discover.

12

The Three Bears

An envelope containing a short note from Colonel Freddie Jones was awaiting Moore on his arrival at the hotel check-in asking to meet him at 12 noon on Tuesday at the three bears sculpture in Central Park, south side of the Metropolitan Museum of Art. The note did not explain any reason for the unscheduled meeting. Tomorrow is Tuesday, thought Moore, and time to settle in at his hotel with an evening meal and a sound night's sleep to recoup his mental energy after the long hours of travelling.

It was next morning. Refreshed and having breakfasted on eggs Benedict and hot coffee, Peter Moore walked out from the hotel lobby and into the noise of a Manhattan morning. It was 10.00 o'clock and he felt the chill in the air from the sharp breeze blowing off the East River, funnelling up 42nd Street. The sun was not visible to Moore as he orientated himself. The long shadows from the buildings interspaced with narrow shafts of sunlight squeezing between the skyscrapers fell across the moving traffic in undulating waves, adding to the vibrance of the city streetscape. Moore looked up, momentarily distracted; dazzled by the stainless steel and glass of the Chrysler dome and spire in iconic brilliance against the azure sky.

Operation FURY

It was the sound of an irate cab driver blasting his horn that brought Moore back to matters in hand. Regardless of how much planning went into an operation, it needed to be confirmed on the spot when possible, by reconnaissance and on foot. Moore was wearing a sensible pair of shoes, not quite Army issue, but good enough, for he was about to walk Fifth Avenue or rather that stretch which ran from 44th Street to 86th Street and the route the parade would take in four days time on March 17. Peter Moore had made his way along 42nd Street and was now walking up Fifth Avenue. He had just passed the Rockefeller Center where Atlas looked down from his elevated position. Well, thought Moore to himself, he's not the only one with the universe on his shoulders – or at least part of it. All the brand names in gilt and silver associated with the rich and famous came into view. Tiffany & Co was the star; Audrey Hepburn and her alfresco breakfast, George Peppard and that darn cat without a name! All the images he had seen over the years in the cinemas back home in London's Leicester Square were now a reality. Taking in the tourist attractions was not part of his task but he was beginning to feel relaxed and sensed that somehow he was in familiar territory. Moore's pace slowed to suit his mood as he headed Uptown.

It would be somewhere between 85th and 86th Streets where the parade would slow to a stop as it reached its finishing point. It would be then when events would hit the news bulletins, New York style – instantaneous and without detail. The New York Police Department caught up in the panic and immersed in the bewilderment of what had happened. The press, TV and radio reporters descending like excited school children with their exigent questioning of officials. The Mayor, the Police Commissioner and anyone else foolish enough to step up and provide instantaneous answers - was it a lone gunman, a grudge by some insane person or

The Three Bears

organised crime, the Mafia or another group who had taken exception to the Senator for an unknown reason? And beyond doubt, parallels would be drawn with the Kennedys. Who were the conspirators in the assassination of yet another representative of the people? The press with extra copy; pages filled with quotes from eye-witnesses, facts, opinions and visual images. The cafés and bars would be the source for the spread of the television news reports. Car radios turned up to grip the occupants with every syllable of conflicting speculation.

Following on and adding to the confusion, MI6 will enter the game with Operation SPEAKEASY and the *black arts* of subtle deception. Disinformation will be the currency, previously scripted for groups of two or three agents, discussing openly within earshot of the patrons frequenting the multitude of bars and restaurants of Washington and dropping a hint here or there to known security advisers to the Washington administration.

> *It's a feud within the IRA – a coup by the Marxists. My cousin back in Ireland is in the Garda Siochana. They are convinced it's rivalry and jealousies between the Officials and Provos spilling over into the States…..*

Manufactured rumours, embellished to sound like fact by the conspiracy theorists talking with conviction on the late-night shows. The television hosts introducing their programmes with…*tonight, we have a former FBI Special Agent who is sure that the assassination was carried out by Irish terrorists….A leading expert in such matters is convinced it's the IRA.* MI6 had decided not to include in their black propaganda operation any suggestion of Protestant paramilitary involvement. They assessed that both the UVF and UDA had neither the capacity nor inclination to extend their terrorism across the Atlantic and if others mentioned the possibility of involvement by Protestant paramilitaries, all to the good. It would add to the plethora of speculation. All would be welcome, playing in to confuse and deflecting from the truth of the covert British operation.

The Irish Ambassador in Washington was to receive, via his residential mail box, an envelope containing a number of revealing photographs of late night shenanigans with him and two young ladies enjoying cocktails and neither of the young ladies, his wife. A note accompanying the photographs would advise the Ambassador not to issue any public statements on the Senator's demise other than what normal protocol requires. In Washington the innocuous images would not make the newspaper gossip columns. It was not quite the honey trap, but back in Catholic Ireland, the photographs showing the Ambassador living it up would be published with exaggerated innuendo. The Ambassador would not take the risk; he would be compliant. He was not a spokesman for the IRA and could not make any statement absolving the IRA from involvement and how would he know anyway? By saying nothing on the matter, his silence would be construed by the State Department that he or his government knew something. The Irish Ambassador would be summoned by the State Department and asked directly...*a United States Senator leading a St Patrick's Day parade and the Irish government knows nothing and has no comment to make about his murder*...annoyance and mistrust would claim the day.

Peter Moore had walked along the winding path in Central Park that ran north, parallel with Fifth Avenue. He found the meeting place without difficulty. The majestic family group of shiny bronze set back off to the right of the path and partly surrounded with leafless shrubbery, gave the impression the three beards had just emerged from the edge of the wood into the open clearing of sunlight. It was surprisingly quiet with an absence of

The Three Bears

children who ought to be milling about in excited inquisitiveness. Moore was about to sit down in one of the adjacent seats when he heard, coming from behind, the familiar voice of fellow-officer and close friend.

'Good morning Peter, or is it now good afternoon? Am I late?' said Colonel Freddie Jones as he approached, glancing at his wrist watch.

'Good morning Freddie; not at all, I am probably slightly early,' replied Moore.

'It's odd Peter, why human beings sometimes put their interpretation and apply their own values to nature. Bears don't form family groups nor take weekend picnics together. Bears are generally solitary creatures. It's the male who doesn't find family life appealing. In fact, he sees the cubs as getting in the way of his love life and would kill them at the slightest opportunity. Rather than be called grizzly, more appropriately he should be called grisly. No matter, the children seem to find the family group amusing and not altogether frightening.

'To the matter in hand Peter, I am sorry the note was short on detail but I need to discuss it first hand and have your views and input. It's Artemis.'

Moore interrupted. 'What's wrong Colonel. Has something happened?'

'No, no, Peter. Everything is fine. Artemis will be here as scheduled; sometime this evening as you know. It's a slight change to her operation on the day I need to discuss. From the briefings in London and out of all the locations suggested, it was my apartment that was judged the best position and provided the minimum of risk to Artemis being spotted by a hawk-eyed police officer. We all agreed on that. Even Six thought it ideal as it kept their people and ours separated. My eighth floor apartment is in that building over there. Being at the side, it's not perfect for sighting the target over the top of the Guggenheim but that was factored in at the time and accepted. The slight compromise is within the capabilities of a marksman, or more correctly, a British army trained sniper.'

'Yes Freddie, you can rest assured on that, Artemis will be fine.'

'The adjoining apartment to mine, of which I have seen the inside, directly overlooks Central Park and has a corner French window to the living space. This window gives a more direct line of vision to the parade route as far down as 79th Street, opposite the three bears. If Artemis were to target from this window position, it would give a longer sighting range, reduce the angle to almost square-on and provide a greater time frame to zero in and wide of the target; an almost perfect sniper position. What do you think Peter? Is it wise to change the plan at this late stage into the operation?'

Moore did not answer straightaway. He was thinking through Freddie's proposed new scenario.

'Yes Freddie. It sounds logical, an added bonus to increase operational efficiency. Artemis would need to decide for herself, but what about access to the adjoining apartment and its occupants, your neighbours?'

'That's what gave me the idea in the first place. My neighbours, the Hoffman's, are away in Europe for six weeks visiting relatives and are not due to return until the middle of next month. They were not too happy to leave a key with the building's commissionaire and asked if I wouldn't mind looking in occasionally. They knew I worked at the UN and I suppose felt they could trust me. It's the plumbing system Peter. There have been a few leaks in some of the other apartments over recent months, so the Hoffmans were a bit apprehensive leaving their apartment unattended. I suggested they close off the valve to the main supply

The Three Bears

but they were more concerned with the apartments above them flooding into theirs. Nice people, so I could hardly refuse. There is access leading to the rear door of their apartment off the service stairs. Everything factors in, except for one problem. How do we key in and advise Artemis?' I am off to Washington first thing in the morning before Artemis arrives mid-afternoon. I don't want to upset things by hanging back. I need to keep to my out-of-town cover schedule. It's your operational control Peter and it means you will need to make contact with Artemis.'

'Yes Freddie. I agree completely, we should stay with the operational plan, but it's worth considering. After all, that's why I am in New York to cover for such an eventuality of any change to FURY. It means breaking into what was agreed – a solo run on her part from beginning to end without interference from anyone, including me.'

'Good Peter. I suggest in the morning after she arrives when she has recovered from the travelling, is wide awake and able to appreciate and take in everything. Agreed?'

'Agreed Freddie, besides, Artemis needs to be at the apartment when the instrument is delivered by Debbie Rutherford, sometime around eight tomorrow evening.'

'I would suggest that you both meet at the front steps of the Museum at ten on Thursday morning. There are usually quite a number of tourists milling around at that time and you can both mingle with the activity. Besides, with the new scenario, it will also give you the opportunity to walk the kill zone down to 79th Street and discuss the options.'

'OK Freddie, but in the end it will be down to Artemis to make the final decision on her preference for apartment - yours or the Hoffmans.'

'I will leave the Hoffmans' key plus a note for Artemis in my

Operation FURY

apartment telling her to meet you on Thursday morning at ten on the steps of the Museum, but nothing on what we have discussed. I should be off now Peter and back at the UN for a scheduled call from Paddy Wingfield. Sorry we can't have lunch but you can get a light meal at the restaurant to the side of the Guggenheim. I use it myself on occasions. It's a cold day and I would recommend the soup, it is first class.'

'One other point Freddie, are we being followed over to our left?'

'No Peter that is Rex and George. They are shadowing us. Part of the security provided for me by our people at the UN under MI6 control I believe. I know it's the middle of the day, but this is Central Park after all. Rex is keeping an eye on us while George keeps an eye on Rex. George by the way is the one on four legs.'

Peter Moore gave a broad grin at the ironic reversal of names and thought to himself, Freddie is joking, but said nothing. Perhaps MI6 has a sense of humour after all – a dog with a codename.

'Right Peter, I suppose the next time we will see each other will be back in London for the debriefing of FURY.'

'Yes, Freddie. Good afternoon.'

Both men parted, aware of their own imminent roles to play in overseeing FURY to its successful conclusion and hopefully denying the IRA the illegal supply of weapons and finances from the obliging Irish-American Senator and his so-called aid relief fund.

13
Operation JAZZ BAND

Debra Rutherford had left earlier that morning from Pennsylvania Railway Station on her way to the Canadian border or rather to Plattsburgh, a small city of 18,000 in population and 300 miles due north of New York City. Situated on the shores of Lake Champlain, Plattsburgh was ideal for a rendezvous, being only twenty-five miles south of the US/Canadian border. It was home to the US Air Force Base of Strategic Air Command's primary wing on the East Coast. Strangers would not stand out with the comings and goings of military personnel and their families. Besides, Debra Rutherford would only be staying overnight. Her mission: to meet with her MI6 colleague Greg Redington to collect the instrument. She had with her, a small overnight suitcase and of prime importance, an empty saxophone case tailored internally to transport the instrument without damage back to New York the following day.

In all respects the case was in appearance the genuine article complete with silver nameplate. *Sounds Alive: Manufacturers of Musical Instruments: New York City and Chicago.*

Rutherford was two hours into her journey. It would be mid-afternoon, around 3.00pm when she would arrive in Plattsburgh and take the short cab ride from the railway station to the rendezvous at the Hotel Lake Champlain where she had reserved a room. The hotel was a popular location for the well-to-do of Montreal for vacations and the long weekend break. It was early in the season and quieter during the week, but there was always enough activity and Rutherford could easily blend in as just another traveller up from New York.

Rather than Rutherford cross the border into Canada as part of operation JAZZ BAND it had been agreed with careful planning in London that Greg Redington, MI6's man who worked out of the High Commission of the United Kingdom in Ottawa, Canada, would be brought in to co-ordinate the first stage of the operation. A few days before, on March 12, as a subterfuge he had donned the uniform of a Captain in the Canadian Military Police to officially oversee an overnight stop of the British SAS at Montreal Airport. 'D' Squadron had been in transit to BATUS (British army Training Unit Suffield) situated a 100 miles to the south of Calgary, Alberta. Redington's contact had been Warrant Officer David Whittaker, whose responsibility had been to oversee the safe transportation into Canada and the transfer of the instrument personally to Redington. The Warrant Officer had duly handed over the instrument concealed inside an aluminium rectangular box, sized to fit beneath the front bench seat of Redington's vehicle.

It was now for Redington to transport the instrument across the border into the United States without detection. There was the unknown of being stopped and his vehicle thoroughly searched by American Customs. Redington had anticipated such a scenario and had gone to considerable effort to deter a zealous official. If customs were intent on a thorough search, it would take a screwdriver and a strong wrist action. Redington had secured the aluminium box complete with its contents, firmly within the front bench seat-well, covering this in turn with a flat steel sheet cut to fit snugly to the exact profile of the well and spot welded it in

Operation JAZZ BAND

position. When necessary at the appropriate time, the welds would be broken with a sharp chisel and hammer. On inspection, it would appear to be part of the floor pan of the vehicle. Not content with this, Redington had in addition, welded brackets to the front frame of the seat and secured them to the sub-frame with screws. Three brackets each with three screws. His intention was to make the removal of the seat a slow and awkward business. He anticipated, or rather hoped, that an inquisitive official would not be bothered. The necessity of first removing the seat then having to refit it, complete with screws to its original state, would be laborious – hardly necessary for a search.

Redington had carried out a 'dry run' a few weeks earlier without any vehicle search. He was at least familiar with the procedures and would cross over at the busy part of the evening between 5.00 and 7.00 as a Canadian citizen on a short business trip. He would meet covertly with Debra on the evening of the 15th; at the hotel as pre-planned, hand over the case containing the instrument to her and complete his part of Operation JAZZ BAND.

The train was slowing down as Debbie heard a voice somewhere in the background. 'Next stop Plattsburgh in five minutes.' It was the raised voice of the conductor as he passed along the carriage. Having enjoyed a light lunch in the lounge car, Rutherford had fallen asleep after returning to her carriage car seat at around 1.30pm. Hell, she thought, trying not to panic. This wasn't factored in when planning the operation. The brightness pouring into the carriage car from the outside, made her eyes tingle and sting as she struggled to some semblance of alertness. Through bleary eyes she realised it was snowing. The flat whiteness extended beyond the immediate view of the frozen lake into the distance and interwove with the monochrome dove grey sky, falling to earth at an undefined horizon. Nothing of movement

Operation FURY

could be detected across the panorama of gently falling snow as the Montreal-bound train whistled its imminent arrival at Plattsburgh. An odd location for a strategic air force base, thought Rutherford. Perhaps, ironically, that's what is meant by the precarious military stand-off of the 'Cold War.' The snow ploughs requiring to be scrambled before the bombers[30] could rumble along the airstrip, laden down with their deadly nuclear pay-loads and into the air on the way to predetermined military and civilian targets in the Soviet Union. It would be the same for the Russians; the horns like the seven trumpets at Jericho sounding out across the desolate Siberian airbases signalling that mutual annihilation was to begin.

Debbie Rutherford had taken a cab from the train station and checked into her hotel by mid-afternoon. All had gone off without incident on her journey from New York, apart from her unscheduled cat-nap. She was now seated in the hotel dining room and finishing her evening meal with a cup of black coffee, accompanied by the added comfort of a Peter Stuyvesant. It was 8.40 as she glanced at her wrist watch in the quietness of the room where she agreed to make contact with Redington. Debbie had asked for a table which would give her a clear view through the open doors of the dining room to the lobby. The dining room was not as busy as when Rutherford had first entered at around 8.00. A few tables away sat a man in his mid-fifties, more interested in his magazine between sips of coffee, than the surroundings. It wasn't Redington; his physical description didn't come close. The only other guests left were a young couple, engaged in conversation while exchanging loving smiles. Was that the young woman's second or third glass of red wine, wondered Rutherford, as the waiter popped the cork from another half bottle. The dining room would be closing at 9.00, and she was thinking Redington was leaving it rather fine. Perhaps something had gone wrong. Held up behind a snow plough, clearing the main highway route from Montreal, or worse, Redington's car skidded and he had been involved in an accident. Well, whatever it was, there was nothing she could do.

Just then, the waiter interrupted.

'Would you care for more coffee madam?'

'Yes please, if I may. The dining room closes at 9.00. Is that correct?'

'Yes, madam, give or take five or ten minutes. If you prefer, I can bring your coffee through to the lounge bar.'

'No thank you. I prefer to finish my coffee here if that's OK.'

'Certainly madam, just as you wish.'

The hotel cuisine may have been a touch too French, but the coffee was definitely New York Yankee!

Debbie watched as the waiter walked off, gyrating as he negotiated the tables and chairs on his way back to the kitchen. She could not resist a half smile at the thought of waiters dressed in their clip waistcoats and obligatory tight pants reminded her of Spanish bullfighters! It was the noise filtering from the reception that ceased her fantasy of the young waiter and brought her attention back on track. The voices were not quite audible to make out what was being discussed. The man standing in conversation with the receptionist had set down a small canvass travel bag, along with a silver coloured rectangular metal case. It was the clink of the box being set on the hard tiled floor, running along the desk front which gave the first indication that Redington may finally have arrived. Neither had ever met, but they had spoken briefly by telephone. From his physical description of 5'10", slim build and mousey brown hair, Debbie could not quite tell as the man at reception turned down his overcoat collar and removed his red scarf – hardly dressed like a waiter or bullfighter, more like an ordinary business man as she had expected.

Operation FURY

It was the silver metal case that was the tell-tale. It is bound to be Redington, thought Rutherford.

Those planning Operation JAZZ BAND, had decided that the two MI6 officers should not make public contact, just a covert acknowledgement of one another in passing. It was down to Rutherford to initiate the contact. She could just see the female receptionist pointing in the direction of the dining room, obviously giving directions to the newly-arrived guest. As he walked towards the dining room, Rutherford could now see and make an assessment. He was the right height and she gauged he was of slim build from his open overcoat. It is him, she decided – bound to be him. Rutherford was last to leave the dining room as she anticipated her next move. Both met face to face at the dining room doors. Rutherford dropped her room key and allowing Redington to respond by picking it up.

'Your key, I believe. Room 405. Is this yours?'

'Yes, thank you, how kind,' as she extended her hand, feeling the coolness of Redington's slender fingers as he pressed the key into her hand.

'My pleasure.'

Contact had been made.

Rutherford was half way along the corridor on her way to the elevator when she heard the young waiter explain apologetically that the dining room had now closed but he was sure the Chef would rustle up a snack of hot soup and sandwiches along with a pot of hot coffee and send it up by room service.

On leaving the dining room, Debbie made her way directly to her bedroom. She had settled in and was sitting on the bed reading, or rather leafing through out-of-date magazines provided by the hotel, waiting patiently for her MI6 colleague to follow up on the initial contact. It was 10.25 by her travel alarm, on the bedside unit.

Operation JAZZ BAND

Rutherford tried not to become agitated by the apparent indifference of her colleague – not even a quick room-to-room phone call to let her know what his intentions were. Again she could do nothing but wait. If she fell asleep, too bad; it had been a long day.

As Rutherford eased off the bed, there was a knock on the door. Giving a sigh of relief, at last, she thought. The man has shifted his ass into gear. As she peeped through the door spy lens – yes, it was him and holding the silver metal case. Debbie opened the door.

'Hello Debbie Rutherford. I hope you haven't become anxious.' Redington entered the room, squeezing past her and walked towards the bed, dropping the case onto it with obvious relief.

'No, not anxious, just concerned for the hand-over,' biting her tongue.

'Sorry, I got held up on the route down. A truck skidded and jack-knifed, blocking one lane and holding up the traffic, I thought I was going to freeze to death. The unpredictable car heater wasn't working. After seeing you in the dining room I went to my room and took a hot shower to get some heat back into my bones. I'm on the floor below, room 309. Well there it is. The instrument secure in its metal case and delivered without damage. It's now your responsibility,' as Redington gestured with his open hand towards the bed.

'Do you know what precisely it is and what it's for?' continued Redington.

'No, to both questions,' retorted Rutherford abruptly.

'Are you not a bit curious?'

'I wasn't told and I didn't ask, except as explained to me that it is essential to a particular operation and I was to keep it with me at all times, even when I went to the bathroom.'

'Yes, that's how it was explained to me. A bit over the top, but orders are orders.'

'Yes Greg, they are. Let's just get on with it and transfer it, whatever it may be' as she lifted up the empty saxophone case on to the bed. Debbie started to undo the top buttons of her blouse. The silver chain around her neck caught on one as she attempted to undo the clasp.

'Can I help?'

'No, not with those cold fingers, I can manage thank you.'

'Let me help,' and without waiting for an answer, Redington quickly undid the clasp, removed the chain complete with its attachment of a small key and dropped it into her waiting hand.

'There we are. I couldn't have managed that with cold fingers, could I?'

'No I suppose not.'

With anticipation, Rutherford placed the key into the lock of the metal case. Turning it, the lock clicked open and with both hands, she opened the lid. Both looked at one another with glum disappointment. The case did not reveal what the instrument was. Whatever it might be, it was hidden from view by a rigid foam packaging, clipped with tightly bound tape running both across and lengthways. There was no way of breaking open the inner encapsulation without cutting loose the tape.

'Well that's that. We are not meant or required to know its secrets. Help me ease the package out and transfer it over. It wouldn't do it by itself Greg.'

'OK, just ease it loose at your end Debbie.'

The package fitted neatly into the saxophone case as they both carefully eased it down.

'Tailor made, a perfect fit. Perhaps it's some kind of electronic surveillance equipment – a listening device for spying on some delegation at the UN. It's probably a MAMS.'

'And what's that Graham?'

Operation JAZZ BAND

'It's a microwave activated microphone system Debbie, and if properly installed out of sight, is virtually impossible to detect. A clever little bugger you might say.'

'It's not the only clever little bugger, is it Graham?'

Redington gave a broad smile to counter Debbie's jibe.

'What's the point of speculating? Close the case and I'll secure the lock. There we are. Perfect. Next stop New York.'

Rutherford raised her arms behind her head to re-fix the chain key. Redington moved forward to assist, putting his hands on hers and attempting to take hold of the clasp. Their mutual fumbling caused the silver chain to slip forward and disappear beneath the front of Rutherford's blouse. Redington moved his hands instinctively forward to catch the chain from falling. It was then he noticed Debbie's fullness, partly visible by her half-open white silk blouse, gently undulating to the rhythm of her breathing. His hands stopped in mid-air as he realised where they were going.

'Check is it Greg? I assume you play chess?' as Debbie's green eyes met Redington's full gaze moving upwards in response.

'What? I suppose – well I am a bit out of practice. Anyway isn't it white to move first, Debbie?'

In that case Greg let me help you a little. I said check not checkmate. With deliberate slowness, she undid the remaining buttons of her blouse and pulling it out from under her skirt revealed her slim waist; like a magnet drawing Redington's arms around her. His slender hands slipped beneath the top of her pants and downwards over her smooth curvaceous hips. Debbie felt the warmth from his caressing hands permeate into her buttocks and a tingling pulsation between her thighs as Greg firmly drew her close.

'You are not as out of practice as you may think Greg – and it is still your move.'

It was next morning and Rutherford was back in the dining

room, this time finishing her breakfast. In less than three hours' time, she will have checked out from the hotel and be at the station in good time to board the New York bound train at 12.30pm. It had stopped snowing during the night and there was a tinge of blue to the sky. As Debbie looked out through the dining room window over the freshly banked snow drifts and across the frozen lake, she began to imagine what it would be like in summer. Lake Champlain, no longer sparkling with icy crystals in the low winter sunshine, but glinting with floating argent discs like an Impressionist painting on a tranquil summer morning as the sun rose above the Green Hills of Vermont at the far shore of the lake.

But Lake Champlain had not always been so peaceful. Debbie had been reading an article on the history of Plattsburgh the previous evening while waiting in her room for Redington to make the follow-up contact. The article described the early nineteenth century Plattsburgh with its population of around 3,000, when the British Red Coats in the War of 1812 crossed from Canada into the northern states of America to capture and control the waterways of Lake Champlain and confront the defending Yankee militia and regulars of the Army forces. The battle finally won by the Americans in the naval engagement and retreat of the British army ensured Plattsburgh and Lake Champlain remained American territory. The rumbling thunder of battery artillery as the opposing war ships came broadside on and clouds of fusil smoke in the naval skirmishes of the Battle of Plattsburgh[31] were now long silent and had floated away into the distant past.

There had been no sign of Greg. Had he left earlier that morning on his journey back to Ottawa? More likely he had taken an extra hour to catch up with his sleep. After all, he seemed somewhat exhausted when he left her at around 1.30am to return to his room. Greg may be her MI6 colleague, but under the necessary veneer of the job, she found him warm and more intimate than the other men she had encountered while posted to the UN. She sensed there was no underlying motive. She had felt completely at ease with his arms wrapped around her and her legs entwined with his strong undulating body in that hour of unscheduled intimacy the previous evening. That's that. Debbie's thoughts moved on and she slowly surveyed the room. No, Greg had gone. No sign of the loving couple either. Her gaze was caught by 'Magazine Man' as she had labelled him the previous night in the dining room. There he was once more seated in the corner transfixed to more reading material, hardly lifting his head to acknowledge the waitress as she poured his coffee. Debbie looked at her watch. Time to move and return to her room to complete her packing and double check that all was secure with the saxophone case which she had concealed and locked away inside the wardrobe.

She was now at reception. 'Yes Madam, cash is fine. Did you have a pleasant stay at the hotel?'

'Yes thank you. It is nice to be inside in the warmth and looking out at the snow in such cold weather.'

'Yes Madam. It will be another month before the snows finally disappear.'

'I would like to come back again in the summer, if I can and spend a little longer.'

Debbie handed over her room key and checked out.

'Can you order me a taxi cab please? I need to be at the Amtrak Station by 12.30.'

'Yes of course Miss Rutherford. Oh! Miss Rutherford. An envelope was left for you by a Mr Redington when he checked out. It was around 9.00 this morning. I had just come on duty and I rang your room to let you know but there was no response.'

'That's OK. I think I may have been on my way down to breakfast at the time.'

Operation FURY

'Here we are Madam, your receipt and envelope.'

Debbie sat down in the lobby to wait for her taxi cab. She decided to open the envelope in case it had something to do with Operation JAZZ BAND.

Debbie – sorry to leave without seeing you but I need to find a garage to have my car heater fixed for the long journey home. I had a sense I was being watched in the dining room at breakfast, just a feeling. A middle-aged man, who was reading at one of the tables, seemed interested in me. So be cautious on your return to New York

I have reserved a double room for the end of June, so if you are at a loose end and need some summer comfort, let me know.

Greg R.

At the bottom of the notepaper, Redington had sketched the scene of a snowman playing a saxophone and a figure of a young lady listening intently.

The train arrived at Penn Station on schedule and Rutherford felt relief to be back in New York, nearing the completion of the operation. She struggled awkwardly with both cases as she attempted to step on to the platform.

'Can I help?' came a voice from behind.

Rutherford turned around, startled as she recognised the man who had just spoken. It was 'Magazine Man' from the hotel dining room. She remembered Redington's note telling her to be cautious. There had been no sign of the man on the train journey down and she had forgotten all about him. But now there he was. It took a few seconds before Rutherford answered as her instinct automatically moved to orange alert. 'Magazine Man' was much taller than she had imagined him to be back at the hotel; at least six feet perhaps more and heavily built.

'It's fine. I can get a porter to help me, thank you.'

Operation JAZZ BAND

'No need. Save yourself a few dollars,' as his hand moved forward to take hold of the saxophone case.

Damn it, thought Rutherford, as she quickly moved to stop his advance to grip the case.

'Well perhaps,' as she handed him her small suitcase. No need to start a fuss, probably he was just being helpful. Besides, there were too many people around for him to make off with the saxophone case and its contents, if that's what his underlying motive was. This is an MI6 undercover operation. There was absolutely no possibility Rutherford was about to blow it. She remembered her former instructor when she went through the unarmed defence training course on her way to becoming a field operative. Be defensive first. If that doesn't deter an attack, then be lethal. Am I going to have to put that stuff into effect? Rutherford realised her vulnerability as the adrenalin surged through her body. A carefully aimed punch to the throat would be her physical force retort if 'Magazine Man' was determined to seize the instrument case. Defensive or lethal, Debbie Rutherford MI6 did not much care. She would claim self-defence if unavoidably detained by the New York police.

Rutherford began to wonder as they walked along the platform. Was she being too suspicious, even paranoid? Should she perhaps mention that she had seen her temporary companion at the hotel in Plattsburgh? Better not, as she wasn't interested in polite conversation which would not in any way ease her apprehension.

Rutherford and 'Magazine Man' were now standing on the sidewalk beside the taxi cab rank. Rutherford opened the rear door of the next cab in line.

'Thank you for your help,' somewhat relieved nothing had occurred and unarmed combat had been unnecessary.

'Magazine Man' set the suitcase down on the sidewalk.

'My pleasure Maggie to be of assistance,' and without waiting

Operation FURY

for a reply, he immediately turned and walked off, removing a folded up newspaper from his overcoat pocket and disposing of it into an adjacent trash bin. Rutherford was stunned rigid on hearing his words.

How does he know my cover name? How was this possible?

It was the voice of the cab driver that diverted her thoughts.

'Hey lady, do you want this cab or not?'

She quickly bundled the two cases and herself into the back of the taxi.

'Upper Fifth, Guggenheim Museum please, I'm in a bit of a hurry and there is an extra five for you.'

'Sure lady.' The yellow cab sped off into the evening Manhattan traffic.

Rutherford's heart pounded and her stomach churned with pulsating nerves. How was it possible for 'Magazine Man' to know her cover name? His accent was Canadian, not American. Was he from the Canadian Security Intelligence Service who somehow had found out about Operation JAZZ BAND, and what business was it of the Canadians anyway to involve themselves? Surely Redington had not been compromised. The CSIS would have no reason to compromise a British Intelligence Officer as a double agent. Relations between the two services were cordial as far as she was aware. Canada was a close ally, as was the US. But then, there she was, carrying out an MI6 operation probably without the knowledge of the CIA or FBI. It was Redington's note after all that had alerted suspicion of 'Magazine Man.' Rutherford was at a loss to put logic to it, except one other possibility. 'Magazine Man' was MI6; a background under-cover chaperone to provide protection for Rutherford and more importantly the instrument; one of those MI6 fire arm Protection Unit officers that remain in the twilight of an operation. It would be vital for such a person to know the cover name of the person or persons being protected if instant contact became absolutely necessary. That is why he had used her cover name; there was no other explanation. He had slipped up as he broke off his protection duty. On the other hand, it may have been deliberate. In the end, was it just a field training exercise to assess Rutherford's capabilities on how she would respond to sudden situations? And was Redington part of the sham or was he too being assessed? Whatever the purpose of JAZZ BAND, it was not a sham. At least part of it had its diversion as Debbie reflected the previous evening's events with Greg and the pleasures of their intimacy. As the cab driver weaved his way through the traffic, Rutherford was committed to complete the final part of her task and safely deliver the instrument. In less than ten minutes time Debbie Rutherford's part in Operation JAZZ BAND would be over. She had mixed feelings of relief and concern as she stood in the apartment lobby near the Guggenheim Museum, the address to which final delivery for the case and its unknown contents was to be made.

'Hello, I have a delivery for Miss Hamilton, apartment 802. It is the saxophone she ordered from '*Sounds Alive*'.'

'Yes Miss, if you wouldn't mind waiting here I'll just ring the apartment.' As he picked up the phone, the Concierge gestured for Rutherford to take a seat opposite his desk.

'That's OK Miss. Miss Hamilton says you may go up. Apartment 802 is almost opposite just to the left as you step out from the elevator.'

'Thank you.'

Rutherford set down the saxophone case across the apartment door and pressed the buzzer. She did not wait for the door to open but immediately turned towards the elevator to make her way out. As she pressed the elevator button, the apartment door opened. A young woman bending down picked up the case. She looked up

Operation FURY

towards Rutherford, smiled and without waiting for an acknowledgement; she closed the door to apartment 802.

Rutherford was now standing on the sidewalk as she adjusted her overcoat and turned up her fur collar against the coolness of the evening. Operation JAZZ BAND was over and it was home to her apartment for a hot bath and a few drinks to relax allowing her to gather her thoughts before operational debriefing the next day by Head of Station Max Westcott. It would be then that Rutherford would raise the subject of 'Magazine Man,' friend or foe? She stepped onto the road to hail a cab, totally unaware as to the events that would unfold the following day. It would be then, Debbie Rutherford would come to realise her involvement, in assassination.

Three 'long' months after their first encounter, Debbie Rutherford and Greg Redington met again at Hotel Lake Plattsburgh. On this occasion it was not on another joint MI6 operation, but for them. Greg and Debbie spend a week together watching the summer sun rising over the silver blue waters of Lake Champlain before Redington returned to London. Debbie followed shortly afterwards. Her two-year posting as MI6 field officer, amongst other duties at the UN, was of the highest quality as reflected by her Head of Station's staff assessment. Shortly after returning to London, she was promoted and reassigned to the all important Russia Desk. A few of Debbie's colleagues, 'slower knights,' resented her promotion. They watched, 'secretly' hoping she would someday make a wrong move and drop from the chess board.

A year later and with great surprise to her MI6 colleagues, Debbie Rutherford quietly became Mrs Greg Redington. It remained to be seen if Debra 'Maggie' Redington would have all the attributes which she displayed in New York and someday become Head of the British Secret Intelligence Service – Director-General MI6 with the exclusive privilege to sign orders in green ink.

14
Artemis Arrives

It was thirteen months previously, when Major Moore first became aware of Artemis on that fateful February Saturday, back in Belfast. Moore had accompanied Inspector Montgomery to the home of Patricia Hamilton to inform her parents of their daughter's murder.

It was in the home of Patricia Hamilton while Montgomery was endeavouring to explain the circumstances of her death that Moore had noticed, sitting on the mantelpiece, a photograph of Patricia's sister in Army uniform. It transpired that her elder sister had joined 15 Parachute Regiment of the Territorial Army while attending Aberdeen University in Scotland, four years earlier. It was in her final year and as Moore was later to discover, she was interested in making a full-time career in the Army on leaving University, hopefully with a degree in Russian and English.

Peter Moore had quietly befriended Artemis at Patricia's funeral and had subsequently offered to help if he could, in furthering her career. His long-term motive was to persuade her in the future, to join Army Intelligence Corps and eventually work in Ulster within the indigenous population in the dangerous emerging covert game of undercover intelligence gathering and counter-terrorist operations.

Operation FURY

When Operation FURY was in its initial planning stage, Major Moore never considered Artemis for the task she was now trained, conditioned and committed to carry out. Of the three or four possible military marksmen candidates, none seemed suited to operate in what would be a civilian environment. They were professional soldiers trained to operate in military zones of conflict and any one of them unwittingly could compromise the top secret operation. It had not been since the First World War that British army had used snipers and this left Moore with limited options. After long thought, he had a flash of inspired genius – the possibility of using Artemis, specifically trained for Operation FURY. Females had not been used for such purposes since WWII when Special Operations Executive had a number of female trained agents to carry out covert missions in occupied Europe. SOE had been disbanded at the ending of WWII with a number of agents and staff being absorbed into MI5 and MI6. But that was over twenty-five years ago and unlikely that any of the 'Baker Street Irregulars'[32] would be suitable or for that matter, at their age, willing to volunteer.

In the exclusively male-orientated realm of special forces, the SAS and SBS, a female was an object of desire; someone to get drunk with, then shagged and usually forgotten about. Female liberation was not a concept within the British army. Sniper training for a female would be treated as 'simply not on; plainly stupid and out of the question.' But there was always the exception and Major Moore would insist upon it. His single-minded determination had gained the support of Colonel Jones and in turn his influence with Major General Patrick Wingfield ultimately proved positive.

Moore recalled the last day of training at the target 'kill zone,' a section of undulating scrubland at the Weapons Training Unit

Artemis Arrives

where he had witnessed Artemis' capabilities; a final test on her resolve to become a proficient sniper. Failure to complete her final task would mean she could not be used for the operation and Moore's reputation of judgement in selecting a female would be questioned by Army command. Major Moore, along with Artemis' instructor, Sergeant 'Taffy' Edwards, had installed themselves inside the observation post, some 500 yards from where an Army transport lorry had pulled up a few minutes earlier. Sergeant Edwards picked up and switched on the mobile field radio phone.

'Corporal Hamilton, your only and final task this morning is to eliminate the single target which will be presented shortly and some distance forward from your present position'

'Yes Sergeant. Can I assume the target will not be the driver of the lorry that has just pulled up?' came the muffled reply.

'No Corporal, the driver is not the target, I repeat, *not* the target; nor for that matter, any of the other Army personnel. You are to hold back and observe only, until the vehicle has off-loaded and driven clear from the area of the kill zone.'

'Understood Sergeant. I'm holding off until further instruction.' Sergeant Edwards gestured to the Major that he may wish to observe with the binoculars hanging on the hook to his left. Moore adjusted the focus of the binoculars and brought the view into clarity. The back flap of the lorry dropped down, immediately followed by six squaddies in sharp order who proceeded to remove the load; a large wooden crate. The obvious weight caused it to thump and squelch upon the soggy ground as the soldiers struggled with their task. One squaddie proceeded to open the front gate of the crate while two others kicked the side panels. Moore nodded his approval to the Sergeant, as both watched in silence until the lorry complete with personnel had moved off and was clear of the zone.

Operation FURY

'Corporal Hamilton, you are now free to move to eliminate the target and in your own time. You have the field Corporal,' came the instructions from Sergeant Edwards.

'I have the field Sergeant Edwards.'

Eight seconds later the hefty bulk of a pink sow keeled over onto its side – stone dead.

Artemis was not told of the intended task until completion of her Sniper training course. She was asked to volunteer and given twenty-four hours to decide.

Corporal Jennifer Hamilton, codename Artemis, became the first female in the British Armed Forces to receive intensive modern weapons training: the first female professional Army Sniper to be deployed in covert operations. Ironically her first bullet to be fired with deadly accuracy would be to eliminate a civilian target; nonetheless, an enemy of the British state.

* * *

It was Thursday morning and Major Moore was walking up the steps leading to the main entrance into the Metropolitan Museum of Art. He had decided that morning, rather than walk the same route he had taken to meet Freddie Jones at the three bears, he would take the subway from Central Terminal to 79th Street and walk the short distance from Lexington Avenue to the Museum.

Moore had spent part of Wednesday in his hotel room going over calculations of distance and time frame estimates for targeting-in the Hydra from the position of the Hoffman's French window. He doubled-checked everything and was sure he had factored in all the relevant aspects. Moore concluded the Freddie Jones' suggestion of using the Hoffman apartment was the better option except for one major concern. Artemis would be exposed to a

Artemis Arrives

greater risk of being observed and discovered. To reduce this risk to a minimum, Artemis would need to position herself within the room, several feet back from the window while still being able to sight through to the target. This was a judgement and adjustment that could only be made by Artemis on the spot. Peter Moore had calculated and was sure – as sure as he could be – that the optimum distance from the French window to the target should ideally be close to 400 yards, provided it was not windy on the day. If there was anything more than a light breeze, then the range would need to be reduced by perhaps as much as fifty yards. Moore would go over all the points with Artemis but in the end, it would be down to her fine-tuning and her skill that would ultimately matter on the day. Her skill based upon what she had learned on the intensive training course at the Army Weapons Training Unit, where her natural ability proved exceptional. Psychological introjection was an essential element of the programme. There was no difference between a plywood profile cut-out and breathing flesh and blood; they were one of the same – a target. In this, Artemis was no different than those who had preceded her; proficiency was only proved by death. Artemis had yet to zero-in on a breathing human being, squeeze the trigger and kill.

Before leaving for Washington, Colonel Jones had spoken to Frank, his apartment block concierge. He would be away unavoidably on business for the next week and that his niece was arriving later that day. She was to be in New York for some musical event and would be staying at his apartment for a few days so there was no need for concern as he had already provided his niece with an apartment key.

As Moore climbed the steps of the Museum he saw Artemis waiting just to the left of the main entrance and obviously avoiding the flux of gathering visitors. Moore could not avoid the throng himself as he was forced to wait for a gaggle of teenage school girls to cross his path. He could not fail to notice that liberated femininity, or what he assumed that to be, had infected the New York female teenager. The schoolgirls' self-awareness, emerging from the twilight of sleepy innocence into the daylight of conscious early womanhood had expressed itself in the daring shortness of the school girl skirt. No longer pleated, nor gently flouncing with modesty below the knee, but deliberately shortened to mid-thigh, encircling slender silky limbs of shapely perfection. Moore felt uneasy; inwardly embarrassed that he was distracted by self-inflicted voyeurism.

'Come along girls and stay together at all times,' instructed one of the school mistresses. Moore suddenly realised - children! There were bound to be children taking part in the parade. No one had considered this, including himself, when planning the operation. Hopefully there wouldn't be any at the head of the parade and this would be restricted to the leading members, organisers and guests which would include the Hydra. If Artemis mentions it, thought Moore, then he would dismiss it as being unlikely and irrelevant to the operation. Moore continued to climb the steps weaving a path slowly upwards in the direction to where Artemis was waiting. She spotted Moore and immediately started down towards him. Both met, exchanging smiles, but there was no embrace between officer and corporal.

'Good to see you Jennifer; how are you. I trust all is OK with you?'

'Yes Sir. Everything is fine so far. The Colonel's note was a bit unexpected. It didn't say much and actually nothing at all, other than to meet you here. Do we have a problem?'

'No Jennifer, there is nothing to be anxious about. The operation is still live and all is on course. Possibly a slight modification which Colonel Jones and I believe would be to overall

Artemis Arrives

advantage for the operation and give you better positioning on D-day. But look, let's walk a bit and I'll explain. Somewhere quieter, through the park and I'll buy you a New York hotdog. They are actually quite good and better than you would expect for alfresco fast food.'

It was almost mid-morning by the time Moore had explained everything in detail and both were now walking along Fifth Avenue. Artemis had listened intently, only interrupting Moore on a few occasions for clarification on some important point.

'Sorry, I hadn't forgotten to ask. Has the instrument arrived Jennifer?'

'Yes. All is in order, perfect. All we need now is for the Hydra to play his part and present himself tomorrow.'

'I think we should break off contact now and I'll let you go off on your own to make a decision on which apartment is better suited for the operation. Here are a few notes and calculations I worked out yesterday. They may be of some assistance to you or you may prefer to work things out for yourself. Anyway, here you are.'

Moore slipped a half folded envelope into Artemis' coat pocket.

'Well, I believe that's it. Everything is covered and stay calm and aim true. After all, it's only another target. You will be fine.'

Jennifer smiled and as she turned to walk away, Moore added, 'See you in Montreal on the 18th.'

'Yes, and with operation accomplished.'

15

Montgomery Arrives

It was the day after Major Moore had arrived in New York that on the morning of the 14th, Chief Inspector Montgomery left Belfast on the connecting flight to Glasgow and from there, onwards to New York. Moore and Montgomery were unaware of each other's movements and therefore their separate reasons for being in New York. They were never to cross one another's path, although momentarily they would be within a few hundred yards of each other, three days later. Montgomery was exhausted by the long day of travelling and the time difference made it even longer. After checking in to his hotel off West 42nd Street, he had a light meal and was in bed by 9.30.

Montgomery was awakened the next morning at 7.30 by the unfamiliar din of traffic noise from the street below, filtering in through the partly open window of his room. As he showered and dressed, he wondered what response he would receive from the FBI. Would they have a positive approach in pursuing, apprehending and ultimately extraditing Dermot Patrick Ryan back to the UK? Chief Inspector McClatchey had already sent the official paperwork. Montgomery would be on hand to provide any necessary additional detailed information. After breakfast he made

Operation FURY

his way to the Federal Plaza in Downtown Manhattan. What seemed over-the-top security checks, Montgomery had been escorted to the FBI offices, by a slim, red-head who did not engage in conversation. Hand gestures were her only means of communication. Not even a hint of a smile. Perhaps she had bad teeth, thought Montgomery. He felt slightly nervous in the unfamiliar domain and the red-head hadn't helped. Within a few minutes the door opposite to where he was sitting, opened.

'Good morning Chief Inspector Montgomery. I'm Special Agent Sorrell Dinkalow. Welcome to New York and the FBI.'

'Good morning Special Agent Dinkalow - CI James Montgomery Royal Ulster Constabulary.' Both men smiled affably and shook hands.

'Right, Chief Inspector, if you would like to follow me into my office we can get to know each other and of course I can learn a bit more about your fugitive from justice, Dermot Patrick Ryan.'

Dinkalow was a small man, well-dressed in a grey three-piece suit, white shirt and jazzy tie. He spoke rather loudly with a mild New York accent. Montgomery immediately got the impression he would be efficient in approach to everything and was unlikely to engage in small talk. Montgomery was led into what was a spacious office as he casually surveyed the room observing the ambience. The stars and stripes draped from its pole, was conspicuously placed beneath a photograph of the President. Flanked on each side of the portrait was an assortment of images and memorabilia of what was obviously Dinkalow's progression through the service; symbols of his dedication to the Bureau meticulously arranged with artistic flare. No ambiguity here, thought Montgomery. Americans like to remind themselves of who they are. Dinkalow's office was a visible enthusiastic reverence to the federal state and to the maintenance of its laws. Pointing to a

Montgomery Arrives

comfortable chair, facing what was obviously Dinkalow's uncluttered desk, he asked Montgomery to sit down.

'I'll take your overcoat if I may. This building can become quite warm by lunch time and my office catches the sun most of the day. The air conditioning on occasions, struggles to cope.'

Air conditioning, thought Montgomery – at home it was simple; open a few windows to get rid of the haze of cigarette smoke.

'I know a little of the problems of Northern Ireland or Ireland from the television and newspaper reports. Do people actually kill one another merely over religion?'

'Yes, that's part of the whole sorry state of affairs – driven by hatred,' replied Montgomery in a low voice hoping that he did not need to expand further on the situation.

'I have an older brother who served in the US Navy during the war. He was stationed at Londonderry for a while and married a girl from Limavady after the war ended. They both settled up-state and from conversations with them, I know a little about the country. The RUC, that's a British police force and An Garda Síochána completely separate. Is that correct?'

'Yes, regional and county police forces with Chief Constables in charge all operate under the Crown. Cooperation on occasions can lack efficiency but with this terrorism there are more reliable and regular communications. The Garda is the police force of the Republic of Ireland, totally separate. Cooperation at times can be spasmodic. It is more about the politics which tends to put a damper on them locating suspects. Extradition can be a problem. Their courts are reluctant to grant extradition requests. When terrorist suspects go on the run, it is usually over the border into the Republic. They tend to lay-up in safe houses, usually in remote country areas and man hunts can be a waste of time and resources at least that what the Garda tells the RUC. The US seems to be a new venture for these people, lying low and hoping they can be forgotten about.'

'I have received the details on Ryan from Chief Superintendent McClatchey and have subsequently spoken with him by phone so I will start by bringing you up-to-date on our position.'

'Yes. That's fine,' replied Montgomery.

Dinkalow opened the file on his desk and began to refer to its contents.

'Dermot Patrick Ryan passed through immigration into the United States on 2nd March. There was no reason to detain him or refuse him entry. As you are aware, our Central Bureau of the Department of Justice didn't receive an Interpol arrest warrant until nine days after he entered the US. We subsequently followed up on the Brooklyn hotel address he had given on his visa application. It was carried out by two of our agents under a normal routine check so as not to arouse suspicion. He checked in to the hotel on the same day as he entered the country. According to the hotel staff, the maid stated Ryan hadn't slept in the bed after she changed the linen and cleaned the room on the 9th. That was five days ago. The hotel is a bed and breakfast establishment and Ryan paid in advance until 18th March. The hotel still has his passport and his clothes were in his room. We are assuming he will need to return to collect his passport and belongings on or before the check-out date of the 18th. Our agents asked the maid to let us know when Ryan returns. She was promised a generous tip for a simple phone call. The maid will stick to the arrangement if she wants the other half of the $10 bill. You are aware when we apprehend Ryan he could challenge the arrest warrant and extradition before a Federal Court Judge. If that were the case, then he could be in custody for weeks. It may mean either you remain in the US or return home and coming back for the court hearing. You really do need to be here to attend the hearing to

Montgomery Arrives

answer any questions the court may have. If extradition was granted, then you would be required to escort him back to the UK.'

'That will not be a problem. The RUC is determined to have him returned to Belfast and stand trial for the brutal double murder, Special Agent Dinkalow.'

'When speaking with Chief Superintendent McClatchey, he believes Ryan is involved with the IRA but there is no mention of this on the arrest warrant.'

'No, we have no firm evidence other than he has been seen in the company of IRA members. I can vouch for this personally. The RUC believes Ryan to be an important member of the IRA.'

'There is growing support for the IRA in the United States, particularly here in New York and across the river in New Jersey, not only from the Irish but also some sympathy from members of government. Nothing official of course but we need to tread cautiously. I don't want the FBI stepping on Senator's toes if it can be avoided. There are a number of groups and well-to-do individuals who the FBI believes are connected to and involved with the Irish Republican Brotherhood. It is these people who are pushing the agenda for financial support – fund-raising events, things of that nature. Dare I say, Chief Inspector, we believe guns are part of the agenda of support. The FBI, along with other federal agencies, is taking an active interest. Gun-running is a federal crime.'

Dinkalow paused for a few seconds, looking directly at Montgomery.

'Do you think Ryan is here in New York to make contact with members of the IRB and obtain guns?'

'Yes, it also crossed my mind. It is a reasonable proposition. Unofficially we believe Ryan is someone with the know-how on that type of operation. Someone deeply embedded within the IRA and probably at the top end of their command structure. The RUC classify him as very dangerous and dedicated. He is a professional terrorist, rather than someone on the periphery of things; a top dog to be reckoned with and a murderer without conscience. We are adamant that Ryan is unaware the RUC knows of his whereabouts. He may feel safe here in America.'

'If Ryan is connected to the IRA in Ireland as the RUC firmly believes, then there is the possibility of him making contact with their supporters here in the US. That would put an added complexion on the whole situation. Ryan, travelling on a British passport,[33] doesn't fit with connections to the IRA. If Ryan is Irish, how is it he is travelling on a British passport?'

Montgomery explained that the RUC has reason to believe Ryan was born in England of an English mother and an Irish father which made him eligible to claim joint British and Irish nationalities. Montgomery did not elaborate on Ryan's British army record. That was confidential, between him and Major Moore and besides, it was unnecessary in assisting the FBI apprehending him for extradition.

'From what you say Chief Inspector, and what we know, he entered the US on a valid British passport. Would it be in order to suggest he may also have with him an Irish national passport? Would that be a reasonable possibility?'

'Yes, that's a possibility, but I don't know if he has indeed an Irish passport.'

'Well I think in that case, we should check with the Irish authorities to make sure. I'll do that straight away after our meeting.'

Montgomery nodding to indicate his agreement, felt a bit stupid that he had not checked up on the possibility of Ryan holding two passports. He consoled himself that it was the urgency of obtaining the international warrant and making the arrangements for travelling to the US. It simply did not cross his mind.

'With these two murders Ryan is suspected of committing,

makes him potentially a dangerous alien. The sooner he is apprehended and extradited from the US, the better. Rather than rely solely on the hotel maid for information, I have earlier this morning set up a twenty-four hour undercover surveillance unit to watch the hotel. If and when he turns up, he will immediately be arrested. We will give it until the 18th; it is all I can do for now, Chief Inspector. I will of course advise immigration of the situation and that we hold an international arrest warrant on one Dermot Patrick Ryan, British national and possibly also travelling on an Irish passport. As you can understand I can't directly involve you in any FBI operational aspect of the arrest of Ryan. I will let you know of any development that arises. You are here until the 18th I believe.'

'Yes the 18th. I fly back on a mid-evening flight. I am staying at the Whitney Court Hotel, off 42nd Street. You can contact me there.'

'OK Chief Inspector Montgomery. It is good to meet you and make face to face contact with an officer in the RUC. I shall contact you, hopefully with positive news before you leave.'

'Thank you Special Agent Dinkalow for the FBI's commitment to Ryan's apprehension.'

On his way back to the hotel, Montgomery reflected on the exchange of views with Dinkalow. He realised the implications of the FBI position. If Ryan was indeed in the US to organise a weapons shipment for the IRA and the FBI caught and arrested him in the act, then he would probably receive a prison sentence and extradition would be put back until his release. It could be years before he was brought before the Northern Ireland courts. Montgomery felt despondent. It always seemed that when he was close to capturing Ryan, he managed to step out of reach. Either by calculation or luck, Ryan was a Harry Houdini figure – there was always another miraculous escape from avoiding capture. With the assistance of the FBI, hopefully his luck would finally run out.

16

Undercover For Drinks

It was 8.30 by the time Montgomery had finished enjoying his morning shower. The phone rang. Montgomery was sitting on the edge of the bed and was in two minds whether to answer the ringing phone. He reluctantly stretched across to pick up the receiver.

'Hello, room five twenty.'

'Good morning Sir. I have an outside party on the line. I am putting the call through, said the female voice at the other end in a thinly cultured New York accent.

'Yes, OK, thank you.'

'Hello, Chief Inspector. It's Sorrel Dinkalow. I hope I am not disturbing you.'

'No Sorrel.' What can I do for you?'

'James. As you, or rather we have had no luck so far in locating and apprehending your suspect, I thought of an outside possibility. A last change before you're off back to Northern Ireland in a few days. As you know, it is the St Patrick's Day Parade tomorrow and there is a pre-event get-together of the Irish clan – local dignitaries and organisers of the parade, and I am informed it includes overseas invited Irish guests. I was thinking we might have some of that 'luck of the Irish' and perhaps spot your suspect Ryan. It's a long shot, nothing more. What do you think James?'

'I'm beginning to think that he has moved on out of New York, but if you feel it's worthwhile, I'm open to any suggestions you have.'

'Thank you James, I'll take that as a yes. We will need to treat it as an undercover operation and with your Irish accent and my New York charm, we will fit in OK. Nothing to be concerned about. One of our administration people here in the office has a second cousin who manages the restaurant grill bar. It's called 'Rossa O'Donovan' in midtown, just off 8th. She can secure us a table for four. I'll pick you up from your hotel around 8 o'clock. It's not black tie, so may I suggest to dress nice James? It's a bit up and up and we don't want to be outclassed by the dignitaries and honoured guests. 8 o'clock it is then James.'

Dinkalow rang off and before Montgomery could ask the obvious questions.

A table for four and honoured guests. What had he just agreed to? thought Montgomery. Ah well, Special Agent Dinkalow said it was an undercover operation. At least he can claim his share of the tab on expenses and the thought that 'Red Tom' Ryan might, just might turn up gave Montgomery a sense of nervous anticipation. After so many months, the prospect that he would apprehend Ryan at last was the only reason he was in town.

It was approaching 6.30pm and after a light lunch around midday, Montgomery had rambled at right angles up and down the Avenues and east and west along the streets of linear midtown Manhattan. The daylight filtering down between the skyscrapers was beginning to fade as he made his way east along 42nd Street and back to the hotel, a few blocks past Times Square. The constant traffic noise and fumes from the endless taxis were giving him a headache. Before his undercover operation with Dinkalow, he needed to shake it off. Montgomery, after taking Dinkalow's

Undercover For Drinks

morning phone call, had decided there was not much else to do but to take the day for himself. Besides, he hadn't anticipated the evening's venture so was limited in his scant suitcase wardrobe. The sales assistant at Macy's had insisted that the green tie was the only one in store to match the green and white striped shirt Montgomery had selected, after some dithering. Back home his wife Catherine usually assisted with his attire for social occasions. Montgomery was on his own and he hoped the hotel valet service would remove the creases and the odd stain from his suit after the rigours of the eight hour transatlantic flight and the grime of New York. The shirt and tie would be fine along with the cleaned and pressed suit. 'Dress nice' – as Dinkalow had quaintly put it. Montgomery could imagine and hear CS McClatchey dispensing last minute instructions to an undercover squad and telling them to dress nice – a pink shirt and flares from Carnaby Street in London, for an early morning raid on the suspected UVF Belfast headquarters on the Shankill Road.

It was 7.55pm as Montgomery stepped out of the elevator to see Dinkalow sweep through the revolving door entrance into the hotel lobby. Montgomery raised a hand to catch Dinkalow's attention.

'Right James, good evening. You look the perfect Irish gentleman for our undercover operation, while simultaneously putting a hand to Montgomery's arm and ushering him to a more quiet area of the lobby. As it's an official operation, I'll explain in order to keep everyone right and within the law, if I may James. We must eliminate the possibility of any confusion arising.'

'That's fine Sorrel. I can appreciate the situation.'

'First name terms only. My cover name is Neil. I'll introduce you to the other members of the team in the car. Cheer up James and let's go.'

Although his blinding headache had passed, Montgomery felt a nervous tension on being involved undercover in unfamiliar territory of a foreign city. He would need to be alert and also outwardly relaxed so that he would not stand out. A difficulty at the best of times, Montgomery was much taller than most, if not all of his RUC colleagues, standing a pencil-thickness under 6'4".

Dinkalow, or Neil as Montgomery would refer to him from now on, directed him to the rear seat of the car while he seated himself in the front.

'Well James. I'll introduce you to the other members of the team who have been fully briefed by me earlier today. Audrey, whom you are sitting beside, is our senior administration staff officer, strictly not a field agent, but volunteering to join in and help out. It is her cousin who organised a table for us at tonight's event. So, Audrey will be your date, only of course for the purpose of undercover James. With the numbers there this evening, we are assuming that not everyone knows everyone else. Except Audrey may know a few which is another reason she has come along to ensure we blend in.'

'Hello Audrey. I'll be relying on you to look after me.'

'Yes, James Montgomery, and I on you.'

Both fused together with mutual smiles.

'My date for this evening is Susan who is the only female special agent assigned to the FBI New York office. Susan, like me James, is armed as is also our driver Frank. Frank will remain in the cab and will radio for back-up support if we need it. Lastly James, if you do spot our suspect Ryan, then leave it to us to make an arrest. Along with Audrey, you must move well away from the remainder of the operation. It's for your own safety. If Ryan is here and we can arrest him, then he most likely will have friends with him. We don't need nor want a Belfast-style shoot-out here in the middle of Manhattan.'

'OK Neil. No point in my getting in the way. I'll be more than pleased if Ryan is brought into custody. Audrey and I will step well to the side and leave it to the FBI.'

'Good, everyone is clear on what's what. Right Frank, let's go and good luck for a positive outcome.'

It was fifteen minutes later when the party of four was shown to their table by Audrey's cousin, the functions manager at Rossa O'Donovan's. The table was towards the back of the room diagonally opposite to the top table, but ideal to observe the mingling and seated guests; in excess of 150 according to Audrey's cousin. There were areas which were dimly lit while the top table by contrast seemed to be flooded with light, no doubt emphasising the importance of those dozen or so dignitaries and city officials seated on the podium.

The Chairman, the Grand Marshall of the St Patrick's Day Parade was centrally placed with the auxiliary Bishop of the Archdiocese of New York to his right, while the unmistakable presence of the distinguished guest of honour, Senator Patrick D. McCartney was to his left; smiling and gesticulating with the occasional wave to someone recognised in the main body of the room. To his left was the First Deputy Commissioner of NY City Police Department. Everyone seemed relaxed and the mood was congenial, resembling a large family reunion. Dinkalow's FBI undercover team had missed the Senator's grand entrance some twenty minutes earlier in the evening, to the apparent spontaneous applause of the gathering of the clan; a few well-placed flunkies had led off the engineered adulation.

The evening's function was supported by a buffet of Irish salmon with everything. It was well organised with each table party in turn joining the line for the fare. Waiters intermingled in the throng, their trays laden with tinkling glasses of the various brands of Irish whiskey on the rocks. Dinkalow seemed to be in his element, at ease with the occasion, totally different, as Montgomery had assessed him to be, the dedicated and calculating professional FBI agent. It was Dinkalow who had ordered the first round of drinks giving the impression that his party was there for the merriment of the evening. But it was a front; there was the absolute necessity to remain sober and alert if an arrest was in the offing. Following on from everyone having satisfied themselves in partaking of the various platters of the buffet, came the speeches. The Chairman was pleasantly short; while the Senator's theme was to raise funds for those suffering in occupied Ireland...*each dollar raised here tonight will go towards providing relief to ease the hardships being endured by our Irish brotherhood in the six counties. Funds will be used to help in organising defence for Irish Catholics living in the Bogside of Derry, Ballymurphy and Ardoyne in Belfast and many other besieged areas throughout the North. Such defensive measures as are necessary against the Protestant extremists in their murderous campaign. I ask everyone to please give generously for those families left without the breadwinners of the Catholic households of Belfast and Derry: husbands and fathers taken from their beds in the dark of night and imprisoned without trial by the British army oppressors...* The Senator's oratory skill in working an audience was unmatched. To rapturous applause, almost in tears, he raised both arms in acknowledgement of intending commitment from the gathered clan. He soaked up the adulation as if he was the very reincarnation of Saint Patrick. Naturally he had not mentioned that a large portion of the funds raised would be diverted to purchase arms for the IRA.

Montgomery and Dinkalow had listened in silence, each keeping his thoughts to himself. Senator McCartney had barely settled back into his seat when the ceilidh band blazed forth in full volume. Within minutes the wooden dance floor vibrated in rhythm to the stomping feet of the dancers, and Irish jig followed

Undercover For Drinks

Irish jig to the infectious notes from the fiddles, penny whistle and thundering bodhran.

Montgomery concentrated on the matter in hand as he systematically scanned the tables hoping to spot Ryan. He chatted with Audrey; occasionally diverting his gaze to someone walking close by in hope of making a positive identification. Disappointment slipped into the evening as time passed and Montgomery was certain that Ryan was not at the gathering and felt sure he would have seen him by now.

'Neil, it looks as if we are out of luck, a dead end. Ryan's not here. Perhaps a waste of time.'

'No James, it's just one of those outside chances which have proved negative. Surely back in Belfast you must reach dead ends in cases.'

'Aye Neil, more times than I would admit to. This whole Ryan business has been a series of blind alleys – chasing shadows in the dark. Part of police work I suppose, but nevertheless, still disappointing.'

'Let's give it another ten minutes or so James. Why don't you take a walk around and have one last look at the far end of the room before we call it a night.'

'Right, Neil, I'll do just that.'

'If you see him James, come back immediately and leave it to Susan and me to decide when to make an arrest.'

Montgomery was up on his feet moving off between the tables, slipping past the edge of the dance floor and endeavouring not to be obvious as to his motive. He was about to call it quits when he noticed what looked like a familiar stumpy figure from the past heading towards the secondary exit at the back of the functions room. There was no mistaking the profile. It was Sean Wallace! What's he doing in New York, Montgomery thought in disbelief. He instinctively began to follow him in pursuit – only realising, as he lost sight of him through the doors, there was nothing he could do. The RUC had not requested an international warrant through Interpol for his arrest. There was never any reason for one. As far as Montgomery knew and with good reason, Wallace had been hiding out in a safe house in the suburbs of Dublin. Wallace had vanished once again; escaped. Perhaps it was just imagination, his mind playing tricks in his desire to find Ryan – an association of images of suspects planted in his memory for the brutal double murder a year earlier. Montgomery thought better of it, not to mention Wallace, to Dinkalow. There would be no point. The stuffy atmosphere, tension and frustration was causing Montgomery's headache to return. It was time to call it a night and Wallace would have to wait until another time in another city. Eventually, Wallace would return to Belfast, drawing him back like a magnet to the killing zones of the narrow streets and alley-ways of the city and more British soldiers and RUC officers to be murdered in the armed struggle.

Little was said on the way back to drop Montgomery off at his hotel, except for Dinkalow who felt he should try and ease the obvious disappointment.

'I am sorry James we didn't have a better outcome, but after all it was a long shot. Tonight's get-together was only one of a number of similar pre-St Patrick's Day events throughout the city. It was the main one, so I assumed it was the one that Ryan was most likely to attend.'

'Not to worry Neil, it's fine. I'm grateful to the FBI and all involved, particularly Audrey for arranging it with her cousin.'

'That's OK James. I rather enjoyed your company and the experience of being on an undercover assignment. It's a change from being in the office all the time.'

'You're off back home the day after tomorrow James?'

Undercover For Drinks

'Yes Neill, the late evening flight on the 18th.'

'Well then James, as you're here in New York, why not take in tomorrow's parade? You never know, Ryan might show up. Call into the office in the morning, say between 11.00 and 11.30 and we'll take a walk over to 44th Street and watch the start - sometime around noon.'

The undercover cab pulled up at the hotel and Montgomery bid everyone goodnight.

'See you in the morning James.'

'Yes, I'll be there.'

17

Operation FURY
Authorisation to be Rescinded

LONDON

MORNING 11.48 GMT – 17 March

'Excuse me General; it's the Permanent Secretary at the Foreign and Commonwealth Office on the telephone wishing to speak with you – he insists it's urgent.'

Major General Patrick Wingfield was Chief of Defence Intelligence and didn't normally receive telephone calls from the Foreign Secretary. His direct political boss was the Secretary of State for Defence. He wondered if he ought to take the call or stall and call back.

'Would you mind telling the Perm Sec I'm not immediately available and take the message. I'll call him back within the hour. Thank you Wendy.'

'If I may General, he sounds rather insistent. Slightly agitated I would say.'

'Right Wendy, if it's urgent – I suppose I should. Give me a few moments before putting the call through and bring in the Ops

Operation FURY

FURY file before I speak with him. It's probably about FURY.'

'Yes Sir, I will need the combination for the safe. Remember you changed it yesterday afternoon?'

'Yes, Wendy, of course you will.'

The General quickly wrote down the combination and passed the piece of paper to Warrant Officer Lloyd.

'Shred it please when you have opened the safe.'

'Of course General,' replied Wendy in a higher octave of her voice. Why would she do otherwise and she thought the General sounded a bit fluffed. In her three years as the General's Personal Assistant, Warrant Officer Wendy Lloyd had never known the General to show displeasure or react to what she referred to as 'fluff balls' from others, they had no affect on the General's composure. It was less than a minute that had elapsed for Lloyd to open the safe and after handing the file to the General, she was now putting the call through.

'It's Sir Keith Summers, General. I'm putting him through to you now.'

'Good morning Sir Keith; Wingfield speaking. What can I do for you?'

'Yes General Wingfield. Good morning, the Foreign Secretary wishes to see you as soon as is possible. It is somewhat urgent – important,' came the abrupt reply.

'May I ask the reason, Sir Keith – you are on a secure line?'

'Well General, it's Operation FURY. The Minister needs to have a word, and in person. Are you available? Can you come over to the FCO; the Minister will fit you in at say, 2.30pm today?'

The arrogance, thought the General. More like a direct order than a request. The General decided to fish.

'Will the Defence Secretary also be at the meeting?'

'No General. It's you and the Minister.'

'And will the Director-General of MI6 be present?'

Authorisation to be Rescinded

'I don't have an answer to that question General.'

'Give me a moment Sir Keith. I believe I have no appointments for early afternoon. I'll just double check.' After a long pause; the General told Sir Keith that he was available at 2.30pm.

With that, the telephone conversation mutually ended.

Wingfield made a file note of the conversation with the Permanent Secretary and gave the file back to the Warrant Officer to return to the safe. He would not be taking the file with him to the FCO. The whole operation was acid-etched into his memory and if need be, every detail could instantly be recalled.

'Wendy, I need to be at the Foreign Office for 2.30pm today. Meeting with the Minister – please arrange transport and a driver. You will be accompanying me and in uniform, Warrant Officer.'

'Yes, General, full dress as ordered.'

'Has Lieutenant Jackson arrived yet?'

'Yes Sir, he has just arrived. He is waiting in the outer office.'

Without raising his head Wingfield looked up and observed that it was thirty seconds before noon by the GMT clock on the wall.

'He is spot on time, sounds as though he could be our man. Show the Lieutenant in.'

'Straight away Sir.'

Wendy escorted the Lieutenant into the General's office and both paused just inside. The Lieutenant was not in uniform but this did not detract from his presence. He was immaculate in his charcoal grey pinstripe suit, pristine white shirt and Parachute Regiment maroon tie. His black leather punched Derby shoes glinting in the artificial light filtering down from recessed ceiling luminaries of the General's office. Framed by the doorway, stood the quintessential soldier, honoured to be in the service of the Crown. 'Telamon of the Argonauts' had arrived, thought the General.

'Come in Lieutenant Jackson, please take a seat.'

Operation FURY

'Thank you Sir,' was the Lieutenant's reply with a voice that could only have been purchased from a hardware store and belonging to one of those petrol-driven chain saws emitting melodious notes from its exhaust.

'I understand Lieutenant, you are just back from a second stint in Ulster; border area I believe...

AFTERNOON 14.25 GMT

It was 2.25pm when Major General Wingfield and his PA Warrant Officer Wendy Lloyd were shown into an anteroom next to the Foreign and Commonwealth Secretary's office.

Lloyd had seated herself in one of the uncomfortable high-backed leather chairs placed against the wall and directly facing the door leading into the Minister's office. General Wingfield preferred to stand. He was somewhat distant as he looked out of the only window of the room into the drizzle and coldness of a winter's afternoon.

The door to the Minister's office opened.

'Good afternoon General Wingfield. I am the Permanent Secretary to the Minister; I spoke with you earlier on the phone.'

'Good afternoon Sir Keith. I am pleased to meet you. It is a miserable day.'

'Indeed, General,' replied Sir Keith as he looked directly at Warrant Officer Lloyd who had stood to accompany the General into the Minister's office.

'This is my PA, Warrant Officer Lloyd. She is familiar with Operation FURY. I can assure you Sir Keith, she has my full confidence in all matters – and besides she is a fully paid-up member of the Official Secrets Act.'

A half smirk passed across Sir Keith's face.

'Indeed General. As we all are – subject to the constraints of the OSA. Please, if you will follow me.'

Authorisation to be Rescinded

As the General entered, the Foreign Secretary rose from his chair behind his desk and walked forward extending his hand to greet the General.

'Welcome to the Foreign Office General Wingfield. I don't believe we have met before.'

'No, Foreign Secretary, I believe not. Let me introduce my PA, Warrant Officer Lloyd.'

'Yes, of course General Wingfield. We all need assistants to keep us on our toes – meetings, endless functions, Ambassadors to entertain etcetera.'

'The Permanent Secretary intervened and gestured to Lloyd that she was to be seated some distance back from the Minister and the General. The office was of such large dimensions that anyone positioned at the back of the room would need sonar in order to pick up what was being said.

'Please General Wingfield, sit here. You don't mind Sir Keith joining us. I need him for details if needs be.'

'Yes Minister, as you please.'

The Minister sat at the head of the table with Sir Keith to his right and one seat down. The General was seated to the left, but three seats down from the Minister.

'Firstly, may I thank you for coming over, and at such short notice. I am most grateful.'

'Yes. Foreign Secretary, I had no other appointments and as Sir Keith mentioned, it was somewhat urgent – Operation FURY.'

'Yes, General, as a Minister in the new government, I am being brought up to speed by Sir Keith on current issues. Matters inherited from the previous Foreign Secretary's portfolio. Operation FURY is at the top of the agenda - and a most serious one indeed.'

Wingfield did not respond, allowing the Minister to continue.

'I am aware that SIS is involved and that JIC Chairman, Sir

Operation FURY

Cunningham Smith personally supported the operation, along of course with the former Prime Minister and Defence Secretary.'

'I am correct in assuming, from a practical view point, that the running of FURY is your responsibility, General Wingfield – you have primacy in all operational matters within Defence Intelligence?'

'Yes, Foreign Secretary that is a correct assessment.'

'Well then, General, I would be grateful for a briefing on the current position, as a new boy on the block, is the American phraseology.'

Wingfield began to wonder where this foray was leading. Was it more than a *'coup d'oeil,'* the Minister was seeking, or was he circling the wagons? The General decided to be forthright in his response.

'FURY' is well advanced. All field officers, both SIS and Defence Intelligence are in place. Completion of the operation is imminent.'

Wingfield was not about to elaborate with further details on dates and timings. Naturally he knew D-Day was the 17th. Today was the 17th and he was not about to inform the Minister.

'Foreign Secretary, if I might add, once our field officers and personnel are in place we do not interfere with their task. They need to be fully focused, without any ongoing advice from this end. We leave it to them on timing and basically we become incommunicado.'

'Where I am coming from General Wingfield, is questioning the policy of the previous government and somewhat drastic counter measures arrived at by them.'

'Foreign Secretary. Operation FURY was, as I understand it, predicated on the basis of a joint memorandum submitted by the former Defence Secretary and your predecessor to the Cabinet Committee of Defence and Overseas Policy and approved by the Prime Minister. It covered immediate policy strategy to counter-

Authorisation to be Rescinded

terrorism activities within the UK and with particular emphasis on the deteriorating situation in Ulster.'

General Wingfield had received a copy of the memorandum stating its terms of reference and objectives. Wingfield felt it was not his place to enlighten the Minister further. This was a matter for Sir Keith to bring the policy document into play in its specifics.

The memorandum to implement policy had two enabling paragraphs:

In the short term to use all means necessary to reduce and eliminate the possibility of modern weaponry including explosive materials (all munitions) being obtained by any and all Irish terrorists operating within the United Kingdom;

To identify any and all international (foreign) involvement in connection with supplying weaponry and finances to and in support of Irish terrorist groups (proscribed list MoD).

'Sir Keith has drawn that to my attention, General. However, there is a policy shift beginning to arise. With the Sunningdale Agreement bringing in a new administration at Stormont in Northern Ireland together with involving the Irish government, the situation should begin to ease from a security aspect but will also have a knock-on effect here on the mainland and terrorist activities will hopefully reduce and fade.'

'That is a political assessment Foreign Secretary. I trust you agree that I should not want to comment on that but for one point, if I may.'

'And what point would that be, General Wingfield?'

'As you have indicated the involvement by the Irish government may well lead to a falling-off of support for the IRA, in particular the Provisionals, but I understand from intelligence reports that there is growing opposition from the unionist community to any formal involvement by the Republic's government in Northern Ireland affairs. This may lead to increasing support for the Protestant paramilitaries resenting such involvement and thus escalating the violence towards the republicans who will counter with more violence while Army endeavours to keep them apart.'

'I doubt it is serious opposition - just bible-thumping by a few political extremists wearing dog collars. Keeping them apart is why the Army is there, General Wingfield.'

'Indeed Foreign Secretary,' replied Wingfield – not wishing to be seen at odds with the Minister's assessment.

'So General Wingfield, taking all matters under due consideration, I feel inclined to recommend to the Prime Minister, that Operation FURY should be cancelled. In turn, I will be required to rescind the Authorisation Certificate issued by my predecessor.

'Sir Keith on my behalf will be writing to the Secretary of State for Defence indicating my intentions. Hopefully the letter will be on the Minister's desk by tomorrow morning.'

General Wingfield showed no other response. His mind partly drifted to FURY. There was insufficient time to call off the operation. It was shortly before 3.30pm by the Minister's wall clock. New York Eastern Time was five hours behind. That made it 10.30am in Manhattan. Within three to four hours' time, the target as per standing orders would be rendered permanently ineffective.

'Thank you again General Wingfield for coming over. No doubt the Defence Secretary will be speaking with you after he receives my views on Operation FURY.'

'Yes, indeed Secretary of State. I have no doubt about that.'

Nothing more was said as Wingfield and Lloyd were shown out of the Minister's office by the Permanent Secretary. Wingfield began to ponder the situation. There had been no attempt by the Minister to find out what he assessed the situation to be. No

Authorisation to be Rescinded

attempt to apologise for his obvious decision to cancel. The Minister had made up his mind. And what about MI6? Did the Director-General know and if so, when?

'These politicians Wendy, some of them expect the senior command of the British army to come up with strategy and solutions, initiatives to counter the terrorist threat to the UK. When we do, they prevaricate and retreat into piety. It's like we are expected to shoot a moving target, wearing a blindfold using only a child's water pistol or cork gun – impossible.'

'Yes General. The Foreign Secretary was having first night nerves. He did not seem to understand that such a late decision could be putting British lives at risk. He didn't even ask.'

'More like stage fright Sergeant,' replied the General somewhat annoyed.

'And what if the PM disagrees with the Foreign Secretary?'

Nothing more was said. Wingfield and Lloyd were making their way across the car park towards the staff car when a single flash from the headlights of a Ford Granada parked opposite caught their attention.

'It's OK, Sergeant, I know the vehicle. I'll just go across. You may wait in the car.'

'Right Sir.'

As General Wingfield reached the Granada, the rear left hand door with perfect timing, opened.

'Good afternoon Patrick. I thought I might catch you here for a quiet word,' came a voice from inside the vehicle.

'Good afternoon Director-General. I thought you usually left surveillance to your staff.'

'Not always Patrick. The organ grinder on occasion needs to exercise. I cannot let the monkeys have all the fun. My driver wouldn't disagree with that. OK, George you can stretch your limbs

Operation FURY

for a few minutes while General Wingfield and I compare notes.'

General Wingfield had seated himself beside the Director-General of MI6 in the temporary committee room of the black leather-upholstered Ford Granada.

'Meeting with the Minister, I believe Patrick. I had mine this morning. A bit like the doctor's surgery. He did tell me he would be seeing you this afternoon for a consultation. I'll be succinct General. I believe you and I are about to be shafted and right up our kilts. Left to retrieve a situation agreed by the former Foreign and Defence Secretaries, the PM, the JIC Chairman and ourselves. Now an instruction on a damn memo pad to abort Operation FURY without the slightest round table input by all concerned. The Minister has no perception of the time and effort used up in planning this operation. It is after all your lead on this, Patrick, which I fully support and Six is committed to. On past form when we catch some 'viper in the firm' – working for the other side – we either let them escape or imprison them and then let them escape. The Americans who catch an enemy spy put them on trial, find them guilty and execute them. And the KGB, much more efficient, interrogating, torturing for days and finally without any pretence of a trial executes them with a 9mm bullet from a Makarov to the back of the head. We don't have the option of these legal niceties. We cannot arrest and question the Senator or put him on trial, but we can follow KGB method of operation. Execute the enemy with a rifle bullet and be done with him. We have our licence to kill – that's our legal and moral authority. I am assuming you agree Patrick. You do have an opinion on what should be done?'

'Well Director. There is not much I can add. You have put it rather well. It's too late even if we tried to call off FURY. As you are aware in less than three hours, we can anticipate the operation will have completed its objective. More to the point the Foreign

Authorisation to be Rescinded

Secretary only talked about rescinding. I have received no written instruction or directive to cancel the operation. My understanding is he will be discussing it, rather writing, to the PM on the matter and I assume only then will a final decision be made. I doubt if the Foreign Secretary has even discussed it with the Defence Secretary. He didn't say and I didn't ask except he did mention Sir Keith would be writing to the Permanent Secretary to the Defence Minister on his behalf.'

'Good Patrick. We are in agreement. FURY is proceeding and not to be interfered with. The JIC Chair, Sir Cunningham Smyth, will smooth things over with the PM. We can rely on his support and I have his reassurance. Enough said. What's the life of a corrupt and rotten US Senator set against the lives of British citizens and those lives of Her Majesty's Armed Forces in Ulster. The Army is taking casualties along the border and elsewhere. The civilian police force is being gunned down on the streets of Belfast. The IRA with their car bomb activities has spread to here, into the mainland. That firmly places the Senator an enemy of the British State and its people. Does the arrogant sod think that three and a half thousand miles of the Atlantic Ocean insulates him from any consequences? If you support the enemy, then you become the enemy. The Senator has become the enemy by his own actions. Our duty is to the protection of sovereignty of this island including its population and I may also add the government.'

'Speaking of the Atlantic Ocean, Patrick, three days ago a CX Report from our New York Station arrived on my desk. It gives details of a positive shipment of munitions; upwards of fifty assault rifles, ammunition and an unknown quantity of gelignite were loaded on to the QEII passenger liner bound for Southampton. Rumours had started to circulate in a few Irish bars in New Jersey that guns were being secretly shipped to the IRA on the QEII. So

Operation FURY

New York decided to install two agents at the docks. What they discovered was that arms were being loaded, along with the liner's food provisions and at the last minute. There is always a rush to load the supplies aboard to meet the QEII's quick turn around schedule. That was eight days ago and three days ago, the ship docked. We had no opportunity to mount surveillance at this end. We have no information where these munitions have ended up. We are assuming they were unloaded along with the ship's waste. Customs don't bother much about waste disposal brought ashore. Very occasionally they make a token check which I suppose is understandable. What is of major concern, we don't know if there have been previous shipments, whether this is the first or tenth.

I have spoken with DG, MI5 and he agrees that if this is a tried and safe route, there could well be more shipments, so we are in the process of setting up joint undercover surveillance at this end. This is a new twist to bringing in weapons from America. Now they are arriving on the mainland, via the QEII. It's most likely a new route into Ireland. I should hardly venture the suggestion that they are for use on the mainland; Bank and Post Office raids in the middle of London by the IRA using automatic assault rifles. The Met's approach on occasions has been less than adequate on tracking suspects due to lack of finance to provide full surveillance operations. It was only when the IRA bombs started to go off in the capital that the Home Office secured additional finance. MI5 should have been brought in earlier to help with manpower and round-the-clock surveillance. Known terrorists hopped on the ferries from Ireland, landed on the mainland without so much as a *'how do you do?'* from Special Branch and disappeared into the throng of the city. We need intelligence on this. It is up to Special Branch and MI5 to become more proactive all round. They will just have to forget about the Marxists, Trotskyists and the dolly mixture assortment of

Authorisation to be Rescinded

wannabe anarchists in the trades unions for the moment and concentrate on the activities of Irish navvies living in Kilburn, more like a suburb of Dublin than London.'

'Have you ever been to Dublin, Director?'

'Not recently Patrick. I thought we had already covered that – that's what the drones are for and very good at it. We have as you know, received top-rate product landing on our Irish Desk from first class officers. It was our resident in the Dublin Embassy who found out about the Irish government planning to send their troops over the border into Ulster.'[34]

'Yes, Jonathan, without such information we may well have been engaged in a full scale war on British territory.'

'This new government is unlikely to appreciate the efforts Six and Army Intelligence have put into this tortuous Irish mess, but I will give them the benefit of their ignorance, for the moment. Not wishing to be offensive General, but some of these politicians couldn't organise a brothel in the middle of an Army camp, after the men had been on a ten-day exercise – and that would include the beer being on free tap; totally incompetent people! There are more than a few politicians who do not realise or would necessarily admit that those in the IRA are absolute in their hatred for the British – raised on it from the cradle. In reply our response cannot be hatred, but it must be absolute. If these funkers like the Foreign Secretary fail to hit this situation with full force in resolve, then the government may as well conclude the inevitable, to withdraw from Ulster and set it adrift. And for what we are doing General Wingfield, it will end up just a bloody waste. Let the Protestant loyalists take on the IRA Marxists in their own backyard - a battle between the intellectually void and the intellectually naïve. The Irish chess match where all the squares on the board are white and all the pieces are black, with the end-game of mutual self-destruction. The Kilkenny cat solution to the Irish problem.'

Operation FURY

Moving briefly to North Africa if I may Patrick, and Libya. We have received an interesting CX from our people in Tripoli. It's scant on detail, but representatives of the Libyan regime along with a Bulgarian arms dealer have met with two Irishmen on at least three occasions over the previous week. The Bulgarian has been identified as a known KGB agent. Tripoli station has been asked to urgently identify the Irishmen and whatever intelligence they can obtain on the meetings. It will prove extremely difficult and dangerous as the Colonel's internal security people are on every street corner. The situation is so bad that we have considered pulling our people out and closing down until quieter times. But we shall see. I'll hold off on making any reference to Libya in my report to JIC, until we can find out exactly what the regime is up to and not rush ahead of the game, but it could be your Hydra is about to grow another head, Patrick.'

'Jonathan, perhaps we should conclude. Nothing more in the meantime except we can look forward to a successful completion of FURY. It will probably make the late evening news and then we can expect the phone calls from the Prime Minister, the Foreign Secretary and my own Minister.'

'And for me, Patrick, to advise the government directly to follow the previously agreed line if they are asked, that the UK government has no knowledge, intelligence or otherwise on the Senator's demise and believe it to be purely an American domestic situation and absolutely not to mention or suggest the possibility of Irish terrorist involvement. That's for the Americans to factor in and with the assistance of our disinformation Operation SPEAKEASY. I'm curious Patrick. One question if you don't mind. Why have you taken to green ink in your communications?'

'Sorry Jonathan. I hope you don't mind. It's mapping ink, a few shades lighter than yours. It is for quick identification; red for the

Authorisation to be Rescinded

Soviets, green for the Irish and of course royal blue for her Majesty's Armed Forces.'

'Well General, I suspect you will be using a considerable number of bottles of mapping ink in the future. I also suspect the Foreign Secretary, in consultation with the Prime Minister, may wish to borrow a bottle to re-draw the Northern Ireland border.'

'No Jonathan, I suspect he may wish to use one of those tiny rubbers at the end of a standard civil service pencil. Did you not notice he had a few lying on his desk?'

Without adding further comment on the subject, the Director-General gave a rueful smile.

'Normal routine for both of us in the meantime. Good afternoon Jonathan.'

'Good day, General Wingfield.'

18

The Wrong Corpse

New York

Senator Patrick Devoy McCartney, codename Hydra – the target, had the gift of the gab, and a memory that would shame a fifty year old elephant. His charm was in abundance and he was on first name terms with everyone, high and of lowly station. Even His Grace, the Bishop on occasions sought out his counsel on delicate social matters relating to the masses, and particularly anything that might adversely impact upon the faithful. His ancestors mentioned on every occasion to impress an audience or when canvassing votes for public office, came from Ireland and settled in New York over 120 years earlier. He was not an American, but an Irish-American and those in close proximity would receive a daily slice of his ancestral connection to the Emerald Isle. When once asked by an elderly man had he ever visited Ireland, his reply was instant. No, for there was no reason to do so because Ireland had visited him and having enjoyed the experience so much, it had decided to stay. The poor sod who had asked the question must have regretted it, at having to listen to family history, delivered firstly with pathos and as each generation came and went, finally with elation as he ejaculated in terms of his own Irish presence upon God's earth. His story was an Old Testament parable capable of mesmerising any Lower East Side priest.

Senator McCartney was no fraud. His paternal great grandparents, along with their young son, his grandfather, had booked one-way passage on the emigrant ship *Urgent*[35] for the five week journey across the vast ocean, outward bound from Belfast to the Port of New York. The year was 1851 and the family had left to escape the ravages of the 'Great Famine' caused by the year-on-year failure of the blighted potato crop, resulting in widespread starvation and ultimately thousands perishing. The Senator's ancestors had survived the disease-ridden coffin ship and arrived in America, exhausted by the winter sea journey with little money or belongings, but with hope and determination to forge a better life in the 'New World,' free from the tyranny of the English landlord. The indifference by the landlords to the plight of their tenant farmers, made the English and England symbols of Irish hatred. This hatred was exported across the Atlantic Ocean and formed part of the inheritance of the Irish immigrant, passed on from generation to generation with exaggerated eloquence of tragedy and tyranny. The Senator could speak the Irish Gaelic tongue fluently and wore it as a badge of honour. He claimed with justification that his ancestors helped establish the Fenians[36] of New York; the Irish Republican Brotherhood[37] dedicated to armed revolution and overthrow of English (British) rule in Ireland.

In 1969, when 'The Troubles' erupted in Londonderry and Belfast, he stepped into the limelight and took it upon himself to publicly speak out against the British and he felt it his duty to involve himself practically, helping to set up and establish The Irish Relief & Aid Fund. By manipulation, guile and the odd bribe he now single-handedly controlled this dubious charity. His kleptomania for greenbacks was limitless. Those who knew of the

The Wrong Corpse

theft and participated as willing volunteers received handsome kick backs and expenses. There were none who were prepared to inform the revenue authorities, fearing the Senator's vicious response through his hired clan of thugs, which included officers in the higher ranks of the New York Police Department.

AFTERNOON 1.15pm – 17 March

Peter Moore was decidedly early for the St Patrick's Day Parade as he emerged from walking along 79th Street and on to the uneven side walk of Upper Fifth Avenue. It would be around an hour before the Parade would finish. There was nothing more to be done logistically. He had covered all the aspects of the operation with military diligence. He was confident everything had been factored-in, over the previous weeks of planning FURY and that Artemis would execute her duty.

He was now sitting relaxed with his coffee, at the back of the restaurant situated at the side of the Guggenheim Museum. This is where he would wait for the next thirty minutes or so before mingling with the spectators and revellers that accompanied the parade.

Moore's thoughts drifted back to the final briefing meeting when the Foreign and Commonwealth Secretary had shown mild apprehensiveness towards the operation. After the meeting, it was Colonel Freddie Jones who had steadied Moore's resolve.

Listen Peter; don't be concerned about the Foreign Secretary. Perhaps I wasn't too diplomatic at the time. He was asking about your experience. I mentioned you had been with Lieutenant Colonel C.C. Mitchell when he was sent into Aden to sort out the mess in Crater, and on the proposed disbandment of the Argyll and Sutherland Highlanders you had transferred over to us. He

Operation FURY

appeared to go slightly distant, walked off muttering something about – Well then, he'll be up to the job and I expect him to do it without the accompaniment of the regimental bagpipes!
The Minister doesn't see the US Senator as a spokesman for the 'Free World.' He sees him for what he is; a third or fourth generation Irish-American who has latched on to the 'cause,' talking up his Irishness for political advancement and personal gain. A twentieth century Boss Tweed, if you like – the Good Samaritan to the hard-pressed. For every dollar he raises for the huddled masses, subjugated under British rule back in Ireland, fifty cents is ripped off for his expenses and administration costs. Money raised from New Jersey up to Boston and back down again to Washington. It extends to Chicago and on over the Rockies to San Francisco. Anywhere and everywhere the Leprechaun is the unofficial emblem of the community. The odd cheque for fifty or hundred dollars from the local dignitary running for office and claiming Irish ancestry. Mostly, it is two or three dollars cash given willingly by the gullible; induced by false stories exaggerated to the point of myth.

Peter Moore and Freddie Jones had seen the CX intelligence reports. For all involved, at Defence Intelligence, the Senator was a gun-runner. Guns and explosives used to murder British troops, police personnel and slaughter British citizens on the streets of London and the towns of Ulster. Moore had his *'licence to kill'* and he wasn't about to waste it. He thought why would the political classes in Washington give a fiddlers damn about the demise of the Senator and besides the Republicans hold the White House. As for the Democrats, they will blame it on another Soviet KGB conspiracy or a mentally deranged lone gunman. Operation FURY was live and Major Peter Moore would look to his orders and see it through to the death.

From the comings and goings of the restaurant, the crowds

The Wrong Corpse

were beginning to assemble. It was time for him to join in as just another enthusiastic tourist. Moore stepped out once again on to Fifth Avenue, rather pleased that he was sporting his shamrock sprig. He was even more pleased that he had declined the green coloured hokey-pokey being sold by a street vender dressed in the guise of a leprechaun and hoping to turn a quick buck. The parade was now visible as Moore saw a slightly elevated space behind the crowds, which he gauged would give him an uninterrupted view of the leading dignitaries as they arrived at 86th Street. Within a few minutes, Moore had reached his selected observation point as the parade advanced to within 100 yards from where he was now standing. There seemed to be some commotion developing and the parade stopped abruptly; someone had fallen to the ground. Moore's thoughts turned to Artemis; had she prematurely pulled the trigger to complete her mission? He suddenly spotted the Senator's unmistakable bulky presence.

The Senator was on one knee stretching over the prostrate, motionless body. From his elevated position, Moore could just see him through the muddled panic. He went rigid. What had gone wrong? All the planning, the weeks, the meetings and personnel involved. Above all, the politicians. The Americans did not register for Moore. It was back home; the Minister would be none too pleased. Well, thought Moore, holding back from speaking aloud – bollocks to him! The unrelenting pressure from his colleagues in Defence Intelligence; 'perhaps he should resign,' would be the mutterings from his co-conspirators, distancing themselves to protect their careers. Operation FURY had failed. The wrong corpse lay on Upper Fifth Avenue.

Major Moore had instantly jumped to the conclusion that Artemis had cocked up and the operation was now a disaster. He felt his whole body jitter with disbelief. It was a few seconds before he gathered his thought processes. What was he to do? Leaving Artemis to her fate, whatever that entailed was sidestepping the situation and how would she react – panic, expose her position and get caught? Moore's overwhelming instinct was to make his way to the apartment, find out what had gone wrong and see what he could do, but he could be further risking the chance of discovery of the British operation. With second thoughts, Artemis for the moment would be on her own. Artemis' extraction from the operation had been pre-planned but this was down to MI6 to expedite. Their task was to recover the weapon and oversee Artemis' safe passage from New York and on to Canadian territory. If Moore interfered at this stage, he could cause more harm and blow open and expose the whole secret operation, bringing the British government into a diplomatic hail-storm row with the US government. Moore had made his decision. He would immediately return to his hotel, ring the telephone number, only to be used in emergency and ask for 'Maggie,' the contact name he had been given by Debra Rutherford on his arrival in New York.

Some feet back from an open French window of an eighth floor apartment, above and behind the Guggenheim Museum, the stage setting had not altered - Artemis had yet to play the finale. For she, like Moore, was unnerved by the unscheduled act. Through the riflescope, she saw a microcosm of panic play into the scene. Artemis had been through her ten weeks of intense training. She remembered the words of her SAS instructor Sergeant 'Taffy' Edwards. *Always be ready for the unexpected. If it does not interfere with the task, ignore it; stay focussed for your own protection.* Artemis reacted as if 'Taffy' Edwards was at her side and talking her through the unexpected. The psychology as part of her training was steadying her nerve. Artemis adjusted her composure which extended into her rifle, fused together as one in aligned symmetry of zero precision. Artemis was ready.

The Wrong Corpse

'Turn around Senator McCartney - and I'll take your breath away.'

As if by direction or telepathy, the Senator obliged. With a slow out-breath, Artemis squeezed the trigger. The muffled flash and sound came half a micro-second after the .224 Remington launched with maximum velocity from the black instrument; the Aug HBAR-T Sniper rifle. The bullet hit the Senator square point below his nose. The force jerking his head violently backwards, his body as if by slow motion, fell and slumped over the already lifeless corpse. A tooth dropped out of the Senator's shattered mouth and rolled on to the ground. The bullet had internally tumbled downwards, severing the Senator's spinal cord just below the foramen magnum, exiting from the neck, ricocheting off the road and travelling on beyond the emerging necropolis. The Good Samaritan was dead. Operation FURY had indeed succeeded. As the Authorisation Order read, the Senator had been *rendered permanently ineffective* - an abrupt end to his life and to the Saint Patrick's Day parade.

But there had been someone else involved with their own agenda – another gunman. Artemis had only fired one round. The bullet that had rendered up the first corpse - that of Sean 'Butcher' Wallace - had come from elsewhere; nothing to do with Artemis. With self-control and without panic, Artemis scanned the room to ensure everything was as it had been when she first entered to check out the suitability of the Hoffmans' apartment the previous afternoon. Her last act was to secure closed, the French window which she had only two minutes earlier sighted through to the target. Door knobs were wiped clean as she exited the apartment through the kitchen lobby service entrance. Artemis was now inside Colonel Jones' apartment. She undid the screws of the bath panel and eased it free. Wrapping the rifle in a towel which she pushed tight to the back wall behind the bath, and quickly replaced the panel. Artemis ran both water taps and stripped off her clothes,

Operation FURY

dropping them into the hot bubble bath as she stepped in to absorb the warmth and rid herself and her clothes of any gun shot residue. The warm effervescence tingled her skin and she began to relax, soaking up the quietness of her solitude. If anyone from the Police Department called to investigate and check out the use of the apartment as the possible location of the gunman, then Artemis had the perfect cover-story. She saw and heard nothing of what had happened eight storeys below the apartment at the St Patrick's Day Parade on Fifth Avenue.

* * *

AFTERNOON 12.30pm – 17 March

Dinkalow and Montgomery had taken the sub-way at Dinkalow's direction as the quickest way to move Uptown. They were now standing at the corner of 59th and Fifth and could hear the noise as the parade made its way up Fifth Avenue. Rather than wait, they decided to move ahead. It made more sense as they reasoned a suspect could be more easily spotted as they walked along scanning the crowds of spectators rather than having to deal with the distraction of the razzmatazz of the parade at the same time.

Since his arrival in New York, Montgomery was beginning to have niggling doubts that Red Tom Ryan was actually here; a wild goose chase with nothing at the end to show for his five-day trip, other than a hefty expenses sheet. Was his sixth-sense and determination as a Belfast police detective about to let him down? Well, if it was down to luck, then he would take it gratefully. If, by the end of the day, there was nothing positive to indicate that Ryan was in New York, then he would have to accept it and go home. From a few pointed remarks made earlier that morning, Montgomery realised Dinkalow was coming to the same conclusion, Ryan was no longer in the city and had

The Wrong Corpse

probably moved on. Dinkalow had given Montgomery all the assistance he could expect and on occasions he had taken the lead. After all, it was at Dinkalow's suggestion they visit Rossa O'Donovan's for the function the previous evening. Montgomery moved off ahead of Dinkalow along the Park sidewalk.

Dressed in an overcoat having the appearance of one size too small and of dubious quality, there was no mistaking Sean 'Butcher' Wallace; out of place in the front rows of the well-groomed civic dignitaries leading the parade. Montgomery had been correct when he instinctively knew and had momentarily spotted Wallace the previous evening. Senator McCartney was strutting along to the left of Wallace as the parade was coming within sight of the finishing point at 86th Street junction. Montgomery began to wonder that if Wallace was in New York, then it was probable Ryan may also be taking part in the parade. He scanned each face in turn as the procession of participants passed by, hoping to catch sight of him. Up front, the parade stopped and some of the marchers began to break rank.

'Someone has collapsed at the front,' said an unidentified voice. It was Sean Wallace who had slumped onto the ground.

'I think the parade is over and is breaking up,' added another which added to the confusion.

Suspecting he could have missed Ryan, Montgomery started to walk up towards the front of the parade.

'The Senator has been shot; Senator McCartney has been shot' came a loud outcry, followed by a chorus of groans from those closest; a second body to add to that of the lifeless Wallace.

The verbal alarm seemed to freeze those within earshot, not sure if it was true. Nervousness gripped the immediate scene. Those spectators watching from the sidewalk became agitated and disbelief came over everyone as they began to realise what had happened. The scene lay silent after two single shots, sixty seconds apart, inaudible above the chatter and clamour of the parade, moments earlier. Two contorted bodies lay like stone as if mimicking the nearby rocky outcrops of Central Park. The leafless trees of late winter with their tracery of branches hanging over like a grey veil of death and the warm rays of the sun suddenly shielded by the mingling clouds, as if they were mourners gathering for the wake. Who would be next? Dead before they would hear the sound of the shot. None came. The silence remained, gripping with fear those crouching and laying prostrate on the cold uneven surface of Upper Fifth Avenue. At the edge of the Park, a pair of squirrels danced in early courtship, oblivious to the events which had taken place. The instincts of life were theirs to enjoy and they intended to play their part to the full. Not so for Senator McCartney and Sean Wallace, for they no longer would enjoy God's earthly domain. Eventually, back in Ireland, the 'Butcher' would be lamented as a martyr, with maudlin lyrics to the accompaniment of the haunting sound of the penny whistle and backdrop of Guinness-swigging volunteers. Sean Wallace would have his place in republican mythology as another patriot and hero of the cause.

Montgomery had now reached the front of the parade to see two bodies lying on the ground, an image he had seen before that reminded him of the double murder at the petrol station the previous year. As he looked around to find Special Agent Dinkalow, he felt a sudden hammering thud against his chest. Grasping for breath as the invisible kinetic force dissipated through his upper body, he stumbled backwards, thumping the side walk on his rump as his head involuntarily jerked backwards against a lamp standard. The Chief Inspector lay motionless, unconscious or dead; another target for a Sniper's bullet.

The Wrong Corpse

'Chief Inspector, what's wrong? James, James are you OK? What on earth is happening here?'

Dinkalow pulled open Montgomery's overcoat and jacket, pressing the palm of his hand underneath and sweeping it across Montgomery's chest. Dinkalow felt the print of hot metal singe the tips of his fingers. As suspected, he realised what had happened. Montgomery had been shot. The bullet had penetrated his clothing and spectacles case in his inside jacket pocket but had been stopped as the bullet lodged between two metal plates of Montgomery's protection vest, which Dinkalow had insisted he wore earlier that morning before going off to observe the parade. With both hands, Dinkalow eased Montgomery's slumped head upwards and resting it against the lamp standard; he felt a trickle of warm blood seep between his fingers.

Dinkalow rose to his feet, turned around and looked up, surveying the buildings with their multiplicity of windows, like cats' eyes looking down upon Upper Fifth and eerily onto the spot where he was standing. Was he the observer or was he being watched by the gunman; the sniper, sighting him up as the fourth target, who minutes earlier had deployed his skill with deadly precision upon the unknown man and Senator McCartney? But Chief Inspector Montgomery had survived the sniper's bullet; stopped by the protection vest Dinkalow had wisely insisted he wore.

But why Chief Inspector Montgomery? He was not taking part in the parade. Was he more than a spectator on the sidewalk, someone the gunman knew from Belfast? Was the gunman Patrick Ryan? It was a possibility, thoughts that hooked onto Dinkalow's investigative instincts. His gaze dropped to ground level and thinking only a fool would shoot from a low position; hardly an advantage point for a long-range killing. Was it the high-back van parked just beyond the Guggenheim with its sign 'Furniture

Operation FURY

Removals' that arrested his scanning eyes as one of its rear doors opened, just enough for a slender figure to step down onto to the road? Dinkalow narrowed his eyes, vainly trying to acquire the North American Indians' superior vision. He could just make out a few features; the figure was male, tall with his dark hair, tied back in pony-tail fashion, looking strangely out of place. Dinkalow concluded it was Ryan.

He was too far off, as the figure weaved amongst the endless yellow cabs; swarming bees heading Uptown for a rich source of pollen. Ryan was gone – vanishing like the Leprechaun into the shadows of the shamrock, with his mystical power who could always escape and avoid capture; but for how long? For no one can escape God's plan, born before time and far beyond the stars.

London

EVENING 22:25 GMT – 17 March.

General Wingfield and Warrant Officer Lloyd had returned to their offices in Defence Intelligence of the MoD. It was 6.45pm when Lloyd left for the evening. General Wingfield left somewhere around 7.15pm and had been dropped off by his driver at his home in Richmond-upon-Thames. He was slightly anxious but was endeavouring to relax with an extra large measure of Scotch and soda after his evening meal.

As he watched television's late evening news, he glanced at the clock on the mantelpiece. It was 10.25 and there had been no mention of anything remotely to do with the American Senator. Perhaps he did not merit newsworthiness in Britain. Still, he was well known in Washington for his views on Irish affairs and had given an interview to *The Times* newspaper suggesting that the British should leave Northern Ireland for good. He had been both

The Wrong Corpse

praised and denounced in equal measure for his outspoken opinions. Wingfield wondered if the operation had gone wrong. No, FURY had been too well planned in meticulous detail, but human error was always the unknown factor. The only other possibility was that the Senator had cancelled his guest of honour appearance at the St Patrick's Day Parade. He was well liked by Irish-America and no more so than by New York's Irish immigrant community and it would have been a public relations necessity for him. Wingfield's thought process was interrupted…

And finally we are just receiving reports from our Washington Correspondent of a shooting incident in New York. Senator Patrick McCartney has been fatally wounded while participating in the New York St Patrick's Day Parade. One other unnamed man who had been standing close to the Senator also died at the scene. Our Correspondent says reports from New York are calling it an assassination of one of America's leading Senators. Senator Patrick McCartney is well respected in Washington and has sat on the Foreign Affairs Committee. Although he did come in for some criticism last year for his reported comments that the British should leave Ireland for good as soon as possible and without delay. Our Correspondent says there is considerable speculation as to who carried out the shooting but nothing specific or official has been announced by the administration. We have no further details of the incident. We are coming to the end of this news bulletin and just to recap on our latest report from Washington of the shocking news that US Senator Patrick Denvoy McCartney has been shot while participating in the St Patrick's Day Parade in New York. It's good evening from everyone here in the ITN News studio.

Fearing the teeth of the Hydra
Herakles with a single sweeping arch of his mighty sword
severed one head from its body
And the light, shining evil from its eyes
of green emerald, blackened into darkness.

Operation FURY

Eight months after the assassination, MI6 informed the CIA that on receiving reliable intelligence from one of their agents embedded within the Republican Movement, the man known as 'Red Tom' Ryan, is believed to have carried out the assassination of Senator McCartney. Ryan was shot and killed by the British SAS in an unrelated undercover operation in County Monaghan, Republic of Ireland.

Secret Intelligence Service understands it was a contract killing of the Senator, sanctioned and organised by the Provisional IRA: reason unknown.

The CIA advised the White House which, after careful consideration, decided against releasing specific details of the Senator's killing to Congress and informing the American people. All papers remain classified.

D-Day Minus 4

Four days before the New York St Patrick's Day Parade, a closed meeting was held chaired by the Prime Minister. Those present were: The Foreign and Commonwealth Secretary; Defence Secretary; Chairman of the Joint Intelligence Committee, along with the Director-General MI6 and Chief of Defence Intelligence. The Secretary to the Cabinet Office was also present.

The following two paragraphs formed the Prime Minister's Directive:

1   *The Director-General MI6 and Chief of Defence Intelligence in their areas of responsibility are ordered to immediately and without delay, suspend Operation FURY, along with all associated support functions and without risk to or compromising any and all operational personnel involved who are embedded on US territory.*

The Wrong Corpse

2   To draw down on and suspend all covert intelligence gathering on US citizens, who are suspected of involvement or assisting in IRA terrorist activities within the United Kingdom of Great Britain and Northern Ireland.

The Foreign and Commonwealth Secretary issued a Certificate countermanding the authorisation of Operation FURY under the authority of the Prime Minister's Directive.

On the eve of St Patrick's Day Parade, Artemis, with the assistance of MI6 officers, crossed the US border into Canada. She returned to her unit in the UK and was reassigned. Artemis received promotion to Sergeant.

Two months after the PM's Directive, Major General Patrick C Wingfield resigned.

MI6 complied with the strict letter of the Directive, but retained its main Agents (assets) who were run from Canada. Intelligence reports were filed under Ottawa Station and tagged 'restricted access Director-General and Head of Section only.' MI6 never submitted a single CX intelligence report on IRA activities (within the US) to the Joint Intelligence Committee; resuming only after there was a change of government. Illegal arms[38] and finances continued to flow from across the Atlantic Ocean for the IRA from supporters and sympathisers who were unquestionably citizens of the United States of America. MI6 never recovered its efficiency within the US.

It was to be a decade later in the early 1980s before the US authorities; the FBI, along with the Treasury, Alcohol, Tobacco and Firearms Division of the IRS finally got to grips with theft, illegal purchasing and exportation of weapons – gun-running to the IRA in Ireland. Throughout the 1990s further arms, including state-of-the-art sniper rifles were smuggled into Ireland from the US, by the

Operation FURY

Provisional IRA. Other Republican groups also smuggled arms as late as 1999.

Time Moves On

After twenty-two years in the RUC, Chief Inspector James Montgomery retired. He was awarded the Police Medal for his dedication in serving the people of Northern Ireland throughout many years of the Troubles. His wife Catherine was unable to persuade him to emigrate 'to the far side of the World' – Australia. Along with their family they moved to Canada. None of the family has every returned to Northern Ireland. Catherine and James still live on the family farm bought shortly after their arrival in Canada – no doubt in the stillness of a clear evening sky, watched over by James' boyhood friend Orion. They continue to have weekly visits from their children and grandchildren.

And what of Clancy the cat? He stayed behind and took up residence with Catherine's brother, Sam. Clancy died peacefully in his sleep and his ashes were sent over to Canada and buried on the farm.

'Red Tom' (Dermot Patrick Ryan) was shot dead by his former British army comrades in an undercover operation in County Monaghan. Legend has it that Artemis led a small Special Air Service unit who crossed the Irish border after receiving information from a double agent in the Provisional IRA. 'Red Tom's' body was disposed of in a deep pit near a disused farm building. It is believed without ceremony.

Peter Moore continued in Army Intelligence and was mainly responsible for formulating and writing the manual for counter terrorist undercover operational procedures in Northern Ireland. He reached the rank of Colonel and received the Queen's Gallantry

The Wrong Corpse

Medal before retiring in the early 1980s. Peter Moore's whereabouts are unknown. James and Catherine receive a Christmas card each year, but without a return address.

And from across the sea the figure of this resplendent soldier may one day appear.

* * *

19
Epilogue

Whistleblower

The following words were written by former Security Service intelligence officer Annie Machon in her book: *Spies, Lies & Whistleblowers MI5, MI6 and the Shayler Affair.*

In fact it would be true to say that the British State had no strategy for bringing the terrorist conflict in Northern Ireland to an end.

Certainly little was done to detect and cut off the flow of support to PIRA, which came principally from the US and Libya, until well into the 1980s.

If the British government had been serious about stopping the conflict, it would have set up a dedicated organisation to defeat PIRA. Instead, it failed to rationalise its response and continued to rely on a piecemeal group of organisations. These included, with shifting degrees of involvement and responsibility; the Army, the RUC (the Royal Ulster Constabulary, now renamed the Police Service of Northern Ireland), MI5, MI6, the Metropolitan Police Special Branch (MPSB), SO13 (the Met's Anti-Terrorist Squad), the 40-odd Constabulary Special Branches (SBs)...and HMCE, all with their own chain of command, all duplicating each other's work and stepping on each other's toes, all with their own discrete archive of records.

Operation FURY

Operation Banner (1969-2007)

Operation Banner was the British Armed Forces longest campaign in its history, lasting short of a few weeks, for thirty-eight years. The commitment involved the British army, backed up by the Royal Air Force helicopter support unit. The Army was initially sent in to support the civil police force, the Royal Ulster Constabulary comprising 3,200 male and female officers. The RUC was becoming overwhelmed in having to deal with escalating violence and rioting. One battalion of garrison troops[39] was sent into Londonderry to relieve the RUC. In Belfast, serious rioting broke out between sectarian factions which included petrol bombings and gun battles. Spasmodic rioting spread to many towns throughout the Province and the death toll had risen to eight. On 20 August 1969, Lieutenant General Sir Ian Freeland GOC Northern Ireland Land Forces, by agreement between the Westminster and Stormont governments became responsible for security matters. The Ulster Special Constabulary ('B' Specials) fell under the GOC's command while a reorganised RUC was to continue with its normal role of policing![40] The Army was now embedded in the Troubles, endeavouring to restore order and protect Northern Ireland's population against opposing republican and loyalist paramilitary terrorism. Within six months of additional troops arriving in the Province, the British army joined the RUC as the IRA's selected enemies.

> *A war on terror is not a strategy per se. For terrorism is no more than a means of fighting, the strategy must address the politics behind that terrorism.*
>
> *I served three tours of duty in Northern Ireland, and have witnessed the British army's engagement in the Province almost from the start. For many of those years, violence there threatened*

Epilogue

the territorial integrity of the United Kingdom itself. Now we have a real prospect of a settlement. At the time of writing, it is planned that the British Armed Forces will go non-operational in Northern Ireland on 31 July 2007.[41]

Northern Ireland 1968-1998

Armalites by the crate-load from Irish-America; Avtomat Kalashnikovas by the boat-load, Semtex by the tonne, and the abject failure of the Irish Republican Army in its 'armed struggle' to remove the British presence, and subjugate the British unionists of Northern Ireland and subsume them into a one-party unified Irish socialist republic.

Acknowledgements

In the writing of this novel, the author acknowledges the use of source material from the Public Record Office of Northern Ireland and the University of Ulster's Conflict Archive (CAIN).

In the Introduction chapter, the text is copied from the (declassified) signed letter 14.8.69 4.45pm from the above records, reference HA/32/2/55. The following is the text of the document: *the attached copy of a warning message* given by telephone at 3.15pm and referred to in the 4.45pm letter.

FORMAL MESSAGE TO MR. CAIRNCROSS OF THE HOME OFFICE GIVEN TO HIM ON THE TELEPHONE AT 3.15 p.m. 14TH AUGUST, 1969

Mr. Cairncross was asked to alert his Ministers to the imminent possibility that a formal request might have to be made this afternoon for the assistance of troops in Londonderry. The formal grounds on which this request would be made were spelt out as follows:-
If troops are not called in the situation as we see it is likely to be –

(1) a compelled retreat of the police from their present position in William Street to Victoria R.U.C. police station which they will have to defend if necessary with firearms; and
(2) occupation of the centre of the city by a riotous mob with the prospect of arson and looting, extensive damage to property and injury to the populace.

(Initialled)

I should also wish to thank those friends and family members whose recollections, reflections, advice and suggestions were invaluable.

Notes

1. The Americans in 1977 were to give up their radio station base at Lough Foyle in Northern Ireland. Perhaps reasoning the base was no longer strategically important in defence of the US and as they became more reliant upon the advancements made to the capabilities of their nuclear submarine fleet operating within the northern Atlantic Ocean, their under water detection systems and military spy satellites. The British would have to rely upon the Royal Navy for defence of all their sea ports and territorial seas including those pertaining to Northern Ireland.
2. Christopher Andrew. The Defence of the Realm. The Authorised History of MI5. (The Penguin Group, 2009).
3. Jonathan Bardon. *A History of Ulster*. (Belfast. Blackstaff Press. 1992).
4. Max Hastings. *Daily Mail*. 31 July 2007.
5. 'Towards the end of 1971, the then Home Secretary for Northern Ireland, Reginald Maudling, said that he could foresee a time when IRA violence could be reduced to 'an acceptable level.' Alex Ashe. *An Acceptable Level of Violence*. (England. Authors Online Ltd. 2002).

   In December 1974 the Provisional IRA Army Council announced a ceasefire which extended into the New Year. There were further attempts to negotiate with the British government, who refused to make any public statement of

Notes

intention to withdraw from Northern Ireland. The ceasefire gradually broke down and again it was back to a full blown IRA campaign which extended to the British mainland with a bombing offensive.

6   Information and details on Armalite assault rifles. Duncan Long. *Assault Pistols, Rifles and Submachine Guns*. (Boulder Colorado. Paladin Press.1986).

7   Vehicle borne improvised explosive device (VBIED) as it is known to the security forces in Northern Ireland and to everyone else as the car bomb, frequently used by the IRA to harass and murder not only members of the police and Army but also civilians throughout Northern Ireland for thirty years. Ammonium Nitrate Fuel Oil (ANFO), a compound of modified Net Nitrate, farmers fertiliser and diesel formed the deadly explosive mixture (fertiliser bomb) packed into the boot of a car, and in turn driven to its target where it was armed with the timer set to detonate somewhere around forty-five minutes. This type of explosive packed into a truck was first used by protesters of the Vietnam War in the US in 1970 at the University of Wisconsin resulting in one employee being killed. The recipe for the bomb was listed (found) in the pages of the Encyclopaedia Britannica. Source: Kevin Toolis, *A Bloody History of the Car Bomb* (Mail on Sunday Supplement. 27 July 2008).

8   The following statement was published in the *United Irishman*, March 1962: The leadership of the Resistance Movement has ordered the termination of the campaign launched on December 12 1956…The Irish Resistance Movement renews its pledge of eternal hostility to the British Forces of Occupation in Ireland. It calls on the Irish people for increased support and looks forward with

confidence in cooperation for the final and victorious phase of the struggle for the full freedom of Ireland.

9   Mick – derogatory term used to describe a Roman Catholic.

10 On 9 August 1971, the British government, under intense pressure from Northern Ireland Prime Minister, Brian Faulkner, gave way and introduced internment. Over 300 suspected IRA members were rounded up by the Army and imprisoned without judicial process. Rather than curtailing the violence it had the opposite effect. The reaction amongst the Nationalist/Republican population led to out and out guerrilla war, directed in the main against the British army.

11 In 1970 the RUC had sound intelligence information that the Provisional IRA had begun to organise into a military structure comprising a (Belfast) Brigade of three Battalions and several hundred volunteers which covered and controlled most of the Nationalist areas of greater Belfast. The Official IRA was less organised, with fewer volunteers and less influence and control.

12 Army parlance.

13 SLR (L1L1) self-loading rifle – a British military variant of the Belgian FN FAL design, firing a 7.62mm calibre bullet.

14 Republicans and members of the IRA who informed on their associates to the RUC had their files marked with a double vertical orange strip and became known as Orange Republicans (ORs). Loyalist informers' files had a double horizontal pink strip and became known as Pink Prods (PPs). The term agents (high-grade assets) who were run by RUC Special Branch were given specific code names to protect their identities. Unlike the ORs and PPs, they

Notes

received protection from their Special Branch handlers. The intelligence provided was generally high quality and was invaluable in counter terrorist operations.

15 Extradition: The Irish courts treated extradition warrants from Northern Ireland and Great Britain, for terrorist related crimes as political offences. Relying upon the Republic of Ireland Extradition Act 1965, terrorist offenders could avoid extradition to the UK. In 1982 in an unprecedented judgement the Supreme Court ordered the extradition of a suspect in the alleged murder of a postmistress. Chief Justice, Mr O'Higgins: 'the judicial authorities on the scope of the (political) offence have in many respects been rendered obsolete by the fact that modern terrorist violence, whether undertaken by military or paramilitary organisations or by individuals or groups of individuals, is often the antithesis of what could reasonably be regarded as political, either in itself or in its connections.'

The Extradition Act 1965 was amended in 1987 and again in 1994. Dáil Éireann, Volume 439, 22 February 1994 (341).

16 The IRA lacked a proper command structure and failed to formulate an overall strategy. It was infected with personal rivalry and was without positive leadership. Political republicanism was equally fragmented and always at loggerheads with itself. The 'armed struggle' was no more than a paramilitary movement; not an Army supporting a unified political base objective. In 1969/70 the IRA irreconcilably split into two factions with the formation or the Six County Northern Command which became known as the Provisional IRA, the remaining faction taking on the name Official IRA.

Operation FURY

17 In May 1970 Taoiseach Jack Lynch, sacked Charles Haughey and Neil Blaney alleging they were using government money, secretly, to purchase and import arms to Dublin which were to be sent north for use by the IRA. Haughey and Blaney, along with Captain Kelly (Army Military Intelligence), John Kelly and Albert Luykx were brought to trial. The charges against Blaney were dropped; the remaining defendants were acquitted in October 1970. Apparently the arms shipment, sourced in Vienna, never arrived in Ireland.

18 It is considered money from the Department of Finance (Irish government) was indirectly used to finance the emergence of the Provisional IRA.

19 On 30 January 1972, thirteen civilians were killed by the British army. The incident became known as Bloody Sunday. On 3 February 1972, the British Embassy in Dublin was gutted by fire and on 22 February, the British army Parachute Brigade at Aldershot, England was bombed by the Official IRA killing seven people. The Provisional IRA escalated its armed struggle against the Army, police and civilians.

20 Diplock courts were established by the British government in Northern Ireland in 1972. Trial by jury was suspended due to potential jury intimidation. The courts consisted of a single Judge who decided on the verdict based on the evidence presented.

21 HMS Rorqual launched 1956. Paid off 1977.

Presently under construction HMS Astute and HMS Ambush are two Royal Navy nuclear-powered hunter-killer submarines which are fitted with silent propellers

Notes

undetectable to sonar. The submarines will be armed with cruise missiles and Spearfish torpedoes which can be fired from lateral tubes. *The Mail on Sunday.* (5 October 2008).

22 'Several consignments of weapons and munitions in waterproof wrapping were submerged by a Soviet intelligence-gathering vessel...The consignments, picked up by a fishing vessel manned by what the KGB called 'Irish friends' (Communists) who were unaware of their contents, went undetected by the British intelligence community...Vasili Mitrokhin defected in 1992, bringing with him intelligence on them [arms] from KGB files.' Christopher Andrew, *The Defence of the Realm. The Authorized History of MI5.* (The Penguin Group. 2009).

23 The term, assault rifle, only applies to weapons which have 'selective fire,' i.e. capable of both semi-automatic and fully automatic firing.

24 In July 1942 the German armies surrounded on three sides and attacked Stalingrad. Fierce fighting ensued throughout the city against the defending Soviet Red Armies who were forced back towards the Volga River to their rear. Close quarter intensive engagements continued. Eventually after severe losses on both sides, the Soviets gained the upper hand. A combination of brilliant strategy by Marshall Zhukov and generalship of General Nikolai Vatutin, the freezing cold as winter set in along with the Luftwaffe's failure to resupply the Germans, Generalfieldmarschall Friedrick Paulus surrendered. Estimates of the death toal and casualties of the German and Soviet armies along with those of the city civilian population caught up in the fighting exceeded 1.7 million souls. Stalingrad had been reduced to rubble by what the

Operation FURY

German High Command termed 'Rattenkrieg' (Rat war). Stalingrad was renamed Volgograd in 1961.

In early 1977 the IRA in a chilling forewarning was to declare it would 'remove the British presence, even if it meant reducing Belfast to rubble...' The IRA was over-optimistic in its imminent strategy. It had acquired the necessary weaponry, including large quantities of high explosives, but was insufficient in number of volunteers. The IRA statement was to be supported by a recruitment drive which proved inadequate. The Republican population was not sufficiently motivated to engage the British army in an all-out Belfast Rattenkrieg.

25 The Ulster Defence Regiment became operational on 1 April 1970. The Ulster Special Constabulary (A, B and C Specials) were gradually run-down and disbanded. 'The Ulster Defence Regiment are better equipped, younger and better soldiers than the 'B' Specials' – Sir Arthur Hezlet, *The 'B' Specials, A History of the Ulster Special Constabulary.* (London, Pan Books Ltd. 1973).

26 In March 1972 the British Prime Minister prorogued the Northern Ireland government at Stormont and introduced direct rule from Westminster. The Chief Constable of the Royal Ulster Constabulary became responsible to the newly appointed Secretary of State for Northern Ireland. General security operations of the RUC fell under the control of the GOC British army Northern Ireland.

27 For over 105 years the Metropolitan Police Special Branch had lead responsibility for dealing with (Irish Republican) terrorism. In 1992 the British Home Secretary decided that this would end and that the Security Service (MI5) would

Notes

have primacy for investigating all Irish terrorist activities throughout the United Kingdom. Known as T Branch, it comprised of four main sub-sections in four geographical areas: London, Southern England, Northern (including Scotland) and Northern Ireland. There were at least twelve T desks ranging from investigating arms trafficking to running undercover agents.

28 .223 Remington (5.56mm). Full Metal Jacket (FMJ) .224. In the 1970s NATO agreed a standardisation (5.56mm NATO) to replace the (7.62mm NATO) SLR ammunition used by the British forces.

29 In 1942 when the US entered WWII their military formed the Office of Strategic Services (OSS). After the war in 1947, the OSS transformed into the Central Intelligence Agency (CIA).

30 The American B52 bombers were gradually being replaced by Inter-Continental Ballistic Missiles with their nuclear warheads as the main weapon (deterrent) of the Cold War stand-off between US and USSR.

31 The Battle of Plattsburgh, also known as the Battle of Lake Champlain, September 1814. The successful victory by the Americans denied the British (Canada) the exclusive control over the great lakes and territorial gains of the New England states.

32 Special Operations Executive (SOE) was given the sobriquet 'Baker Street Irregularies' as its headquarters was at 64 Baker Street, London, and named after Sherlock Holmes' fictional group of helpers.

33 The British Nationality Act 1948 recognised dual nationality in Eire/Ireland: British subject and citizen of Eire. Persons

Operation FURY

in Northern Ireland became citizens of the United Kingdom. When the Irish state quit the commonwealth becoming the Republic of Ireland, the United Kingdom – the Irish Act 1949 – deemed it not to be a foreign country. Its citizens could not be aliens in United Kingdom law.

In 1971, Ireland and Great Britain – for the purpose of passport controls – become a common travel area. There does not appear to be an equivalent provision in Irish law. Austen Morgan. *The Belfast Agreement. A practical legal analysis.* (London. The Belfast Press Limited. 2000).

34 In 1969 the British government on discovering the Irish government's plan to move elements of their Army into Northern Ireland, informed the Republic that: if such an incursion were to happen it would be treated as an act of war: the British army with all force necessary would move to expel such incursion: Royal Navy would deploy to blockade the former 'Treaty Ports' and close down all their trade with the United Kingdom. The blockade would have caused considerable damage to the already precarious Irish economy. It was this threat that the Irish government was persuaded to withdraw their troops already deployed close to the border and to abandon their plan.

35 Ship *Urgent* Belfast, Ireland to New York 25 February 1851. James Pollock, Master, delivered 198 passengers safely. There were no recorded deaths on voyage. Reference Immigrant Ships Transcribers Guild 2 January 2005. *www.immigrantships.net*

36 Fenian (Féne) - name of ancient inhabitants of Ireland.

37 Irish Republican Brotherhood (IRB) – secret Catholic society formed in 1858 from other groups, i.e. Young

Notes

Ireland Movement and Phoenix National & Literary Society. Eventually the Fenians; the IRB became known collectively as Clan na Gael throughout the US.

38 In 1971 the Royal Ulster Constabulary captured a quantity of Provisional IRA armaments of US source. This included approximately 750 Armalite modern assault rifles, over 150,000 rounds of ammunition and upwards of two tonnes of high explosive.

39 In 1969 the normal garrison of British army troops in Northern Ireland consisted of a single brigade of three battalions totalling around 550 Army personnel.

40 Over the period 1969-1970 the British government implemented recommendations of the Hunt Report (3 October 1969), to: 1. Disarm the RUC. 2. Reorganise and modernise the RUC along the lines of British police, i.e. rank and promotion structures. The Chief Police Officer's designation was changed from Inspector General to Chief Constable in November 1969. 3. Disband the Ulster Special Constabulary; with the formation of the Ulster Defence Regiment as part of the British army.

41 General Sir Mike Jackson. *Soldier. The Autobiography.* (London. Transworld Publishers, 2007).

Lightning Source UK Ltd.
Milton Keynes UK
UKOW06f0225040415

249096UK00001B/18/P